UNDER HIS GUIDANCE
THE WHITE ROSE TRILOGY

STACY VON HAEGERT

Under His Guidance

The White Rose Trilogy
Book Two

Stacy Von Haegert

Dragon Crest Publishing

Nashville, TN

Under His Guidance
Book Two: The White Rose Trilogy
by Stacy Von Haegert

Cover Art:
Dawne Dominique
Edited by: Lara Zielinsky

CONTENTS

I

London
1839

EDWARD'S STORY

*E*dward swirled the brandy in his glass as the last tinges of daylight filtered through the branches on the great oak tree. The encroaching night snaked in from the western shore of the lake, its smooth, feathery mist leading the way. A crisp breeze, with a hickory smoke breath from a nearby fire, caught a falling leaf and danced it gracefully down to land beside his black polished boots. The delicate foliage added to the symphony of colors he had been admiring, each leaf singing with their own individual voice. Brilliant golden tenors and sensuous burgundy baritones all lent a song as another beautiful autumn day came to an end.

Too bad he had missed it all, sleeping off the previous night's bender. Edward sighed. He really should take his brother's advice and try to rise at a more appropriate hour.

He shook off the unpleasant thought like a chill. He had no idea how Perkin stayed so... damn... perfect. Alas, such a lifestyle was not for him; Edward Kingston was far from perfect.

Besides, there was limitless enjoyment reaped in the skilled art of being bad. On that thought, he rapped his walking stick on the ground. A grin etched the corners of his mouth as he turned abruptly, eager to start his affair with the night.

Out of the corner of his eye, he saw Henry take a long drag off his cheroot before discarding it on the ground. The two began their silent trek back up to the manor. No words were needed between them. It was time to begin the hunt for the next great scandal.

They matched strides twenty paces down the lane like a pair of stalking lions. As they drew near the house, a carriage appeared. A footman hopped down from the rolling transport and opened the door before the carriage wheels could make their final rotation. Both gentlemen climbed inside.

Henry tapped the roof and the sleek black rig pulled away. "What shall it be first? Dinner, cards, and women. Or the races to start? Followed by dinner, cards, and dancing."

He lounged back in the seat across from Edward and stretched his arms behind his head, lacing his fingers together at the base of his skull. "The order matters not to me as long as the end result remains the same. A few lovely ladies, gifted with questionable morals, draped across our arms."

Edward could feel the corners of his mouth pulling upwards. "I fancy both options." He smiled. "The night is young and as we know, full of delights."

Punishing hands groped at her. A pungent liquor-soaked tongue stabbed around inside her mouth. Vile threats spit poison into her ears.

Morgan jolted awake, choking on the dryness of her throat. Her eyes darted around the carriage in a frantic effort to re-familiarize herself with the surroundings. Her heart pounded heavy in her chest and her skin crawled, as if a spider had unfurled itself in her hand.

She shook her head, forcing away the lingering imagery of her much-too-vivid nightmare. She was safe. In a carriage bound for London. *He was not here.*

Her mother and maid were still asleep on the other seat of the carriage. Morgan exhaled slowly, not wishing to alert them to her personal hell. The last thing she wanted was to bring any more worry to them. Her mother had been through enough after losing Morgan's father, having to hastily remarry, and then being forced to live with the life that followed those tragic set of events.

Morgan's stepfather, the Earl of Vistmont, had seemed agreeable, at first. Having recently lost his own spouse, the two were a logical match. But the honeymoon was short-lived. The earl's well-meaning concern and practical protectiveness over his new bride turned dark and twisted with alarming quickness. Before the ink had barely time to dry on their marriage license, the earl's domineering ways had increased to the point of physical violence.

Morgan watched her mother resting peacefully across from her. It pained her deeply to think that her only repose would, forever forward, be solely found in the confines of her sleep. Life was not fair.

And unfortunately, the strongest usually gave all. As her mother was now doing for Morgan. Bumping along in a carriage on a rutted out old road freedom-bound.

Luckily for Morgan, the earl had not laid a finger on her. That was exactly how her mother intended it to stay. The countess had written to her sister, the Duchess Vandicamp, and implored her to invite them to the city, where Morgan could be "educated on some of the finer skill-sets befitting a lady."

Her dear aunt had graciously accepted, practically beside herself with the prospect of introducing a new debutante into the lucrative world of London's elite bon ton. Morgan hoped the Duchess would not be disappointed when she alighted from their dilapidated carriage.

Morgan glanced at the empty seat to her right. The fabric was threadbare and had an odor that could best be described as cat piss—though she knew it was likely comprised of various stenches—all of which a young lady should know nothing. At least the compartment was in better shape than the outside of the carriage. The transport looked like it had fared poorly in more than a few races and might have even been submerged at one point in time.

Morgan cringed as she considered what a truly noteworthy entrance they would be making on Grosvenor Square. Just another way her stepfather could inflict shame on her mother. The earl had agreed, reluctantly, to allow Morgan a turn at London, but there was no way he would allow them the use of one of his finer rigs to get there. Those he saved for entertaining his whores.

Morgan rolled her eyes. At least she would be free of the earl's dreaded household. She resigned herself to think no more of the vile man. Her stepfather was not worthy of her time or attention. Besides, there was plenty more pressing matters to contemplate.

Foremost, she had much to learn before the season got underway. Once she became engrossed in her education, Morgan would make sure she applied those lessons to all aspects of social obligation. By chance, she might be successful in finding a gentleman that would think her agreeable.

Morgan felt herself nod affirmatively. Any arrangement would be better than the life she was leaving behind. She would appreciate her winter away—not just from her unpredictable stepfather, but from his horrible offspring as well. *Roderick.*

A familiar chill crystallized across her skin like ice over a pond. She pulled her shawl up tighter around her shoulders. Despite her resolve to look only to the future, her thoughts dragged her backward yet again...to her stepbrother. Or as she referred to him: the Devil incarnate.

Throughout the first year of their parents' marriage, Roderick had merely taunted Morgan with nasty, degrading snips here and there. Everything from her simple country upbringing to the way she held a teacup. Apparently, she had hands like a man and the grace of a butcher. He had also taken great pleasure in encouraging his boorish friends to do the same. There was not a day that went by that she hadn't been made to feel inadequate in her home.

However, it had not stopped there. Roderick's torment only intensified when her body dramatically changed over the course of one summer, from lanky teenager to voluptuous woman. Her upbringing ceased to matter much now. Her stepbrother suddenly seemed to seek her out everywhere she went, his jeers becoming even more perverse, filling her ears with all sorts of sexual innuendo every chance he was afforded.

If her maid, Bertrice, had not interrupted them the night before they left for London...Morgan knew he would have made good on his threat to show her *just what* her body was made for. "To give pleasure to men," he had rasped, after having dragged her into the kitchen pantry and pinned her against the wall.

She had been truly terrified for the first time in her life but did not tell a soul save Bertrice, who had witnessed the abuse first-hand. Her loyal maid had reluctantly sworn secrecy, and Morgan had spent the rest of that night in two vastly different states of mind. One half in tears, feeling utterly helpless, and the other half wanting to fight, vowing to be the best deuced debutante London had ever laid eyes on. The latter, however, was her only ticket out. For if she ever did return to her stepfather's residence, her honor, and thus her life, would be over.

All will be fine, she reminded herself for the millionth time, if she could get to London and quickly secure a husband. That was about her only hope. Apart from running away to America.

Morgan rested her head against the seat back. There was no way she could survive in America. She was no more suited for living on her own than she was suited to be the Queen of England. She sighed. No, she was trapped smack dab between two vastly different worlds. Not born an aristocrat, and not born a farmer. She would have to go with her most obvious choice of escape...marriage.

To accomplish that she would need to take her studies very seriously, for she was severely lacking in some of the finer skills expected of a lady. Her needlepoint was subpar, her musical talents were mediocre at best, and her dancing was deplorable. She required desperate help. Thankfully, her aunt had already hired instructors. Morgan could embark on her education as soon as they arrived in London.

At least she was pretty. Or rather, that is what her mother and Bertrice claimed. Roderick's friends had confirmed this ideology when they raked her over with hungry, roving eyes. As disconcerting as it was, Morgan assumed that at least the feeling of being basically undressed by a man's gaze meant one was not altogether unappealing.

Still, she was not the ideal bon ton beauty. As her stepbrother had crudely pointed out, she had the body of a 'doxy' and no 'proper' London gentlemen would find her desirable as a wife.

She knew she was unfashionably curvy for being only eighteen years old. Morgan did not know what a paramour's body looked like, but she suspected the rogue knew what he was talking about.

Morgan continued to mentally tick off her physical attributes and failures. She was of medium height, with good skin, but her fiery auburn hair was just as unfashionable as her overly developed figure. She looked *too* Scottish, another of Roderick's claims. Her shapely legs were probably her best feature, but she could not exactly flaunt those about town. All in all, Morgan suspected she was average— much like her lot in life.

She looked out the window and was pulled sharply from her reverie. The first glimpses of the city were coming into view. Her mouth fell open. This was nothing like her little village town.

Morgan was immediately captivated with the bustling landscape. People darted everywhere, moving in and out of the impressive stone buildings that seemed to grow right out of the ground, as though they had been rooted in the soil for centuries.

As the carriage ambled along, the practical and more rudimentary exteriors began to give way to newer, more artistic detail, each delicate carving of the craftsman's tool telling of the fortune that had gone into the beautiful homes. Extravagant entryways now stared down at them, like imposing guard dogs questioning their intrusion and silently judging their worth. It was both intimidating and exquisite.

The coach hit a bump, jostling Bertrice and her mother from their slumber.

"Oh, Mother!" Morgan exclaimed. "You can practically feel the city breathing, can you not? It is as if every individual heartbeat on these streets is joining together to make up one gigantic beast." She clapped her gloved hands enthusiastically. "This city, London, is where I am meant to be."

She looked back at the two older women sitting speechless across from her and smiled. "This beast of a city is our savior!"

II

*H*er gaze followed the morning light as it crawled across her bedroom floor, lighting the fine silver threads of the oriental carpet so that each strand seemed to come to life, dancing before her.

Morgan glanced over at the grandfather clock. She really should get out of bed. She had been awake for an hour now but every time she tried to rise the same results were yielded. The warmth of the linen kept pulling her back into its soft, snuggly embrace.

She gave it one more attempt and pushed the blankets off. The chill in the air was all the prompting she needed to hurry herself over to the bell pull and ring for Bertrice. Teeth chattering, she donned a robe. Despite the frigid London morning, Morgan could not recall the last time she had slept so soundly. She supposed not feeling the need to lock and prop furniture against her bedroom door at night had a large part to do with that.

She padded over to the wardrobe and perused her limited gown selection. She could wear the traveling dress from yesterday again, or the day dress intended for high tea gatherings. *Curse her evil stepfather.*

He had not even allowed any new gowns to be made for her

9

season in London. Her jaw set in aggravation as she recalled his hateful words to her mother over the subject. "Let your sister buy them. It is the least she can do considering you came with such a pitiful dowry."

Morgan pulled down the yellow tea dress. At least it would serve perfectly since the only thing on her calendar today was *tea...*

The sudden reminder snapped into her mind like the cracking of a whip. Eloise, the young girl next door and Morgan's very first visitor, was set to join her for tea today. She looked back over at the clock. *In fifteen minutes!*

She squeaked and hurried to the bed, discarding the robe and her nightgown faster than she could have imagined possible. A knock fell on her door just as she slid her day shift over her naked body.

"Come in!" she called as she stepped into her skirts.

Bertrice entered, quickly assessed the situation and gasped. "Tea!"

"I forgot." Morgan turned over the fastening of stays to her nimble-fingered maid.

"I as well," Bertrice confessed in her thick Irish accent. "The duchess's house runs much faster than the earl's. I feel as though I am running around like a chicken with me head cut off."

Morgan chuckled at the colorful analogy. "I suppose we will both have to get accustomed to the new pace." She shimmied into the bodice and turned for Bertrice to button up the back. "Less we find ourselves headless."

Morgan was thrilled at the opportunity to make a friend. She did not have any at the earl's estate. She smiled happily at the petite young lady sitting beside her on the sofa.

Eloise had arrived for tea an hour ago and Morgan could say without pause that she was positively delightful. Her new friend was a pretty girl with blonde hair, blue eyes, and dainty bone structure; the perfect example of what an English beauty should be. To Eloise's surprising credit, the young beauty seemed completely unaware of her lovely appearance. This made Morgan curious if most debutantes were innocently unknowledgeable. Or, if Eloise had simply not had any putrid step-relations filling her ears with nasty appraisals.

Eloise had a spunky sense of humor to boot, keeping Morgan jubilantly engaged. For the most part, their conversation centered around one main subject: Eloise's new dancing master. Apparently, the man was an Adonis and poor Eloise could not concentrate a whit on the patterns when in dance frame with him. She finally stopped chattering on with an unladylike huff.

"Maybe you need a new dancing master?" Morgan offered.

Her new friend looked at her like she had just spewed tea from her nose. "Heavens, no! He is too wonderful to look at. And, the best dancing master in the city." Eloise added the last with a measuring nod.

"Well, then..." Morgan smiled over the rim of her teacup. "Perhaps you can simply be bad at dancing and insist your mother employ him more often."

Eloise wagged a raspberry scone in the air. "Now that is a marvelous idea!"

"I daresay you may need a lesson every day until you get your two left feet working properly."

"For three hours a session. Until he falls madly in love with me." Eloise popped the scone in her mouth and leaned back into the sofa, contemplating the idea more thoroughly as she chewed.

"I foresee a proposal at the end of this story." Morgan reclined back, joining her new friend in her fanciful daydream. She had not been this carefree in years. It felt good to simply be a girl enjoying the company of another girl. No pretenses around them. No parental or societal demands. No mocking, hateful men...

Morgan rolled her head to the side to look at Eloise. "Jane Austen would be envious."

"If only we were but characters in a marvelous novel," Eloise's voice grew more wistful. "How nice it would be to flirt unmercifully with whomever one chose, regardless of rank."

And there was the reality of it. The pin to the balloon. The reminder that their lives were not their own, and that fanciful daydreams only lived within the pages of great fictional books.

Morgan's mother was living proof. Without society dictating the path, her mother would not have felt obligated to marry Lord Vistmont. And Morgan would not be running like a scared hare from her fox of a stepbrother, willing to marry the first kind man she came across, regardless of love. Maybe she could land a tolerable older man who would not live long.

She looked up from that depressing thought and found Eloise newly rearranged on the sofa and boring a hole through Morgan's forehead with her stare. "Where did you drift off to?"

"Sorry." Morgan sat up straight again. "Reality just got the better of me." She pasted a smile on her face. "Now, back to your troublesome dance instructor. If you really cannot focus—"

"Logistics,'" Eloise interrupted playfully.

Both women laughed. *It felt good to laugh.*

The parlor door burst open, and Morgan's aunt stomped in, breaking the mood like the sinking of a ship, and wearing a look that could curdle milk.

"I cannot believe the woman is having her blasted party in two weeks. Two weeks!" She glowered, waving about a cream-colored envelope in her hand as she began to prowl the parlor like a caged bear. "She knows it will take more than two weeks' time for me to get you ready for your debut!" The duchess drew her face up so tight, Morgan feared she might pop that unsightly orange turban right off her head.

"You can hire my dancing master, Sir Frederick," Eloise offered helpfully.

Morgan's new friend quickly looked down as the dragon— formerly known as the Duchess Vandicamp—swiveled her head and stared pointblank at her, turban wobbling dangerously.

"Harrumph..." The duchess looked down her nose. "Sir Frederick will not do at all, dear child." She threw up an exasperated hand, either to make a point or summoning God, Morgan was not quite sure, before continuing. "Granted, he has trained most of the bon ton. However, I want a bigger fish other than that boy."

Her aunt continued to pace. "My niece needs the very best...not just in London, but in the world!"

Morgan sucked in a breath and held it. What was the woman thinking? She was not a princess. She was a mere viscount's daughter and stepdaughter to an earl. Morgan wondered if her aunt had been at the brandy already this morning. She looked for signs other than her aunt's words to offer proof of inebriation, which would provide a viable excuse for the duchess's sudden madness.

"Ah ha, I have it!" Lady Vandicamp stopped her assault on the carpet and plopped down on the settee across from Morgan and Eloise, looking back and forth between them.

"The woman is only doing this to get back at me. Lady Printmose," the duchess continued. "She and I have been rivals ever since we made our debut together, and I, of course, shined brighter than she did. Thus, allowing me to secure the first marriage offer... from a duke, no less. Now..."

Lady Vandicamp bobbed her head curtly, a gesture meant to summarize Morgan from toe to head. "Dear Morgan will outshine that hoyden of a niece Lady Printmose plans on shackling to some poor, unsuspecting man."

Eloise twisted a napkin so furiously in her lap that Morgan thought her new friend might rip the innocent material in two. "Lady Rosewood will be attending the ball?" she timidly asked.

Morgan was lost. Who was Lady Rosewood, and why did an old— a very, very old—rivalry have anything to do with Morgan and her apparent need for the best dance instruction in the world? She was just opening her mouth to ask when her mother walked in.

"Helen." The duchess smiled, ignoring Eloise's question. "I have a wonderful plan. I know just who will help us with Morgan."

"I am sorry, Father, I am not sure I heard you correctly. Please say that last part again." Edward half growled, hoisting himself onto his elbows to stare at his father sitting in a Louie XIV chair beside his bed.

His father smiled, the right side of his lip pulling artfully up into the characteristic family trait of amusement. "I believe you heard me just fine. But we will go with the idea that you might still be too foxed to focus if you insist."

"Did you really come here to torture me? I thought I was your favorite?" Edward fell back into his goose down pillows and flung his forearm across his eyes.

"Merely a favor. Besides, I have it on good authority that the girl in question is quite comely."

Edward could hear his father stand and the curtains drawing open. He did not need to open his eyes to see that the Duke was smiling as he did so. *Of course, he was.*

He covered his face with an overstuffed pillow and cursed. "I have ruined more than my share of young ladies this year, Father. I am at my quota, so please..."

A loud knock came from his door. Edward sat up, ready to respond with a well-delivered tongue lashing for whoever else dared rouse him from his slumber. A second time.

Before he could get the words out, his older brother, Perkin, entered and made a face. "My word! Brother...are you brewing ale in here?" He waved off the stench.

Edward sat up and glared at his intrusive relatives. "What do you want? Come to offer me more challenges?" Where the hell was his blasted butler, and why was the deuced man allowing visitors to roam his house? "Boswell!" he shouted.

"Well, I guess, yes. I have news of something you will most likely

14

find distasteful," Perkin said as he kicked a pair of Edward's favorite Hessians out of the way. "Where is your damned valet?"

"Dismissed, just like my butler is about to be. Now please stop abusing my boots and get to your point."

"I thought you sacked him last week?"

His father gave a brisk chuckle. "I thought you let him go twice last month?"

Edward narrowed his eyes. "The damned man's like lice. He keeps finding his way back to further irritate me. I must have been downright rotten in a past life to deserve such insubordinate help in this one."

Perkin grinned. "Ah, a former life, is it? I daresay you earned him in this one."

Edward reached for a pillow and flung it at his brother, who dodged it effortlessly.

"Davenport has arrived in town," Perkin said matter-of-factly, his smile replaced with an unflappable stillness that never boded well for the listener.

And just like that, in true Perkin fashion, the proverbial water bucket had been doused on Edward's head. The room became quiet as everyone allowed the comment to take hold. Davenport—Edward's childhood nemesis—was in London. *Why?*

Last Edward had heard, the man had married, was running his father's estate, and was making a killing off the sale of cotton. Edward shook his head to think clearly. The day was turning into a disaster before it had even started.

"He arrived last night." Perkin lifted a pair of tossed trousers with the end of his walking stick, as if he were hoisting a snake.

"Stop interrogating my clothing, Perkin." He glared at his nosy brother, who just smiled in return. "Where is he staying?"

The door burst open with such vigor Edward feared it might come unhinged. All three men swiveled their heads toward the entry where Greyland, their little sister stood, looking as if barging into a man's bedroom was a completely acceptable means of entering someone else's home. An earl's home, no less!

Edward opened his mouth to chastise her...and closed it. There was no point with her.

She smiled brightly, and rushed in, plopping down on the end of his bed. "I need one of you to have a child!" she stated simply, looking from brother to brother as if she had just asked for a second cup of tea.

Both Perkin and Edward stared, dumbstruck, at their sister.

A fifth voice from the hallway entered the now overcrowded bedchamber. "She means she wishes to have a cousin for little Tristan to play with." Alexander, Edward's brother in-law, offered as he walked in and smiled down at his wife.

"Greyland, sweetheart," Perkin began, as Edward sank back into the covers, wishing for death. "We have been over this. I am much too busy with Parliament to entertain the idea of marriage, and Edward, well..." He waved his hand in a sweeping, dismissive motion, as if the room itself was justification. "Surely you would not wish this on another woman." The corners of his brother's mouth twitched. "Besides, Tristan has a lovely older sister to play with."

Greyland frowned. "Annabelle is almost six years older and quite the lady. She is losing her interest in playing in the mud. Tristan needs another boy to romp around with."

Edward glared at his older brother. "Perhaps if I had a wife, half the free world would not see fit to ambush my bed chambers unannounced at such an ungodly hour." He fixed his eyes on his sister. "So, you do not just require a child, but a male child. To play with my nephew?"

Her green eyes lit up excitedly. "If that is not too much trouble."

"Greyland, love." Alex finally decided to step in. "This would be the perfect definition of placing the cart before the horse. Edward and Perkin do not have wives, nor do they want one."

Perkin chuckled. "And, even if one of us was to marry, I daresay children take at least nine months to arrive after the concep—"

"I think we understand the science." Richard cut in, clearly uncomfortable with discussing what went on in the marriage bed with his daughter in the room, even if she were the only one of his children to have borne one.

Edward sat up and waved them off. "At least turn around so I can finish getting dressed. I am sure it would be too much to ask that you all remove yourselves to the downstairs parlor?"

"Only if you hurry." Greyland persisted, completely undeterred from her course. "Tristan is growing like a weed, and we need to expand the family quickly for solid bonds to form."

She smiled sweetly and allowed her husband to escort her to the door, before turning back with her little nose scrunched up. "And Edward, open a window will you."

Before Edward could respond to his little sister's sarcasm, her husband pushed her gently out of the room. Perkin followed them out.

His father paused at the door, his eyes dancing with elderly gallantry. "My offer is starting to look marvelous by comparison. We will travel over together." The Duke's warm tenor voice wrapped around the corner as he headed on down the hall. "I will pick you up at noon."

Once the door shut, Edward cursed and threw the cover from his legs. Why could he not have a normal family that ignored each other like the rest of English society? He grumbled as he searched for where his butler might have placed his breeches. He really should not have dismissed his valet, but when he had walked in the night before and found the man wearing nothing but his neatly tied cravat, Edward had seen enough...literally.

In hindsight, he really should have thought better of hiring a man his brother-in-law had referred, especially when Alexander made the recommendation while they were both well into their cups—and on April Fools' Day.

Edward rolled his eyes as he rummaged through a pile of clothes. Thinking back on it, not one of his smarter moments. Alexander had said the man had a "familiarity" with clothing that could not be rivaled. *Familiarity*, indeed!

Alexander, the Duke of Ravenswood had never let Edward live

down the night they first met over two years ago, when Edward had cheated the man at cards, engaged him in a bar room brawl in the middle of White's, the gentlemen's club, and threatened him with a morning duel. The blasted man really held onto a grudge for far too long, he mused.

Edward chuckled softly, thinking back on his and his brother-in-law's first meeting as he located a pair of dove-colored breeches and pulled them on. Despite their volatile introductions, the two had become family. More than family. They had become friends, and Edward could not ask for a better husband to his sister, or father to his nephew and niece.

His mirth slipped from his face as he straightened and caught sight of his refection in the mirror. He stared at the grizzly, white scar that ran the length of his chest diagonally from collarbone to hip. The silent reminder of what he had gone through to save his sister from her would-be killer, Alexander's Uncle Derrick.

A year ago, from yesterday, Derrick had kidnapped Greyland and then thrown her into a raging river to drown. Edward had almost lost his own life that night as well. But in the end, it was Alexander's uncle that that drawn his last breath...on the end of Edward's sword.

He pulled a shirt over his head, his muscles tight with a familiar unease. He still could not look at his scar without hearing Derrick's deranged laughter bouncing off the trees like a curse all those nights ago. It was the last sound Edward had heard before the thunderous roar of the river consumed everything else and his world went blind with rage.

Thank God, Alexander had reached Greyland in time and had been able to get her to shore, despite the bullet wound to his own arm. Perkin had taken over then and rushed her back to Greenshire Castle where their father had gotten the physician's help they all required to survive the night.

Correction, Edward mentally amended his earlier sentiment as he moved toward the door of his bedroom. *Thank God, his family was not "normal."*

IV

*M*organ, having just returned from a fitting with the best modiste London had to offer, followed her mother and the duchess up the steps to the front door of her aunt's house. The experience with the rail-thin French dressmaker had been long and humbling, but Morgan had survived being poked, prodded, and discussed at length regarding her every flaw and redeemable asset.

Madam LeMore had started the morning off by demanding that Morgan burn her yellow tea gown she had arrived in. Apparently, the garment was out of fashion, and the color made her look like the underside of a toad. Morgan was not entirely sure she recalled having ever seen the underside of a toad up close. She imagined they looked quite slimy and pale.

Amphibians aside, Morgan took the criticism in stride and mentally made notes. It seemed golds were a must for her skin color. Oranges and burnt reds would be nice as well and her debut dress was to be a warm champagne color that would highlight Morgan's red-hair (apparently not as unfashionable as Roderick had claimed).

Morgan would have at least three new gowns by the end of the week, and she could not be more thrilled for it. Her aunt reminded her of her luck, too. *A lot.* About every street corner, the duchess would restate how fortunate they were to have gotten an audience with the famous dressmaker on such short notice. Morgan and her mother made sure to thank Lady Vandicamp profusely for all her efforts. *And her purse.*

By the time the coach pulled up the drive at Grosvenor Square, Morgan just wanted to take a nap. It was tiresome work being a grateful pin-cushion. She climbed the stone steps behind the duchess and her mother ready to take her leave when they got inside. But before her foot had time to land on the last step, a butler stepped forward and handed her a calling card.

Morgan read it, smiled, and went straight to the sitting room where she found Eloise, a slice of lemon cake in both hands.

"I am so jealous!" the small blonde exclaimed once they were alone. "Have you any idea how lucky you are?"

Morgan let out a long overdue sigh as she plopped down next to her new friend. "Yes, I have been informed. Madam LeMore is the best, and I am akin to a toad in the color yellow."

"A toad!" Eloise gasped. "Did she really compare you to that?"

"At least she was being honest. I will take her assessment gladly." Morgan grinned. "Especially if she can get me looking half as fashionable as you."

"You think me fashionable?" Eloise asked, genuinely shocked.

"Oh, Eloise, surely you have been told petite blondes are the fancy?" She smiled, seeing the blush wash over her friend's cheeks.

"Well, I have heard, but compared to you, I look mousy and not nearly as...dramatic. Why, your dance card will stay full the entire season," Eloise said affirmatively.

"Dramatic?" Morgan considered the descriptive. There were certainly less appealing words. She rather liked *dramatic*. It made her think of something exotic. Or dangerous.

Eloise nodded. "Yes, dramatic. You do not look like you will blend into the wallpaper. Instead, you look like you could compete with it."

Morgan considered her new friend for a moment. "That is probably the nicest thing anyone has ever said to me." She smiled, then tried to look serious. "Now, do not ever call yourself mousy. You are lovely, whereas..."

Morgan leaned forward, taking a lemon cake for herself. "I am afraid my look evokes a rather...less than pleasant reaction in men."

"Unpleasant?" Eloise giggled. "Well, if the new definition of *unpleasant* gets the sort of appreciation that handsome footman bestowed on you when you entered, I will gladly adopt the term."

Morgan shook her head, grinning as she relaxed back into the soft cushions of the sofa. Perry, the cherub-faced, flaxen-haired footman in question, had not been subtle in his attention of her. Especially when he thought no one was looking. According to her dressing maid, the young man was considered quite the catch. And apparently, not overly insecure. A trait Bertrice feared would only end badly if he did not stop ogling the duchess's niece.

Although, it was now whispered amongst the staff that the handsome Perry found Morgan comely, he had not dared speak to her. Just appeared, as if by magic, everywhere Morgan had gone over the past two days.

Morgan knew she should be offended, downright incensed that a lower class man would dare think anything of the sort about her. But she couldn't. Truth was, she was flattered. The thought that she had such an effect on a man as to render him shyly mute, and not barbarically dangerous, simply made her hopeful. Maybe she could find a gentleman that would appreciate her and be kind to her.

"Now, Eloise, what would Sir Frederick say if he heard such a thing?" Morgan teased.

Eloise waved a dismissive hand. "Frederick does not hold a candle to the dancing master your aunt acquired for you."

Morgan sat up so quickly she nearly fell off the settee. How could she have forgotten her biggest concern for the day? Her newly acquired dancing master!

"What do you know of him? All they told me was that he was an earl, but what earl would take time out of their schedule to offer dancing lessons? And then..." She leaned in, her voice barely a whisper. "When I came downstairs last night to get a book from the library, I overheard my mother and aunt talking. They said he had killed someone and was related to a king! And his father has even reclaimed the ancestral name and many titles from the Queen herself."

Morgan rattled on, her thoughts coming faster than her mouth could keep up with. "Is it true that he and his sister taught the Queen the Viennese waltz after having demonstrated the scandalous dance at a royal ball?" When she drew in a large breath, Eloise burst out in laughter.

"How on earth did you manage to keep all that in?" Eloise's eyes twinkled with unfettered amusement. "We wasted all that talk on Madam LeMore. I just assumed you already knew all about the earl."

"Yes. I mean, no. I only know enough to be puzzled beyond reason." Morgan clasped her friend's hands. "Tell me everything you know."

"In that case..." Eloise grinned, clearly delighted with her task. "Yes, on all accounts. Except it was the older Kingston brother who danced the Viennese waltz with his sister the night of the ball. Greyland, the sister, who is now the Duchess of Ravenswood, is considered to be the most beautiful woman the bon ton has ever seen." Eloise lifted a challenging eyebrow. "Not a fashionable blonde, I might add."

"The older brother, the Duke of Dessmark—yes, named Perkin, for the infamous York bloodline—also taught the dance the next day to the Queen and her lord," Eloise said, tapping her finger to her chin and casting her eyes upwards, as if trying hard to remember.

A total bluff, Morgan mused. Of course, she remembered. She probably knew these stories better than her scripture.

"And yes, the Earl of Wellington has killed a man. But only to save his sister when the Duke of Ravenswood's evil uncle kidnapped her and tried to drown her by shoving her into a raging river."

Eloise sat back. "Oh, and the earl is the most desirable man in London. Aside from his brother. Did I leave anything out?" She grinned.

At Eloise's first "yes," Morgan's mouth had fallen agape. And she had sat there throughout her friend's entire monologue holding that same unrefined pose. She finally brought her lips together when Eloise began to laugh anew.

"Stop laughing! The man is coming here to teach me the deuced waltz in less than an hour, and I daresay I am about to suffer from a case of the vapors." Morgan stood and began to pace.

"Oh, do not fret, the earl is very easy on the eyes. And has only ruined the names of four or five ladies this last year. Rather harmless, really." Eloise continued to find utter joy in Morgan's predicament. "You did say you wanted an adventure in London."

Morgan looked aghast at her giddy friend, wishing she had never said any such thing. The two had spent the whole day together yesterday and had shared many, if not all, of their deepest dreams. However, a womanizing rake of an earl was not the sort of *adventure* she had meant. She needed a kind, loving man to save her—not a reckless, dangerous one who might try and ruin her. When Morgan had mentioned an adventure, the most daring thing she had imagined was placing a wager on a horse race.

"I thought you liked me?" She tried for her most wounded appeal.

Eloise relented in her torture. "I am just playing. Why, I would have already swooned to death by now. You are considerably more composed than I would be under the circumstances."

"That is not comforting." Morgan exhaled a breath she had not realized she had been holding. Why on earth would her aunt and mother allow such a man to instruct her? Her palms began to sweat as the worst possible scenarios began to play out in her head.

The body of a doxy. Her stepbrother's words echoed in her self-conscious. *Only good for warming a man's bed.*

Morgan wiped her hands down the front of her skirt. She did not want to give his words power, but she could not forget them. What if he was right? If this earl was anything like Roderick, Morgan would be like catnip tossed at a tomcat.

Morgan shook her head. She could not afford the risk the earl might fancy her the way Roderick did. Why, a man of that stature *just thinking* indecent thoughts would be enough to start tongues wagging if he planted the wrong impression of her. Her name would be marred before she even stepped foot into polite society.

"As I said, he is one of the bon ton's best catches...If he could be caught, but he cannot be. Or rather, *will not* be. Oh, who knows, maybe he will take one look at your unique beauty and fall at your feet." As if to emphasize her point, Eloise dropped her gaze to Morgan's bosom.

Morgan's heart sank. Even her newfound friend was not oblivious to the issues at hand. "This is just a disaster waiting to happen."

Unless... An idea popped into her head. If she could make her lesson with the earl as unmemorable as possible, he might completely overlook her.

"Clothing!" Morgan exclaimed. *Never offer a cat catnip and it would continue to wander on down the alley.* "We must find the most modest gown in the house at once."

"What do you know that you did not impart to your brother? Regarding Davenport being in town." Richard Kingston swirled the brandy in his glass, admiring the amber-colored liquor for a moment before looking up to fix his gaze on his eldest child.

Perkin sat on the other side of Richard's mahogany desk. One long leg had been tossed negligently across his opposite knee as he reclined in the high back leather chair. "I have asked two of my best men to make inquiries around town. Thus far, his only nefarious intentions are against his own pocketbook. He is spending an exorbitant amount of coin on gaming and women. Seems marriage has done little to change him."

Perkin gave a short, mirthless laugh as he shook his head. "However, bad judgment and piss-poor money management aside, it will only be a matter of time before he and Edward cross paths. Lord help us when they do."

That last statement could not be more simply put. Richard's family and the Davenports hated each other. Jonny Davenport was, and always had been, a bully. A tyrant who had taken a great liking to beating up Richard's youngest son when they were children. Edward, being three years younger than Jonny, had been no match for the larger boy.

However, boys grow up. Edward came into his own strength the summer he turned fourteen. His natural athletic prowess, towering stature, and willingness to fight, made for a formidable combination. It only took a couple scuffles for Davenport to realize he was now outmatched. Of course, insecure cowards rarely give up their tormenting ways and Jonny had soon found a new target. Greyland.

Richard's thoughts twisted sharply, the way only a father's could at the memory that came next, hearing his baby girl scream. A shiver chased up his spine as he relived the helpless, desperate feeling of sprinting toward the sound, Perkin at his side. Not knowing what they would find on the other side of the stable.

When they rounded the barn that fateful day, they found Greyland scrambling to her feet, clothing disheveled and covered in mud as if she had been tossed to the ground. Just a few feet away lay Davenport, beaten senseless by Richard's middle child.

Gripped in a blind rage, it had taken both Richard's and Perkin's full strength to remove Edward from atop Jonny Davenport's prone body. The neighbor boy was nearly unrecognizable. Had they arrived only a couple swings later, Edward would have likely killed him. With nothing but his bare fists.

To this day, the horrific image of his son thrashing the other boy within an inch of his life still weighed heavy on Richard's mind. While he could very well understand the emotion Edward must have felt when he discovered Davenport attempting to manhandle Greyland, he could not relate to the vacant look residing in his son's eyes as he stood over the other man, delivering blow after bone-crushing blow. It was as if another person had taken over. A person who felt nothing.

From that day forth, everyone knew better than to provoke the middle Kingston sibling. Edward could turn from fun-loving, carefree charmer to something utterly dangerous in a matter of seconds. Especially if someone threatened his family. As he had proven again last year with Alexander's uncle.

While Richard had not been present for Derrick's murder, he had seen the body the next day. Edward had not simply killed the other man. He had eviscerated him. The amount of strength it had taken, combined with the overkill, proved that Edward's demons had not yet been exorcised. They were just under the surface, waiting.

And that might be what kept Richard up the most at night. Not the knowledge that his son was inclined to bouts of blind violence, but that he had never discovered what it was that made Edward harbor such insurmountable rage. The affable young man smiled the warmest of anyone in a room, but it was a mask. A façade to hide the darkness that dwelled in the unseen recesses of his mind.

Richard wished the boys' mother was still alive. Perhaps she would have known how best to guide their middle child. Though she never said it, Richard always felt Edward had bonded to his mother in a way unlike the other two children.

Greyland looked identical to their mother Elizabeth, but Edward was most like her in personality. Kindred spirits. Whereas, Perkin was most like him. Richard felt a familiar smile tug at the corners of his mouth as his thoughts landed on each of them. *His blessings.*

He lifted the brandy to his lips and looked at the regal blond man sitting across from him. It still astounded him that the once gangly boy had grown into such a remarkable man. Elizabeth would be proud. Past and present troubles aside, and there had been more than their fair share of troubles, all their children had grown into astonishing adults.

Greyland, with her natural wit and timeless beauty, had swept London by storm just a little over a year ago. It had not taken the infamous Dark Duke, Lord Ravenswood, but a day to decide she must be his. Theirs was a true love match and Richard could not be happier for them. They had adopted Annabelle and then been blessed with Tristan, the spitting image of his father. *But...*Greyland would always be a daddy's girl. That thought made Richard's heart swell with pride.

Perkin had risen very high in the Queen's court during the past year. He was, and had always been, the most ambitious of them all. It actually frightened Richard at times how smart his eldest child was. He only hoped that ambition would one day be curbed enough to enjoy the simpler aspects of life. Such as love.

Richard's mind came full circle back to Edward. His charismatic middle child had yet to find his place. He was neither driven by love as Greyland was, nor driven by determination as Perkin was. Although Edward would argue he craved both of those traits. He loved to drink and was highly determined to enjoy the affections of loose women. Richard shook his head as a chuckle rose up in his throat.

"Father." Perkin pulled him from his musings. "I am going to France in the morning. I will be gone for a few weeks. I would like to take the White Rose for the voyage."

Richard followed Perkin's glance down at the crystal glass in his hand.

"The Queen needs some information. Melbrooke chose me."

"Did he now?"

Richard did not trust the Queen's chief advisor. Never had. And the suspicion went both ways. Melbrooke, after discovering *who* their ancestors were, had made it no secret at court that he disapproved of the Queen's acceptance of Richard and his family.

Perkin nodded. "Do not worry; I will keep my ears and eyes open. Thomas and Dalton are going with me."

Richard stared at his oldest son. Perkin had included that last part in an effort to ease his concerns. It did not, but he played along.

"I am surprised Bella is letting Thomas leave. After all, they have a new baby."

Perkin grinned, causing only the right side of his mouth to hitch up the same way his brother's did. The famous Kingston grin. Women seemed to find this a powerfully attractive trait. One that Perkin did not abuse. Edward, on the other hand, took full advantage of the coy smile and employed it unmercifully.

"I believe she threatened him with various medieval forms of dismemberment and torture if he did not return in a month's time." Perkin laughed. "Bella and the baby are staying with Greyland and Alex while Thomas is away."

Richard chuckled, thinking of the petite Bella inflicting any kind of torture on her giant husband. Bella and his daughter had become best friends as soon as they had met and realized they both shared a similar disposition toward avoiding all things proper. Alexander and Thomas were already childhood friends, which was an additional plus.

Perkin had quickly found himself in their fold but had become closest to Lord Dalton Ashlown. Which made complete sense given both men's extreme need for order and discipline. The two had been dubbed "the chess set dukes" by the bon ton, as both men were respected for their intelligence. Yet, like opposing pieces on a chessboard, they had stark differences in their temperaments.

Perkin was personable and outgoing with a lighter, brighter personality. Lord Ashlown was more withdrawn, widely considered to be rather dangerous and mysterious. Richard had to admit the nickname fit them to a T.

Edward had likewise formed a strong friendship with Henry, Earl of Rockafetch, Alex's younger half-brother, who was also an attractive bachelor and always on the lookout for a grand time. The two had their own nickname whispered about by the ladies. *The Devil Duo.* Richard smiled again...yet another well-suited description.

Bella, Thomas, Henry, and Dalton were always around, and Richard considered them all his children at this point. It bothered him greatly that Perkin, Thomas, and Dalton were the ones chosen to go, but he knew there were no better candidates. Mayhap he was overthinking it. He forced a smile and glanced back at Perkin.

"I suppose you know exactly where I will go first in order to find out what this mission is about if you choose not to tell me," he said evenly, leaving no room for escape. He knew his son would not bring the Queen's name into this conversation, at least not past what little he had already stated.

Perkin met his gaze. "There seems to be a large group of men who have invested in a new trading company that is dealing in slaves," he stated without preamble. *Always* right to the point.

Richard leaned back and steepled fingers. He hated slave traders. His distaste for the business was one of the reasons he had left New Orleans, taking his children with him. He hated the idea of making one's living off the sale of human flesh or their unpaid work, and he detested the thought of Perkin getting involved in such a thing, even peripherally.

Those men were ruthless, and they employed only the most savage of pirates to captain and man their vessels. Perkin would need to take the White Rose indeed. She was the fastest ship in their fleet, rumored to be the fastest in all of Europe. Armed with four cannons and quiet as a stalking cat, the ship was deadly.

He weighed his words carefully, knowing they would not make a difference. Perkin's loyalty to England was as impenetrable as Richard's. Besides, once his eldest made up his mind, there was no point arguing against it.

"Just keep your head down and remember not to ruffle Tiny's feathers. He is the best and most temperamental cook we have."

Richard smirked, knowing Perkin was all too familiar with the ship's larger-than-life Italian chef. The man was a master at making do with what he had and keeping rations from running out on overly long voyages. Tiny was also a cutthroat at heart and would be a valuable fighter if their ship should come under attack.

Richard had outfitted the whole vessel with the most loyal and roughest ruffians he could find. He had been in the trade business for too long not to know that a ship's worth was only as good as the men standing to protect it. Knowing that Perkin would travel on the White Rose made Richard feel marginally better.

"I will pen a letter to Captain Smithy letting him know to prepare the rig."

Perkin, recognizing the dismissal, began to rise. "Thank you, father. I will keep you abreast on what I uncover along the way."

Richard stood as well and embraced his son. "I will keep an eye on your brother."

Perkin nodded and gave Richard a wry grin. "Can never have enough eyes where Edward is concerned." He chuckled and turned swiftly, strolling across the marble floor.

Once at the double doors, Perkin looked back over his shoulder. "Do not worry." The commanding tone in his eldest son's voice reminded Richard of himself. He felt his heart swell anew with pride.

Richard smiled. "Tell me that again when you are a father."

Perkin merely sketched an amused brow before inclining his head and rounding the corner.

"One hour." Edward's words were deliberate and finalizing, even authoritarian to his own ears.

"Pardon me?" His father, Richard Kingston, His Grace, the nineteenth Duke of York, and a man you never gave orders to, paused mid-step and looked fixedly at him.

"Nothing. Just woolgathering."

"Earls do not woolgather, Edward," his father said before he resumed his pace.

Edward took the last step up to the Duchess Vandicamp's front door. "I will try to remember that," he grumbled. "During what is sure to be the waste of a perfectly good day."

"Earls do not make unintelligible rumblings in their throats either; try to keep up," Richard said as a very enthusiastic young footman raced up the opposite side of the arched staircase and opened the door for them, the most delighted expression pasted across his face.

Richard nodded to the entirely too pretty lad, and then addressed him by name. "Good evening, Perry."

The footman smiled, all gleaming white teeth. Edward doffed his hat as he passed and was promptly stabbed smack-dab in the ear canal with an ice pick. At least that was the effect generated from the screeching shriek that swept the cavernous and acoustically sound room like a cannonball drilling through the hull of a ship.

Edward shook his head to try and stop the ringing. His father continued on, seemingly hale, toward the source of the sound.

"Your Grace, I am so very happy you are here." A woman cooed, thankfully in a lower pitch than that of a banshee, from the top of the stairs.

Edward, mostly recovered, looked up to find an eccentrically dressed older lady, built like a cauldron, bobbing down the stairs. She wore a ridiculously tall, lime-colored turban atop her head that teetered dangerously with each step, as if the material might be contemplating suicide. And she was talking still, a seamless flow, barely pausing to draw air. Jeweled rings adorned each of her plump fingers and when they caught the light, which was happening a lot since their hostess seemed to be unable to speak a word without fluttering her hands, they nearly blinded everyone in the room.

Lady Vandicamp was certainly...*expressive.* Edward's father continued toward her, across the checkered black and white marble floor, a genuine smile of greeting on his face. Edward followed, still not sure when his father and this larger-than-life woman had met.

"It is so good to see you again." Richard finally got a word in. "This is Edward, my son."

Edward bent at the waist to begin the customary greetings of polite society, which in this circumstance dictated a bow. Upon straightening, and just as he was opening his mouth to offer his own formal greeting, he was nearly yanked off his feet.

He struggled to find his footing as he was pressed firmly into the Duchess Vandicamp's ample bosom. He had no words. Literally, he could not breathe to form them. One minute, his eyes had been cast to the floor; the next, they were fighting for supremacy with a lime-green turban.

A combination of powder and musky gardenia perfume assaulted his nostrils as he was squeezed tighter still. Edward had envisioned dying in a woman's arms many times, but now, presented with the possibility of suffocation, he very much wanted to live.

"Oh, it is so nice to finally meet you, dear boy," the duchess said as she shoved him back, with nearly as much force as she had dragged him in.

Edward had never been more thankful for decent balance. He was sure a good many gently born men had found themselves flat on their ass after such a greeting

"Likewise, Your..." he began, then paused as Lady Vandicamp started circling him, her eyes raking him over from head to toe as if she were doing a tax assessment. Edward cast his father a speculative look, unsure how to proceed. To his shock, his father merely grinned back at him.

"It is likewise, a pleasure to make your acquaintance," he regained his voice. "My father has spoken of you with the highest of praises." Edward shot his father a rigid smile.

"Oh, lovely." She clasped her hands, coming back around full circle to stand in front of him. "What were they?"

"Beg pardon?"

"The praises, dear boy, what were they?" The duchess persisted tersely.

His father finally decided to come to his rescue. "Only that you are the most exciting woman in all of society." Richard smiled warmly.

Lady Vandicamp turned to the duke, sheer joy dancing in her eyes. "Oh my, Your Grace, how you do flatter." She beamed.

"Only the truth." Richard offered his arm and began leading the way down a long hall.

Edward followed, assuming his father knew where he was going and still feeling the aftershocks of ringing bells in his left ear. He might have protested obliging this favor more had he known there was going to be maiming involved. He glanced at a longcase clock.

One hour. All he had to do now was meet this drab young debutante, hope to God she would not swoon at his feet, teach her the blasted waltz, and leave to meet Henry for drinks at White's. *One hour!*

They entered an eye-popping pink and yellow parlor of which Edward was certain no color in nature resembled. While his retinas tried to adjust to the room's brightness—it had been a long time since he had occupied a space that was not dark in color and theme—Lady Vandicamp began introducing them to another woman.

"My lords, this is my sister, Lady Vistmont." She looked at Edward. "The mother of the young lady you so graciously agreed to help with today."

Edward made his introductions, not quite believing the two women were related. Lady Vistmont was a tall and lean, handsome woman, and appeared to be around the same age as the duchess. Age was about the only thing the two women had in common. Unlike her more flamboyant sister, Lady Vistmont seemed rather reserved, modestly prim.

"Thank you for helping on such short notice," Lady Vistmont said, her head inclining in a practiced way, her words even and spaced perfectly.

"My pleasure," Edward answered, gifting her one of his winning smiles. He was pleased to see it met its mark when she demurely smiled back. "I am sure your daughter is..."

"Perry!" Lady Vandicamp yelled, her voice bouncing around the room like a tossed ball, set on knocking over everything in its path. And just like that, before Edward could even contemplate the useless compliment he had been poised to deliver, the young footman appeared.

"Tell Miss Sinclair to come down and greet her tutor," the duchess ordered before heaving herself into a chair. "The earl probably has at least seven sins he needs to accomplish before dusk.

We shan't keep him tarried for too long." She finished matter-of-factly.

Edward stood speechless. There was a first. It was not that Lady Vandicamp was judging him. She was simply remarking on his nature as if she were stating an obvious fact. Like *birds needed to fly. Cows have four stomachs. Known rakes had debauchery to orchestrate.*

Edward was so taken aback by the duchess's appraisal that he almost missed the fact that the footman's eyes slanted downward in a simpering sort of besotted fashion and a wistful smile spread across his lips, right before he remembered his job and bolted from the room. *Ah ha*, so the boy had a tender for one of his mistresses. Likely the young debutante Edward was about to instruct. The day was getting more interesting by the second. At least, he would have an entertaining story for Henry later on.

What if the young debutante had feelings for the young buck as well? Now *that* would be a very entertaining little drama in the making. Star-crossed lovers. Edward mentally rubbed his hands together. If there was anything he liked more than drinking, gaming, and women, it was ferreting out a good story.

Morgan, escorted by her new puppy, also known as the footman Perry, turned around the last corner before the hallway would dump them into the parlor. The parlor that housed the duchess's newly arrived guest, and Morgan's first London challenge. *Three more steps.* She counted them out.

This was it. This was her chance to make the very best worst impression. She pulled herself up tall and sucked in a breath, ready to proceed.

That perfectly held breath came rushing out when Perry stopped so suddenly that the momentum all but slapped her in the back. He spun about to face her. "Miss Sinclair, if you don't mind me saying..." He paused, looking doubtful of his next words.

"Yes?" she said, wondering what the man had to say that was so important that he had chosen this moment to speak it.

"It is just. Well. You see...the earl has a reputation," he muttered.

Morgan smiled up at him. "I know of his reputation, and I will keep that in mind."

"I could stand just outside the door while he is teaching you the dance, if you like?"

He was still not persuaded of her safety; she liked him even more for this somehow. "That is very thoughtful. However, I am sure my aunt will need you for something more important during that time. Besides, I will have Bertrice there as chaperone."

"Of course. Capital idea!"

Perry smiled as he reached to open the door and Morgan was once again struck by how pleasing the young man truly was. Why, if he had been born to the upper class, he would surely be running the bon ton by now. On charm and appearance alone. The Earl of Wellington could not possibly have anything on young Perry.

That rationalization gave Morgan a boost of confidence regarding her first London challenge. The earl was simply a man; no less, and no more, than the footman walking beside her. The only difference was a silly title. If she could think of her dancing master as she did Perry, everything would go smoothly.

"Oh, and excellent choice of dress, Miss Sinclair." Perry nodded approvingly, interrupting her newfound plot.

Morgan smiled as the door started to open. "I told you, Perry. I have heard all about this Earl of Wellington."

A number of issues became apparent when Miss Sinclair entered the parlor. The first one being that she was not at all what Edward had been expecting. He was ready to teach a wide-eyed, unsure, overly conditioned, unbecomingly shy, bewildered, and no doubt mousy, debutante a few basics in dance.

He was not prepared to find that his student seemed to be none of those things. In only her five steps into the study, it was clear that Miss Sinclair was not some simpering wallflower. *Quite the opposite.*

She radiated a quiet confidence. There was a punctuation in her stride. A challenge in the set of her shoulders. And an unmasked intelligence lighting up her hazel eyes.

Best of all was the personality that had clearly gone into preparing her wardrobe ensemble. Lady Sinclair was either taking a page from her aunt's fashion sense, or she had dressed herself according to the company she would be keeping this day. Based on the wrinkle creasing Lady Vistmont's brow at present, it was the latter.

Miss Sinclair was prepared. She had accounted for Edward's reputation with the ladies and actively tried to camouflage and downplay any part of her that might draw his interest. Which proved all of his first observations about her were correct.

A, she was smart. B, she was confident enough to know she would seem appealing to a known cad. And C, *she had no idea who she was dealing with.*

If she thought wearing a gown six times too large would hide the luscious womanly figure underneath... she had a few more things to learn about men. Despite the yards and yards of material, she would not be fooling any hot-blooded man of the bon ton. Certainly no man with questionable morals and half an imagination.

Edward Kingston was both; very imaginative and ethically unsound. No amount of fabric could disguise the fact that this woman possessed a body as bewitching as the head of fiery hair that peaked out from under the horrific headdress she tried to hide under.

First impressions aside, the second noteworthy thing that struck Edward was the way she had been smiling at the footman when the doors had opened. She obviously had something going on with the dimple-faced Perry. Rather, innocent on her part or not, one thing was clear—the duchess's footman had eyes for Miss Sinclair. Suddenly, the previous amusement Edward sought to find in the 'star-crossed lovers' story escaped him.

"Morgan, dear, whatever are you wearing?" the duchess asked.

The third problem with Edward's mental list of issues regarding Miss Sinclair became apparent when she spoke.

"I felt this would work best for navigating the dance steps," she said, her voice poised and controlled as she spoke what he knew to be a lie.

Absolutely too alluring with its hidden seductive layers. *Entirely* too mature sounding. His mind was already undressing her. Edward blinked to get control of his wayward thoughts.

"Morgan, dear," Lady Vandicamp said, and then looked pointedly at Edward. "I assume you will be on a first name basis by the end of the lesson, so we might as well get that formality out of the way."

The duchess regarded her niece again, from head to toe this time. "This is Edward Kingston, Earl of Wellington. I need not add anything else by way of introduction, as I can see his reputation clearly precedes him."

"It is very nice to make your acquaintance." Edward nodded. "Would you like to begin?"

Good, right to the point. He congratulated himself. *Get in, and get out.* This lesson was quickly turning on him. He had expected to be bored, not transfixed. His father would kill him if he mucked this up.

Miss Sinclair smiled, and he realized issue number four... She was not merely desirable in a 'roll about the hay' way. She was *beautiful.*

Lady Vandicamp called for the young lady's maid and within seconds, Edward was being shown down the hallway.

Once in the impressive ballroom, he tried to focus on the task at hand and took an immediate interest in his surroundings. As with the parlor, this room continued the same bold and blinding colors of which the duchess was too fond. The layout was ideal for the more intricate patterns of the waltz. All pillars hugged close to the walls, making for extra room and fewer possible collisions. Always a plus if one did not accidentally crush his or her partner.

His attention was brought around to the two older women and his father as the trio abruptly bid farewell, leaving him alone with Miss Sinclair. Well, and her maid, who had already found a seat and started her needlework. Not the ideal chaperone for a man of his talents. *Issue number five.*

The large doors were drawn slowly to a close by the footman, who kept his sights leveled on Edward, an unmistakable warning to behave. Edward watched the double doors until they were *almost* completely shut. He chuckled to himself. Miss Sinclair would have *two* chaperones today after all.

He turned to face his student. "How much do you know of the waltz?"

Morgan quickly tried to cover up her blank expression with a ready smile. He had asked a question, but she had missed it. She was too lost in his unusual rolling accent and the way his mouth shaped each word before he spoke it.

"Are you familiar with the waltz?" he repeated, a tinge of impatience in his voice.

"Yes. Sorry."

She tried to focus her thoughts on the actual words coming out of his throat, not the throat itself. Her eyes drifted to his Adam's apple, the way it moved...

Drat it! She mentally chastised herself. She had wanted him to find her unworthy of sexual attention, not stupid.

"I have only danced it by myself." She might have to settle for stupid.

He studied her without responding. She should have just scribed the words 'country mouse' in rouge across her forehead. It would have gone nicely with the turban. *Mortification*. There was no better word for how she felt now, having admitted such a thing to this much too handsome man. Morgan knew she should have at least gotten Eloise to show her the basics. And why did her friend not warn her of this man's alluring drawl?

"Very well," he *finally* responded.

"Very well," she parroted back.

"Well then."

"Yes, well then."

"Let us start at the beginning."

Morgan watched him turn his back to her and stride to the edge of the ballroom. *And*, what an exquisite back it was. The man was huge! His shoulders had to be twice the width of hers. She took a moment to study the way the cut of his jacket molded to his muscles, emphasizing his powerful build, before he turned and faced her again.

The earl motioned for her to join him. Her feet felt weighted with lead as she reluctantly trudged toward him. Morgan suddenly hoped, for reasons she was not ready to explore, that she would not embarrass herself further by being an utter failure at the waltz.

When she was within arm's reach, he unexpectedly took hold of her hand. Morgan instinctively jerked it away. The reaction shocked her into an awkward silence. She immediately felt like an errant child. Or worse, a dog flinching from its master. That thought made her mad. *Roderick!* She had him to thank for this skittish impulse.

Morgan stared down at the space between them, afraid to look up and see his reaction to her unseemly response. He would think her more of a fool than he already did. He would pity her inexperience.

Was that not what she wanted? For him to pay no mind to her. To think that she was *insignificant...* If he did, would that not be in accordance to her masterful plan? She should be doing mental cartwheels right now. Instead, she was ashamed. Ashamed that she had let Roderick get so well into her head.

Morgan ventured a glance up. What she saw in her dancing master's eyes was not pity. It was disbelief. Lord Wellington was likely experiencing a royal shock of his own. Undoubtedly a first for the notorious man. If Morgan were a betting woman, she would put all her money on the notion that the earl had never in his life had a woman pull away from him.

"I need your hand to dance with you." He broke the labored silence.

"Might you ask for it next time?" she replied sharply.

He rocked back on his heels, assessing her. "I assumed," he said with clear amusement, "since this was a planned dance lesson that permission had already been granted."

The cad. Of course, he *presumed* he had the right to touch her person freely. Every woman he had ever met likely fell under his charms and leapt right into his embrace. *Well, not this woman.*

Morgan painted on what she hoped was a wry smile. "I will still need you to ask permission before touching me."

"I see," he said. "For the sake of time..." He held up his hand, palm side up. "May I have your hand?"

She lifted her hand grudgingly. He placed it in his much larger one. Morgan immediately felt a warmth spread over and through her palm at his touch. She looked curiously at their joined hands. His fingers and palm completely swallowed hers. She could feel the roughness of his skin, the strength of bones and muscle beneath it. His touch did not feel anything like Roderick's neatly manicured and clammy hands, which he used for nothing but debauchery.

Edward Wellington obviously used his hands for work. This was a man who knew physical activity and partook in it often. Morgan wondered at that. Were his hands calloused from holding back the leather reins of a willful steed? Did he mend fences, as her father used to, on his own land? Or maybe he competed in Scottish caber tossing?

That last thought, the earl heaving massive logs clad in a kilt, made her genuinely smile and she slowly lifted her gaze from his hand to his face. *My word.* She mentally staggered. The man was even more impressive up close. His square-cut jaw and straight aristocratic nose... *And those eyes...*

His eyes were a deep blue, so rich they called to mind indigo. His skin was sun-kissed—another sign he enjoyed the outdoors—and his tousled blond hair was un-styled, falling in soft waves over his brow and curling at the nape of his neck. Her fingers wanted to reach up and touch it, to see if the locks were as soft as they looked.

The earl's lips brought her soundly out of her reverie. The edges of his sensuous mouth pulled playfully into a lopsided grin. She felt as if she was on the cusp of doing the unthinkable...swooning. Just as Eloise predicted she would.

No, Morgan had been dead wrong in her naïve planning. The Earl of Wellington was nothing like the wide-eyed, guileless footman. This was a man not to be trifled with or underestimated. She was doomed!

The moment Miss Sinclair realized Edward had caught her brazenly staring, she bashfully smiled and quickly averted her eyes. It was a reaction Edward had seen a hundred times when a young lady fell prey to his charms. Morgan Sinclair had succumbed to them rather easily, the same as any other debutante.

Except...something about this particular young lady made Edward want to know more. That fact, in and of itself, was a startling revelation. Mayhap, it was the way she had responded to the touch of his hand.

Or maybe she was just that innocent. Edward really had no litmus test to identify chaste women. For as much as he enjoyed claiming 'ruin' for most of the bon ton's young ladies, he preferred more enlightened women. Virgins had never been his pleasure. So, he could not be certain if her sudden knee-jerk reaction to his touch was due to age and inexperience, or something else.

It was a quandary that could be overthought. And Edward, whenever possible, preferred avoiding overthinking. It was best to simply stay the original course. Dancing. That was why he was here after all. Not to be sidetracked into philosophical deliberation over a debutante's hesitancy toward him.

Edward drew her closer, holding her securely in dance frame. He was pleased to find she fit perfectly in his arms. She shifted her weight, obviously uncomfortable with the intimate embrace. *Were all debutantes this skittish*, he wondered. Just as he was about to instruct her on what to do next, she twisted her body again, this time causing her breasts to press against him. The sensation was a definite plus.

He glanced down to see if she was as aware of her new positioning as his trousers were. A beautiful rose-colored blush was rising in her cheeks. *She was!* For some utterly stupid reason, he wanted to recreate that high color on her skin again and again. He pulled her in tighter, and the flush deepened.

She looked up at him and Edward realized issue number six. Her amber eyes held definitive flecks the color of poured gold. He had only seen eyes the like in wolves. They were beguiling.

She was a stunning woman. While not the standard London beauty, she was, nevertheless, intoxicating. With her perfectly shaped body, auburn locks, and... *those eyes.*

As Edward studied her more closely, he saw a few tiny freckles dotted across the bridge of her nose. Suddenly he wanted to know if those beauty marks appeared elsewhere. His pants grew uncomfortably snug.

Edward released her and took a large step back. *Seven, eight, nine, ten.* Too many problems in this scenario. A man could only take so much.

"I believe that will do for today, Miss Sinclair. I fear that I have just recalled another appointment. Please accept my sincere apology."

He gave a small bow before turning away. "Tomorrow, we will

move on to the patterns," Edward said over his shoulder as he reached the doors. "Good day, Miss Sinclair."

Once safely in the hallway, he exhaled and caught the measuring side-eye of the lovesick Perry. Edward offered the footman a rebuking scowl before turning and heading toward the front door. He very much understood the poor fellow's protectiveness, but he really should know his place. It was *not* as champion to the young Lady Sinclair.

No, Edward reminded himself with each heavy fall of his boots-- that would be the right of whatever lord took her as his wife. Miss Sinclair was here to make her debut and find a husband. Perry the footman would not be that man. No matter how much the two might fancy one another.

Edward was not sure why that logic now irritated him. He had come here hoping to leave with at least some entertaining story to relate to Henry. Lady Vandicamp's banshee-like vocal cords and the possible 'star-crossed lovers' scandal now seemed inapplicable. It soured his mood.

Not breaking stride, Edward took his walking cane and hat from the waiting butler. "Pray, tell my father that I will speak with him later tonight. Inform Lady Vandicamp that I will be by for the lesson tomorrow, as planned. And pass along to Lady Vistmont that she has a lovely daughter."

The servant nodded obediently. Edward took the steps at a jog. The men of London would find Morgan Sinclair a force to be reckoned with this season. Just as her mother and aunt had hoped. It would not take long for her to find a husband.

She was just that *rare*. Just as the thought crossed his mind, he felt ill. He needed a drink.

Edward entered White's where, after exchanging brief pleasantries with a few fellow members, he found Henry enjoying an excellent scotch at a quiet table in the back. His friend smiled by way of greeting and used his foot to push out the seat next to him.

Edward poured a glass, downed it in a single swallow, and then took a seat. Refilling the glass a second time, he sank back into the lush leather chair and exhaled.

"That bad?" Henry inquired.

"I did a favor for my father." Edward tipped back the expensive liquor. "It did not go as planned," he added dryly.

Henry leaned forward and replenished Edward's glass. "What favor?"

"Do you know Lady Vandicamp?"

"Of course. She was at every ball my father ever threw," Henry replied.

Edward mumbled an expletive into his glass. "Apparently, I am the only sod in London who does not know of her."

"I find it hard to believe that old Lady Vandicamp could sour your mood so thoroughly that you would abuse good scotch in such a manner." Henry grinned, amused. "Unless she offered to design you a new wardrobe?"

"Not Lady Vandicamp. Her niece."

Henry relaxed his arm atop the manchette of his chair, his fingers dangling the scotch glass precariously over the edge. "Tell me you did not ruin her niece?"

"Of course not." Edward narrowed his eyes. "Despite however much I was inclined to."

"Ah, I am beginning to see the problem." Henry propped his legs on a footstool and proceeded to get comfortable. "Why don't you just cut to the chase and tell me how this all came about. I am aging by the second, and at the pace you are setting, you are going to be drunk in an hour."

Edward leaned forward. "I agreed to help teach her the waltz." He rolled his eyes before lifting his glass to his lips. "I expected to teach some addle-brained, barely out of leading strings, debutante. Not some curvy, redheaded beauty."

"Redhead?" Henry clucked his tongue. "I love women with hair that color. Quite feisty. And this one is not a dull half-wit, either?"

"Hardly dull." Edward did not like the way Henry's eyes lit up. For some strange reason, he felt the need to punch his best friend in the nose.

"And she is comely?" Henry asked, either ignoring or missing Edward's growing tension.

"Indeed."

"As such, you were taken aback by your desire for her?"

Edward huffed. "Yes."

"Because debutantes are never enticing, or smart, or exciting?" Henry motioned for a serving boy to bring another bottle.

"They are never any of those things." Edward sighed.

Henry leaned forward in his chair and studied him for a long moment. "I recall another surprising debutante. One with a quick wit, amazing charm, and outstanding beauty. Whom I first met while she was falling under attack from a group of large Irish clansmen hell-bent on kidnapping her. The young woman ran a knife through a man's neck," he said with an ironic lift of his brow. "You have met your sister, correct?"

Edward pinched the bridge of his nose and closed his eyes. He hated when Henry made sense. "That is not *at all* the same thing. Greyland is different. Besides, she is my sister. I am used to her unusual behavior."

"I see." Henry chuckled. "We are concluding that no other woman in the world could possibly possess any of those traits?"

"Highly unlikely."

"What about Bella?"

Edward threw his hands in the air. "Oh, bloody hell, Henry. I concede!" He exhaled loudly. "I suppose I never considered I would come across a woman like that—one I would be attracted to. It is disturbing."

"Well, do not run off and marry her." Henry wagged a finger. "I still need my running mate."

Edward lifted his glass in toast. "Agreed. Now, where are we off to next? I have four hours until I need to meet my father and discuss taking over his end of the trade endeavors with India and France."

Henry's blue eyes danced. "Well, let us not waste any time. There is a new play and I have a backstage invitation." He smiled mischievously and clapped Edward on the back as they rose. "We will get this little debutante off your mind in the most satisfying way possible."

"That is exactly what I am in need of."

"So, when can I meet this lovely young redhead of yours?" Henry tossed him a puckish smile as they exited White's.

"Never!"

Morgan stood, looking at her reflection in the mirror. Since her dresses from Madam LeMore would not arrive for another week, she was wearing the one she had arrived in two days prior. Apparently, pilfering her aunt's wardrobe was no longer an option, per her mother's scolding after her dance lesson the previous day.

Her aunt, on the other hand, had seemed more amused than anything. But she did remind Morgan how important first impressions were, and then rattled her ear off for over an hour about using one's natural assets to land a proper gentleman. Morgan had refrained from bringing up the fact that the Earl of Wellington was far from a proper gentleman.

She groaned. Besides, it did not matter what she wore. The earl had been so unimpressed with her that he had left mere minutes after beginning their dance lesson. Was she that repulsive? Or was he that put off by her lack of knowledge?

Why did she care? She had purposely tried to appear undesirable, and her efforts had been a smashing success. If only he had been a little less attractive. The dratted man had unnerved her to the point of restless sleep. More than once during the night, she had woken from a dream about him...how it would feel to touch that amazing, devil-take-all smile.

She gave her expression in the mirror an experimental 'I am not attracted to the Earl of Wellington' smile. *Too wide.* She looked like a lunatic. Morgan tried one last time using less teeth. *Too stiff.* Now she looked like a post-mortem portrait.

She sighed and turned from her reflection. No time to worry on it now. He would obviously rather be anywhere other than downstairs in her aunt's ballroom forced to teach a mere girl the steps of a new dance.

Morgan gathered up her bruised pride and set her mind on simply being a better student. Dashing lords aside, she did need to learn the dance and ten-minute lessons would not get that accomplished. She pulled on her day gloves and headed for the ballroom. Today, she would impress the earl enough to at least find her worthy of instruction.

Perry was waiting by the closed double doors that led into the ballroom when she rounded the base of the stairs. "The earl is here to see you, Miss Sinclair," he said gravely.

"Thank you, Perry." She smiled warmly. At least one person in this house other than herself found the earl's presence disconcerting.

Perry opened the doors for her, and she stepped inside the well-lit room. Lord Wellington turned slowly from his rooted position by the window, hands clasped loosely behind his back. In the diaphanous morning light, his body cast a long shadow across the polished marble floor. The sun held his silhouette in its embrace, giving him an almost angelic grace.

Granted, Morgan mused, *the Devil was once an angel.* She forced, what she hoped was a biddable smile, and made her way across the ballroom. Since he was making no attempt to come to her. Before she could muster a polite greeting, he got right to the point.

"Good day, Miss Sinclair. We are going to start with the basics." The earl extended his hand. "May we assume that when I offer my hand to you, it is a silent request for yours?"

She expected that one to come back to haunt her. She bit down on her tongue and did as requested, placing her hand in his. Once again, she was struck by the warmth and strength of his grip, but this time she did not gape at him as if he had morphed into a unicorn. She mentally patted herself on the back for that.

"Your feet are going to draw a box on the floor, starting with your right foot. With each new step, use the foot you did not use last. Right foot to start on the count of one. Then left for the number two. Right foot again for our third count. You may never use the same foot twice. Always alternate them with each new number. Understand?"

"Yes." She silently repeated it in her head. "Different foot, different number. I have it."

He began to move her through the pattern, and then stopped when she stepped on his foot at the count of three. "I am sorry." Morgan felt herself blush. "I thought I started with my right foot?"

"Just to start," he said evenly. "Count it again and remember what I said about a new foot for each number."

He did not give her time to remember before moving her into the pattern again. "One, two, three." He stopped. "What foot are you on?"

"My right foot just landed," Morgan replied, pleased that the answer came quickly.

"Now, that foot has been used. What foot moves next?" His voice was deliberate and slow, as if he were speaking to a toddler.

She ignored the desire to form a quick retort that would let him know just how she felt about that patronizing tone. She did need him after all. "My left foot is free to step," she answered.

"Good." He continued moving her through the pattern. "Keep counting in your mind now and close your eyes."

"Close my eyes?" Her voice came out like a squeak.

"Yes," he replied levelly. "I want you to feel the lead. Our visual sense hinders our tactile sense. If you were blind, you would need me to guide you. My touch would be all you would have. I need my touch to be all that you need now," he intoned, his voice heavy with conflicting undercurrents.

So many undercurrents you could drown in them. Morgan swallowed hard before doing as he asked. She closed her eyes. His words were the most delicately intimate three sentences she had ever heard strung together, and... *the way his voice hovered over them...*

It was no wonder the man left a path of swooning women in his wake. Of course, Morgan knew he was referring strictly to the role of leading and following, but the warmth that pooled in her stomach as she stood there, eyes closed, in his arms, was all the proof her body needed to know that there was a lot more than schematics to it.

She was all *too* aware now that this dancing business was a vertical expression of a horizontal desire. The fact that all of society partook in such an activity—out in the open no less—under the guise that it was customary and polite was just...*hedonistic.*

Before she could think more on it, he was moving them. Suddenly, Morgan felt disconnected from everything around her save him. Her visual sense gone, all she had was touch, sound, and smell. She felt the strength of his arms around her and the power of his legs as they moved between hers. She heard the soft rustle of her cotton skirts as they skimmed the polished floor and brushed against the thicker material of his trousers.

Then her last sense kicked in. *His scent...*a warm masculine smell, almost smoky, akin to the hickory bouquet that clings to one's clothing after standing next to a wood-burning fire, and something sweet, like brandy. It wrapped around her.

She should have been terrified, being forced to trust him as she was. Instead, the heady awakening of her more dormant senses emboldened her. Morgan felt deeply connected to all that was hidden, as if shadows had just made themselves bright. Every little nuance she had taken for granted was now shouting from the rooftops.

It was *amazing!* Succumbing in to the unfamiliar sensations, she relinquished control and gave her body entirely over to him. Before she knew it she was whirling and spinning, dipping and swaying gracefully to the intoxicating rhythm of the dance they were creating.

Art. She dreamily thought. They were making art *together*.

"Miss Sinclair?" he whispered.

Morgan opened her eyes and realized they had stopped. She knew she was smiling, but when she looked up into his eyes, she saw very clearly that he was *not*.

Morgan suddenly felt like she had just been smacked in face with a wet fish. What had she done wrong? He continued to hold her in dance frame without speaking, heat radiating from his body and eyes as hard as coal. She struggled to find words, *any words*. Something to take the intensity of his stare off her.

"Did I misstep?" she asked quietly.

"No." He released her, and though she was soundly on her feet, she felt as if he had dropped her. "You are a natural."

Morgan was decidedly unsure how to take that, so she opted to reply with the only thing she knew for certain. "You looked as if you might have been upset?"

"I would tell you if I were displeased. You did exactly as I asked."

He turned and walked to a sideboard where a pitcher of lemonade had been left for them. Morgan felt his departure as if a chasm had opened between them. A chasm that grew larger with every step he retreated away from her.

"Here, let me ring Perry for—"

He silenced her with a wave of his hand and a light laugh that bounced off the walls, echoing and taunting her, hinting at a more playful personality. A side of him that she was not permitted to know. Morgan suddenly, *and irrationally*, became jealous of all the women who had ever been gifted the sound of that uninhibited laughter.

The earl glanced over his shoulder when he reached the sideboard and smiled, *really* smiled, before he turned back to fill the glasses. Morgan was once again struck by how handsome the man truly was. She felt an overwhelming desire to know him better. She wanted to hear what a side-gripping, immobilizing laugh would sound like pouring from his lungs. *And*, what did the woman look like that could coax it out of him?

That last thought nearly toppled her where she stood. Morgan had assumed *she* was the one that needed to avoid gaining *his* attention. But now here she was unscrutinized, yet desperately wishing to be more thoroughly considered. By God, she wanted this man to find her pleasing. She wanted to be a lady worthy of hearing that laugh!

Edward steadied his hands that had begun to shake when he released Miss Sinclair. He managed not to spill the blasted lemonade while he contemplated why the young woman was having such a strange effect on him. Lots of women had an effect on him.

Just like the pretty opera dancer he had had six ways from Sunday the previous night and then shown out the back door before the sun had risen. She had been a great release from the desire his student had stirred to life in him the day before. So, why was his appetite not sated?

Edward was a virile man, but even he could go a day without. Three, if he had to. For unbeknownst reasons, Morgan Sinclair was causing a different effect entirely. Well, not *entirely*... He wanted her in his bed all right. But he wanted something besides that, and that *something* was foreign to him.

Possession. He felt an overwhelming need have her in a way no one else could. But that was absurd. He had never cared for the idea of taking a girl's virtue for sheer bragging rights. That he had been the man to get there first. That sort of conquest was beneath him.

No, the need to claim her was more in line with how he had felt when he first laid eyes on his favorite horse. His mind circled back to that day at auction. No one was going to outbid him once he saw Elkinema trotting proudly in his pen.

He stopped himself mid-thought. Was he comparing a debutante to an Arabian stallion? Damn, he needed a drink. He shook his head. Still, the simple fact remained that he felt uncomfortably drawn to the buxom redhead.

Quite uncomfortable. He shifted his weight to relieve the pressure building in his trousers and poured a second glass of lemonade, mentally exorcising the *effect* Morgan Sinclair was having on him. Besides, she must think him a complete oaf.

He had done little more than blatantly stare at her when their dance ended, completely flummoxed by the pleased little smile painted on her lips.

She had trusted him when he asked her to, surrendering her mind and body to his skillful administration of the dance. In doing so, her release of control had allowed him to navigate them effortlessly around the room. It had felt magnificent!

Astounding. Intense. Staggering. There were not enough synonyms in the English language to adequately describe how her faith in him had made him feel in the moment. He would have never thought before today that a woman's wholehearted assurance in him and his ability to keep her safe, much less not crashing into a wall and breaking a leg, would prove so *rewarding*.

She had followed him as if she had been trained in the art of dance for years like his sister. But dancing with Miss Sinclair felt *vastly* different from dancing with his sister. He had moved her with ease through some of his most accomplished patterns, and she had followed his lead like a professional.

Except she was not an experienced dancer. She was a novice. Her only ability to navigate the dance so well was due to the confidence she had placed in him.

It was simply awe-inspiring. Edward was not sure he had ever experienced a dance like the one he just shared with Miss Sinclair. She had felt like an extension of him.

That singular thought drew him up short. He definitely needed a stiff drink. Turning back to the lady in question, he found her practicing a turn he had just danced her through.

"It is not nearly as easy without you," she said. "Were there six steps in this, or just three?"

"Three," he numbly answered, still trying to shake off the spell she had placed upon him. "I will write them down and you can practice tonight. We can resume our lessons tomorrow."

She jerked her head up and gave an imperceptible smile. "Oh. Lovely. You will be back again tomorrow?"

"If you will have me. I would like to make sure you have it down a little better," he stated, just as the door opened and the much-too-attentive footman entered.

Perry smiled a toothy smile at the lady and announced she had a visitor. She thanked him and then turned and thanked Edward earnestly for his help.

Edward located a pen and paper, jotted down their patterns for her study, and then took his leave from the ballroom. As he followed Perry past the front parlor, he could not resist a quick glance inside. To his annoyance, he could not see anything but a pair of well-polished black Hessian boots stretching out comfortably from a cushioned chair.

He frowned. *And so, it starts.* He quietly cursed whoever was calling on his pretty young student.

Richard took the long hall to Lady Vandicamp's ballroom. He had been admitted to the house unannounced, the duchess apparently having told her staff that he was welcome whenever he should arrive. Now he wondered over that peculiarity. Did the duchess make the same exceptions for all her guests? Why? What if he had arrived at two in the morning? Not that he would, but still. Could gentleman callers be found wandering the house at any hour of the day? Most peculiar it was.

He passed a pedestal with a life-size bust of Julius Caesar and dismissed all contemplation over the oddities of Lady Vandicamp. He lengthened his strides. All the duchess's eccentricities aside, he really needed to catch Edward before he departed and speak with him about the trade merger. If Richard could intercept him at the end of his lesson with Lady Vandicamp's niece, it would save him tremendous time. Because who knew where he would find his son once the sun set.

On second thought, there were only so many gentleman's establishments in London. It might be easier to locate Edward after dusk. Richard reached the foyer that opened up to the ballroom and stopped mid-stride. No voices could be heard coming from the ballroom. Instead, they were coming from the library, adjacent to the ballroom.

"Do you think this will work?" Richard recognized Lady Vistmont's voice despite the hushed words.

"Of course, it will work. The girl is quite the beauty." The duchess replied confidently.

Richard took a step back, uncomfortable with the possibility of eavesdropping.

"I am just worried we may be putting too much on her. Surely, she will figure out that eligible peers of the realm do not simply traipse around offering up their precious time to help instruct young debutantes?" Lady Vistmont said worriedly.

Those words stopped his retreat. Despite his good upbringing, which told him dukes did not hover about listening to women gossip, he stayed rooted in place. If this conversation involved his son, proper upbringing be damned.

"Lord De Montrey would be a perfect match. He must have taken a liking to her after their meeting in the park yesterday for he sent a letter requesting to call on her today. Of course," Lady Vandicamp said, sounding pleased, "I could not accept his offer. Not without a favor to our Morgan worked into the deal. I happen to have it on good authority that he plays the pianoforte quite well. Therefore, lending his expertise to help refine my dear niece's skill at the instrument while he is here is really no trouble at all. He is probably already in the parlor waiting for her lesson with the earl to conclude."

Ah, so it was *this* De Montrey fellow Richard had passed in the tearoom. They were not discussing Edward. He could back away now and still maintain his upstanding ethical code of not being a spy. Yet... he did not budge. Some inexplicable instinct kept him right where he stood.

"I am not sure she is ready to start entertaining any suitors yet. I thought our plan was only to introduce her to the most eligible men of the bon ton so that the rumors of her upcoming debut could be spread amongst them. Which, in turn, would allow her to make an even grander entrance into society when the time does arrive." The softer, more demure, Lady Vistmont queried.

This *did* involve Edward. Richard stifled a laugh. The ladies would be sorely disappointed if they thought to pin him down.

"Of course, she is ready. The ultimate goal is to get her married quickly, is it not?" A length of silence ensued before Her Grace spoke again, her voice pitched low. "I will not let that bastard husband of yours to turn his fist on her, Helen!"

The words were curt and unexpected. Richard could no more remove himself from his place in the hallway now than he could remove his own head. Was the Earl of Vistmont beating his lovely wife?

Lady Vistmont spoke next, confirming his suspicion. "You are right, she has to get away from him." She replied plaintively. "Oh, I truly misjudged him."

Richard felt his hands curl into tight balls at his sides.

"Now, do not blame yourself. Not even I knew the man had such a temper." Lady Vandicamp assured her sister. "If we can get Morgan married off to a nice man like De Montrey, she will be well taken care of."

A small sob from Lady Vistmont followed the duchess's vow.

"Then we can start our plan to get you away from that dreaded man," she added.

"Do you really think we can untangle the past?" Lady Vistmont asked, sounding hopeful.

"I will die trying."

Richard had heard enough. He would locate Edward later. He turned on his heels and strode from the manor house.

Morgan sat in the study with Eloise, as her aunt went on and on about a particular tea she was procuring from Kenya. She wondered if one day she might have the luxury of being concerned over which beverage to serve for a lady's garden party.

Right now, all she wished for was the ability to decide between which one of her two threadbare dresses she would wear today. It should be an easy choice—the one she had not worn yesterday. Morgan sighed. At least, she had two dresses to choose from. There were plenty worse scenarios for a woman to have in life.

She looked across the room to her mother poised delicately in her chair, back as straight as an alder sapling. Morgan felt the familiar pinch of the muscles between her brows, the ones that created the crease her mother would scold her for making if she looked over at her now, which was ironic considering Morgan only made the face every time she thought of her mother's poor lot in life. The wife to a man who beat her, demeaned her, and barely found the time to provide for her.

Yes, there were *far* worse situations in life. Much worse than worrying over one's choice of dress. Morgan glanced down at her day dress, ashamed that she had fallen prey to such overindulgent and trivial longings. She quickly altered her train of thought. At least she liked this dress. *There. That was positive.*

It was a pleasant shade of periwinkle blue that allowed her curves to be hinted at without displaying them in a tawdry way. And it was all she had, so she simply had no other choice than to like it. One day she would tear it into shreds and shove it down her stepfather's throat.

Well, so much for positivity. Revenge was a more palatable emotion. Her mother picked up the conversation, asking Eloise about a distant relation, which allowed Morgan more time to remain in her own head. *But...* She would think no more on her wicked stepfather, or her own fears of ending up exactly like her mother.

Instead, her thoughts drifted back over her two lessons the previous day. Both of which had gone surprisingly well. Her dancing lesson with the earl had been much better than expected, even if she still feared that teaching her bored him to tears.

The baron on the other hand, her new music instructor, seemed to truly enjoy working with her. So much so, that after their lesson, he had asked her to go riding with him later today.

Her mother started to stand, halting any further woolgathering.

"Talk amongst yourselves, girls," the duchess stated as she rose and headed for the door, Morgan's mother in tow. "My sister and I have plans to make. Boring stuff. Carry on."

Morgan glanced over at her friend when the sound of the older women's footfalls could no longer be heard down the hall. They both broke into smiles.

"I thought they would never leave." Eloise giggled. "Now, tell me everything about Lord De Montrey."

"Oh, Eloise, I am beside myself with nerves for our ride later. I fear I might slip up and say the wrong thing."

Or confess to wanting to commit murder. Morgan chewed her bottom lip as *all* the possible problems popped into her mind. Her eyes darted to her friend, a new worry setting in.

"What if I fall off my horse?"

Eloise laughed. "I think you may be over-thinking this one. He obviously has an interest in you, why else would he have asked you?" Her expression turned nurturing and she patted Morgan's leg. "I have heard that men are really not that complicated. If they like you, they like you."

Morgan smiled. "When did you get so wise?"

"Last night."

"Last night?" Morgan's smile widened.

"I will tell you all about it later. Let us leave it at that I had a very reflective conversation with myself. And...I might have spied on my sister taking high tea with Lord Archdale when I should not have." Eloise grinned mischievously. "More about that later. Tell me about the baron."

Morgan arched a curious brow, but she did as requested. "He is very patient with me and quite nice."

Her friend gave a dreamy sigh and sank back into the cushions. "I am green with envy; however did your aunt acquire two of the most desirable men in London to serve as dancing and music masters for you?"

"I believe my aunt and *dear* mother are working together on this. I am not entirely sure why." She stirred sugar into her tea. "I can understand why they might secretly push De Montrey. For he is wealthy, attractive, kind, a respectable gentleman and not too terribly high above my station."

Morgan paused, contemplatively. "Then there is Lord Wellington who is distractingly attractive, a known rake, wealthy, abrasively elusive, and entirely too high above my station."

Eloise was obviously pondering the two vastly different men. "Surely, your aunt and mother's goal were not to entice the earl. Even though many a title-hungry mama would eagerly set her cap for him." She shook her head, dismissing the idea and causing her blonde curls to bounce. "I do not believe they would wish that arrangement on you. Do you?"

"At this point, I cannot venture even a guess as to what they would, or would not, arrange. They are both slipping around like little spiders, whispering in corners." Morgan rolled her eyes. "De Montrey is the more reasonable match."

"Miss Sinclair, Lord De Montrey is here to see you," Perry's voice rang out from the door.

With an excited squeeze of Morgan's hand, Eloise stood. "Have a wonderful time, and please, come by later with the details."

She turned and made for the door, before stopping and turning back to Morgan. "My mother always tells my sister there are plenty of fish in the sea. Do not find yourself falling in love with the first one to nip at your hook." She nodded fiercely.

Morgan smiled and nodded back. "Sage advice."

Plenty of fish, she mused...*but also sharks.*

Lord De Montrey gave another marvelously beneficial pianoforte lesson before escorting Morgan to his shiny new curricle pulled by two beautiful midnight-black steeds. She took his offered hand and climbed into the open carriage, a tiny thrill tingling her skin. *Her first real adventure!* She was stupidly giddy. The baron stepped lithely up after her and took the reins from the groom.

He smiled over at her, a gleam in his eyes. "Are you ready?"

Morgan thought that was an interesting question, but nodded all the same. The eager team trotted around a corner. They entered a quiet stretch of the park with Perry and Bertrice following closely behind in the duchess' carriage.

As soon as they were a few yards down the tree-covered lane Morgan realized the import of his earlier question. He snapped the reins and gave the two horses their heads. Morgan barely had time to catch her hat before the wind whipped it away. She gasped and looked to Lord De Montrey, who was grinning from ear to ear.

"Take hold of me if you are frightened," he shouted over the pounding of hooves.

Morgan did just that, anchoring herself to his side. She could hear Perry shouting at their carriage driver to hurry up. Without even venturing a glance backward, she knew his words were being eaten up by dust clouds. They would never catch this rig.

After a few heart stopping minutes of jarring bumps and biting wind, Morgan could feel the carriage began to slow. She opened her eyes, not exactly sure when she had shut them. They were nearing a bend in the lane, which must have accounted for the sudden deceleration. *Thank God!* She released the death grip she had assumed on Lord De Montrey's jacket.

"Now, that was exhilarating, was it not?" He gave her a sideways look and grinned. "Thought we might put some distance between us and your chaperones."

Morgan was utterly dumbfounded. Had she read the baron completely wrong? He had been so mild-mannered and tame back at the house, almost dull. She would have never guessed he was a man inclined toward the exhilarating aspects of life.

Just as she was forming a response, he interrupted her thoughts. "A little bird told me on the way in that you were a lady who liked excitement." He arched his brows, surveying her with considerable interest.

Little bird? Morgan laughed as realization dawned. "Ah, was this little bird blonde and about this tall?" She raised her hand to just under her chin.

"I will never tell." He chuckled, training his sights back on the road.

They settled into a natural quiet as the sounds of the park picked up its own narrative around them: a nightingale with a vigorous little song, two squirrels arguing in a nearby tree, and the sound of distant laughter from others out enjoying the pretty autumn day. This could be her new normal if Morgan married a man like the baron.

She ventured a glance at his profile. He was a distinguished, attractive man, with sandy hair and warm brown eyes. She liked him immensely.

Best of all, he did not make the ground feel as if it might fall out from beneath her feet. She was not transfixed by his smile. Was not captivated by his voice. He did not make her yearn to hear what his laugh might sound like when he was taken by joyful surprise, completely at ease. The baron was just the sort of gentleman she needed. *Agreeable. Safe. Kind.*

"We had better let them catch up." Morgan motioned behind them with a toss of her head. "I believe you may just have made two enemies." She grinned.

"Worth it to see you smile." He studied her closely before looking back to the road. "Ah, look who is approaching."

Morgan turned her head to see the Earl of Wellington riding toward them at breakneck speed. Following right on his heels, a petite woman rode sidesaddle, her long midnight-colored curls dancing wildly in the wind as she urged her mount to keep pace with the earl's bay stallion.

As the advancing couple drew near, an unreasonable, and totally unexpected, jealousy washed over Morgan. The two riders slowed their mounts. The raven-haired woman had a high blush from the race and a ready smile that was downright luminous. She pulled up close beside the earl and nodded her head toward Morgan and the baron. She was *beautiful, confident...happy.*

She fought down the green-eyed beast trying to claw its way out of her heart. Of course, the earl would be in the company of a woman like this. He was all the same descriptives as the pretty brunette at his side.

Except happy. As a matter of fact, he looked outright murderous at present. Perhaps he and the lady had been quarreling.

"Good day, Lord De Montrey," the woman said, sounding winded from the run, but her eyes danced.

The energy radiating from the petite rider was infectious. It filled up the whole of the park. Even the sun seemed to dim in her presence. Morgan sat transfixed, as if watching an actor on stage about to deliver her next line. If the two had been bickering, there was no sign of it here.

"Good day, Your Grace." De Montrey nodded, the perfect amount of incline and pause to indicate her station.

The baron then lifted his gaze to the earl. "And, good day to you, Lord Wellington." Another nod, less dramatic. "Have you had the honor of meeting Miss Sinclair?"

"I have." The earl's answer was smooth, emotionless. A stark contrast to the woman just to his right sitting atop her spirited mare.

The lady—*Her Grace*—looked directly at Morgan and smiled warmly. "So very nice to meet you, Miss Sinclair. I am Lady Hamilton, Duchess of Ravenswood. I have heard you are a natural at the art of dance."

Morgan felt Lord De Montrey's gaze land on her expectantly. She opened her mouth to answer just as her aunt's clambering carriage came to an abrupt halt beside the baron's. A flushed Perry leapt out.

"Miss Sinclair!" The footman rushed to her side, tossing an annoyed look at the baron. "Are you all right?"

Morgan felt everyone focus their attention on her. "Yes, quite fine. The horses just needed to stretch their legs."

The earl shifted his steely gaze to De Montrey.

"We merely broke a canter." The baron answered the unspoken question with an unperturbed shrug.

Morgan watched the earl's stare frost over. "You raced this rig with the young lady on board?"

The question held various degrees of warning, but De Montrey seemed to miss them entirely...or chose to ignore them. "Only for a short distance."

"It was all in fun, and now it is over. No harm is done. I am perfectly hale as you can see." Morgan turned a more sincere smile to the duchess. "Thank you! I have much still to learn."

The other woman smiled politely back at her. "You will have to forgive my brother's ill mood." She lowered her voice, as if imparting a great secret. "I was close to beating him, you see. Even being forced to play the dutiful bon ton lady and ride sidesaddle. In a skirt, no less." She made a face.

Morgan exhaled a breath she was not aware she had been holding.

Of course! The title. The famed beauty. The same lilting accent with its smooth edges that the earl, *her brother*, possessed.

This was the woman of whom Eloise had spoken. Morgan took in the sight of both brother and sister atop their mounts, side by side. She now understood what all the gossip was about. They were a force to be reckoned with. And they *did* evoke the feeling that you were in the presence of royalty.

The earl broke her observation when he abruptly turned his horse. "Try and keep to a trot with my student," he said to Lord De Montrey, over his shoulder. "I need her with legs for our lesson later."

He spurred his stallion, kicking up a cloud of dust. Lady Hamilton smiled almost apologetically before turning her own mount into the wind.

"Nice meeting you," the duchess said before giving chase after her brother.

"For the love of everything good and holy, slow down!" Greyland yelled.

Bloody hell! Edward finally took note of his surroundings. He had been so lost in thought over how chummy the baron looked seated next to Miss Sinclair, like a content house cat, that he had passed their picnic spot by a quarter mile. He ground his teeth.

Why the hell did he care? Moreover, if he were to continue asking himself impossible questions: why did it bother him that the idiot had been racing that damn curricle? *With her in it!*

This was ridiculous. She was not *his* ward. It was not *his* responsibility to keep her safe. *No,* Edward reminded himself, Morgan Sinclair was in town to make a nice match. So why did it make his blood boil to see her laughing with a perfectly worthy man?

Edward turned his horse only to come face to face with another hard to ignore female.

"Lost in thought?" His sister drew her delicate brows together in question.

"Yes, sorry. I have much on my mind. What with the looming trade deal, I forgot where I was." He started past her.

"Liar!" She whirled her mare around to walk beside him.

"Whatever are you about, Greyland?" he said, keeping his sights fixed right between Elkinema's ears.

He was not getting caught in that trap. His sister had an uncanny ability to sniff out a truth, or a falsehood, just by looking him in the eyes. The woman really should work for the Queen's guard.

"Edward." He could practically feel her eyes roll. "Do not be obtuse. It is obvious you have feelings for that young lady back there." Right to the heart of it... *like a good assassin.*

"She is my student; I have come to care about some of the decisions she might make. That is all."

"Then why would you not be pleased at the attention she is receiving from the baron? He is a very nice man."

"A very *nice* man who could have gotten her killed with his poor judgment," he said, a bit harsher than intended.

Greyland grew silent beside him, but he knew her lack of a response was not due to his tone. That wheelhouse in her mind was turning. At their picnic spot, he stopped and dismounted, waiting for the inevitable deluge of questions to hit. It took all of seventeen seconds in its coming.

Greyland slid gracefully from her horse without his assistance, something she had stopped needing at age five. "You do not find her attractive?"

"That has nothing to do with it."

"So, you are attracted to her?"

"God's teeth, Grey! What man would not be? You *did* see De Montrey practically drooling on her, did you not?" He finished tying off Elkinema to a nearby tree.

His sister was doing the same with her mare, completely

unaffected by his outburst or his confession. "Then why not pursue her for yourself?"

The question, in all its simplicity, carried the weight of an elephant. Edward unfastened the saddle bag, feigning interest in the mundane task.

"She is looking for a husband. Not a lover," he said after a perceptible pause.

He handed the bag to Greyland, untied the blanket at the back of his saddle and spread it out on the thick grass. Greyland took a seat when he stepped back from his task and started pulling various cuts of meat, cheese, and fruit from the bag. He sat down beside her.

"Oh good, strawberries." He lamely tried to change the conversational direction, knowing his effort was in vain.

Greyland stared at him with a look that could only be construed as pity. "Don't you dare," he warned.

"I will not receive such wretched scrutiny from you today, little sister." He popped a berry into his mouth, hoping to buy himself more time.

Greyland let out an exasperated sigh. "Why must all men constantly deny what is right before their eyes? It would make matters much easier if your kind would just accept their fate."

Edward snorted. "My kind? Does Alexander know how you have come to view men?"

"Once you meet that one person," she said, ignoring him, "there will never be room for another. It is not *surrendering* to allow life to pull you in a different direction than the one you thought planned. It is a grand new adventure. A new chapter to your life."

She fell silent a moment and smiled warmly.

"What if Alex had never confessed his love to me? Can you imagine him, Annabelle, or little Tristan not in our lives?"

"Of course not. That is not a fair comparison."

"Is it not?" she challenged.

"No!"

"Besides," she continued, completely undeterred, "Lord De

Montrey is not as bewitched with the young beauty as you think."
She flipped the narrative on its head.

"Whatever do you mean? What man would not—"

His words trailed off as something behind a nearby tree caught
the sun's reflection, making a bright flash of light under a canopy that
should have none. Nature's brief warning was all the time he needed.
He threw his weight into Greyland, pinning her underneath him
right as the pistol shot sped over their heads.

"What was that?" She gasped, panic flooding her voice.

He slowly lifted his head to scan the landscape. "Do not move."

"Edward, you are bleeding!"

Was he?

He continued to search the tree line, adrenaline hammering in
his ears. They—whoever *they* were—were gone. Edward slowly lifted
himself off his sister.

He felt her pulling on his jacket. "Take it off. You have been shot!"

He looked down at the red stain seeping through his sleeve.

Indeed, he had been.

Edward lay in his bed with his father, Henry, and Alexander all
pondering who had tried to kill him. Or worse, what if they had been
aiming for Greyland? His father and Alexander paced, crisscrossing
each other's paths. Henry sat across from Edward and they both
waited for someone to speak.

Edward moved to adjust a pillow behind his back and
immediately regretted the action when a white-hot fire lit up his left
arm. The bullet had merely grazed him, but the family physician had
been called in to stitch it up. The wound stung like hell when the skin
stretched. Edward had experienced worse, but this might be the first
time he earned an injury that he had not provoked.

That might be the most annoying part of it all. He had no clue who might have done it. *Well*, a few names floated to the surface... His childhood nemesis had just gotten to town, for one. And then there was always the possibility Colin McGreggor had returned to avenge his father and their botched plans to kidnap Greyland last year.

"Could you have made enemies with some nobleman whose wife you might have slept with?" Henry quipped, clearly trying to bring an element of levity to the somber atmosphere.

"I make it a habit to leave married women alone." Edward narrowed his eyes at his best friend.

"Can you two please *try* to think? My wife could have been killed today. What if Tristan and Annabelle had been with her?" Alexander ground out angrily, rightfully aggravated.

Everyone grew still. *Dear God*, what if the children had been there? Edward's hands involuntarily drew into tight fists. An anger he had only felt twice before seized his chest. Whoever had shot at them was going to *die!* He would find the coward and kill him with his bare hands, if need be!

His father, ever the voice of reason, put a hand on Alexander's shoulder. "I think it is best if you take Greyland and the children back to Greenshire until we clear this up."

"Absolutely!" Both Henry and Edward spoke in unison.

Alexander rubbed his forehead as he looked down, shaking his head. "I guess we really do not have any other options. Until we know who the intended target was, and who is behind this, she is not safe here." He looked at Edward. "And neither are you. You should retire to the country for a time."

"That is not an option." He looked pointedly at Alexander, and then his father. "Whoever tried to do this is a dead man. I will not rest until I find the yellow-bellied fool!"

"We will flush him out. I can think of more than a few suspects," Richard said, a hint of malice in his tone. "I have an associate looking into it as we speak. In the meantime, I have posted two Bow Street runners at the front and back of the house."

Edward nodded. "Will you send word to all my day's appointments that I have need to reschedule?"

"All is taken care of," Henry said. "Even your lovely dancing student has been informed." He grinned slyly.

Edward met his friend's laughing eyes. "Thank you," he begrudgingly replied.

Alexander came to the bedside and placed a hand on Edward's good shoulder. "Take care and keep your head down."

His brother-in-law looked more than a little pained. Edward knew it was hard for him to take his leave when danger was still afoot, even though everyone in the room knew that Greyland and the children must come first.

"The greatest assistance you can bring me is to keep Greyland and the little ones safe," Edward assured.

The two men had been through a lot together and Edward knew that deep down, even if he would never admit it publicly, Alexander felt a deep sense of duty to him for saving Greyland's life. Twice now. *Two times too many.*

Alexander half smiled. "I will."

He turned to Henry. "You too, little brother. I know you will not leave his side, but please, be alive when we return." The grin grew.

"I shan't disappoint," Henry replied.

"Tell Greyland I love her and that I do not want her to worry," Edward added as Alexander headed for the door.

"I will," his brother-in-law said over his shoulder. "Get some rest." He quit the room.

"I need to make some more inquires," his father stated. "Let us permit you some rest." He motioned to Henry who stood and followed the duke out of the room.

Edward was glad for the quiet. The sleeping draught Dr. Ferguson had insisted he drink was finally taking hold. He closed his eyes, allowing sleep to claim him. *Someone had tried to kill him and Greyland.*

His breathing grew shallow.

De Montrey was not right for Miss Sinclair.

His mind climbed deeper into nothingness.

*Miss Sinclair should be with someone...someone like...
Me.*

Morgan returned from her outing with Lord De Montrey, Martin, as the baron had insisted she call him. Martin had turned very inquisitive after their meeting with the earl and duchess. He seemed unnerved that the other man was helping her with her dance lessons, and he had even volunteered to assist if she needed a second opinion. Morgan had needed to stifle a laugh at that since everyone knew Lord Wellington, and his family, were famed for having instructed the Queen. Still, the baron's confidence was endearing.

Soon after she arrived home, Perry brought her a message from Lord Wellington stating that he needed to cancel their dance lesson. She was deeply disappointed, but decided not to dwell on it. He was probably drunk somewhere being fawned over.

Instead, she began to think about the adventure Martin had promised her for the next day. He was going to allow her to help him pick out a new horse at auction. She had been so elated by his invitation that she had hugged him.

The baron had seemed startled by the action, but he quickly recovered and returned her embrace, holding her a little longer than proper. Not that throwing your arms around a gentleman in the middle of Hyde Park was proper either, but the impulse had been too strong to resist.

Morgan smiled as she made her way downstairs to meet Eloise. They intended to lay out the details of their own daring adventure today. She practically skipped down the hall when she reached the bottom of the stairs. Life was much improved not having dreadful step-relations breathing down one's neck. Morgan felt young and free, and a bit mischievous.

Tomorrow, the day would be fun, attending the auction, *but tomorrow night...* Tomorrow evening would be one for the books! Morgan and her new best friend were planning on sneaking out to go for a night swim in a nearby lake Eloise knew. The timing was perfect, with half the bon ton in the country. It would be a chilly swim, but that also meant that no one else would be likely planning the same adventure.

Morgan was downright giddy at the opportunity to be scandalous. Albeit only she and Eloise would ever know, thus making it less scandalous on a scale of one to ten. Still, this tiny act of rebellion would be enough to last them both a lifetime. Someday, when they were old, they could look back and marvel at their daring youth.

This was exactly the sort of exhilarating escapade Morgan had hoped to find in the city. She pinched herself to keep from giggling like a crazy person meant for Bedlam as she passed a maid in the hallway. Life was starting to turn over a new leaf for her. Just as she had hoped.

V

*T*he sun shone high in the sky when Morgan stepped out of Martin's curricle. The air was teaming with excitement as grooms led magnificent animals from stalls to rings. Gentlemen shouted from an active auction nearby as others perused the stables.

There were steeds of every size and color, ranging from horses meant for field work to others intended for sport. There was even a sweet-faced pony lazily munching hay in an open pen. Morgan ran her fingers through its thick wiry mane before allowing Lord De Montrey to navigate her through a throng of men arguing over a mule.

Martin led her into the first of two large stables and slowed their pace as they reached a long line of stalls. "Let us take a look at what we may like before the bidding starts, shall we?" He guided her over to a pretty dapple-gray mare.

"Oh, she is beautiful!" Morgan exclaimed, reaching out to pet the horse's soft white nose. The animal nudged her hand and nibbled her fingers. Morgan smiled at the mare's quest for hidden treats. "So lovely."

"Indeed, she is darling. However, you must look for other signs that a horse might be the right choice, and this one's back is too short." The baron pointed at the mare's back. "She is not nearly as covetable as that one." He motioned with his head toward a tall black stallion five stalls down.

"He is a sight. Do you think he is safe?" she asked, watching the giant horse paw the earth. Unlike the mare, he looked none too happy to be there, pinning his ears and snaking his head at every passerby.

"Not at all." A deep, masculine voice came from behind them.

They both turned to see the Earl of Wellington.

The baron opened his mouth and closed it as if he were testing various replies on his tongue, to find the one with just the right amount of indignation.

"Of course, he would be safe. Once someone shows him who his master is." Lord De Montrey actually puffed out his chest.

"He is not safe for reasons beyond that," the earl said evenly. "Come, I will show you." He offered Morgan his arm.

Not sure exactly how to proceed in the face of a polite abduction, Morgan accepted, but she offered Lord De Montrey a sympathetic half smile as she was led away. The baron grumbled something indecipherable, but decidedly vexed, then he followed them over to the prancing stallion.

The earl came to a halt in front of the beast's stall. "You want a short cannon bone on a steed." He pointed to the animal's front leg. "It is the bone between the fetlock and the knee. His are too long. His back is also too long. Unlike your mare with the ideal, short-coupled back."

"Nonsense, this horse is much more elegant and would be prettier to ride." De Montrey nodded toward the impressive stallion. "A man's horse, that one is."

"Prettier to ride?" The earl did not snort, but he came close. "If his back does not snap in two when you jump him the first time. And those rings around his hooves, indicating previous flounder, will surely come back to haunt you in no time at all."

He turned Morgan, still on his arm, back toward the dapple-gray mare. "Your mare," Lord Wellington continued, "has a short back, which will give her extra strength. She has a well-set neck as well, and laid-back shoulders."

He looked at her, as if pausing to wait for her to absorb the information. "You want the shoulders set at about a forty-five-degree angle. Another attribute is that she is not flatfooted like that stallion. Even if that beast over there was sound of foot, he would still try to kill you."

"No matter *how* you try and discipline him." The earl looked pointedly over her head at Lord De Montrey. "For you cannot change any animal's temperament. But you can find the right fit for your own temperament; a perfect match of rider and mount."

"That is your opinion," Lord De Montrey ground out. "Now, if you will excuse us, I am going to bid on that stallion and take the lady with me." He moved to Morgan's other side and grasped her free elbow.

Lord Wellington did not release her.

The baron's eyes shot daggers at him, and he gave a little tug.

The earl acquiesced, but a muscle in his jaw twitched. "Have a care with the lady."

De Montrey blustered. "Are you implying that I do not have her best interest at heart?"

"Yanking her around as if you have a claim on her is *not* in her best interest."

"Why, I would never! You are the one making it appear as if we are dogs set on a bone." The baron glowered down his nose. "Fighting over the lady like heathens."

"I suppose that would make a juicier tidbit for the gossip rags than your rather indecent public embrace yesterday in Hyde Park, would it not?" The earl returned in an absolutely lethal tone before looking down at Morgan. "Good day, Miss Sinclair." He turned abruptly and prowled away.

Morgan was rendered mute. She was having a hard time processing what had just happened. Her mind lit on the only fraction of that exchange that made sense—*the gossip rag*. Her heart dropped. *Was she in it?*

She turned to Lord De Montrey, whose pallor had dropped about three shades. "My lord, how would he know about a silly little thing like—"

"He is a cad; of course, he reads the gossip news," he said, his voice clipped with irritation. "No doubt someone saw the lovely embrace you bestowed upon me and wrote that I am courting you."

Morgan felt suddenly very uncomfortable. "Are you? Courting me?"

He chortled loudly, but there was little mirth in it. "Indeed, I am."

Morgan found air suddenly hard to come by; a ridiculous notion considering there was more than enough airflow around them. Still, her bodice felt tight and her head light. She tried to pinpoint the emotions circling that confession.

She should be happy, elated even, that such a man would choose her. Yet, all she felt was...out of place next to him. Whereas, Lord Wellington had felt...*right*.

The realization came with the impact of a swinging hammer.

"Are you ready to watch me win?" Lord De Montrey asked.

Morgan stared at him. "Win?"

"The horse."

She exhaled, with more enthusiasm than was ladylike. She had never been so happy for a turn in conversation. "Yes." She smiled. "I am sure you will."

Edward stayed close to the stables after the bidding concluded. He wanted to make sure De Montrey did not attempt to celebrate his successful bidding by placing Miss Sinclair atop that giant war horse he had just purchased. The damned fool had all but kissed her when he had outbid the only other two flops in London willing to buy the steed.

Edward was not sure if it was the attention the baron lavished on the lady that bothered him so. Or rather, the sudden knowledge that the lord was not fit to entertain her. The man did not have the commonsense God gave a pigeon.

Was he that ignorant *or,* was the baron just that desperate to impress her? Each possible scenario left Edward with a bitter taste in his mouth. The only two things that were certain was that the man knew nothing about horses *and,* if he kept fondling Miss Sinclair in public, the rumor mill would have them betrothed by the week's end.

Considering what Edward had read in Mrs. Henderson's scandalous gossip rag, the Bon Ton Tattler, earlier that morning—which he did every morning since he was usually in it—the latter was already on a set course. *"A Race to Watch."* He had almost choked on his toast over the headline.

The story stated that a certain, Baron "D", had been seen embracing an unknown young beauty. Little was known of the pretty redheaded maiden other than she was expected to make her formal debut at Lady Printmose's ball in one week.

Edward scoffed. As if that would take a genius to figure out. The shifty columnist had gone on to write that the young lady was sure to be ruined—by either Baron "D" or some other man—before the season was underway if she continued to conduct herself improperly, as she had also been spotted racing curricles in Hyde Park.

He absentmindedly rubbed his tender arm, and then immediately regretted the action. Dr. Ferguson had warned him not to do anything strenuous. Edward supposed that playing tug-o-war with Miss Sinclair counted as being 'strenuous'. He was just about to head for his carriage when he spotted the merry couple leaving the stables. Minus one elephant-sized mount.

Relieved at least for that, Edward rounded the stables. He would have a talk with his naive student tomorrow during their dance lesson and warn her about caution where the baron was concerned. He might also add she should not believe everything she was told, such as how to select a blasted horse. But for now, he had a meeting with Henry, an ice pack, and a bottle of rum.

Morgan removed her jacket and shivered as the chilly night breeze cut right through her thin cotton shirt. She looked at Eloise who had just removed her own jacket and was quickly, and eagerly, unbuttoning her shirt.

"Are you sure about this?" She asked. The idea had been hers. Yet, now that they were disrobing behind a bush in the middle of the park, she was having second thoughts.

"Of course, I am sure," her friend replied, staring down at her task at hand. "I did not sneak out of my house after hours dressed as a stable lad just to cry off."

"You are right." Morgan shivered again as she looked out across the glassy surface of the lake. "It is just a tad cooler than I had thought it might be," she said, stalling.

"Blasted button!"

Eloise cursed the last button on her stolen men's shirt, then gave up, pulling the garment over her head.

"There!" Triumphantly, she tossed it to the ground with the jacket. "And here I thought their clothing was easier." She scoffed, starting to work on getting her trousers undone. "I swear those eyelets are three times smaller than the buttons."

Morgan giggled at her friend's determination, and surprising lack of modesty. "Guess that answers that." She pulled at her breeches. "We are definitely going in."

"Hurry up." Eloise kicked off the trousers. "Lest I freeze to death naked in Hyde Park. How would you explain that one to my mother?" She raised her blonde eyebrows to mark deep significance.

"Point made." Morgan pulled her own shirt quickly over her head.

When Eloise grew unnervingly quiet, Morgan looked up as she fussed with the buttons of her own trousers to find her friend staring at her.

"What?" She laughed, a bit sheepishly. "You have them, too."

"Not like that." Eloise shook her head and kicked off her shoes. "Do men just salivate at your feet?"

Morgan tugged her breeches down and rolled her eyes. "Remember? Doxy, ladybird...those are the names these curves will earn you."

"Well, I would trade figures with you in a heartbeat." Eloise shook her finger. "Besides, you promised not to compare yourself to such women—"

"I know." Morgan waved her hand, suddenly impatient. "It is bloody cold out here."

She gathered her courage, took her friend's hand and pulled her from behind the bush. They darted across the leaf-laden grass toward the pond's edge, looking conspiratorially left and right as they ran.

They reached the water, and without hesitation, plunged in. Both women emerged with gasps, followed closely by thrilling giggles of triumph.

"We did it," Eloise whispered, grinning from ear to ear.

"We did." Morgan laughed and did a back flip.

When she came back up, Eloise went stark white, her eyes huge, and by the single index finger she held up to her mouth, Morgan assessed it was not from the chill of the water.

"What?" she mouthed mutely.

It was *not* Eloise who answered the silent word. A man's voice broke through the still night like a rapier blade. "You there, are you all right?"

The women exchanged wide-eyed horrified looks.

"I know you are in the water; I just want to make sure everything is fine?" the man called out again.

Morgan did the only thing she could think of to do. "Aye, I am hale," she answered into the darkness, pitching her voice as low as she could, in hopes that it would sound masculine.

Eloise clasped her hand to her mouth, whether to keep from laughing, or crying Morgan could not decipher by the moon's light.

"Ah, yes, miss, I see. However, as a gentleman, I must insist on remaining by the shore until you are back on solid ground." After a pause, he added, "I will wait behind the trees, and you have my word I will not glance while you re-robe."

Morgan pointed to the other side of the pond. Eloise took the hint and began swimming away as quietly as she could.

Continuing in her best baritone, Morgan added indignation. "I, good sir, am a peer of the realm and can see to myself. Now please leave me be." She quietly followed after Eloise, swimming silently for the other side and hoping it was too dark to see.

"Unless you want me to jump in after you, miss," he responded, obviously not fooled by her attempts at disguising her gender, "I suggest you swim this way now."

Eloise stopped and turned a worried look to Morgan.

Morgan stilled as well. "Blimey!" She cursed low and abandoned her failed pretense, replying in her normal speaking voice. "How do we know we can trust you?"

After another pause, he said, "On my honor, I will not harm you. I cannot say you will receive the same promise from the group of inebriated young bucks I saw not far down the road and headed this way. I daresay, they might not act as chivalrous when they stumble upon you." There was an odd note of both reproach and amusement when he added, "I actually *am* a peer of the realm. You have my word."

Edward slammed his cup down so hard the coffee splashed out and began soaking into the *Bon Ton Tattler*. He cursed and quickly rescued the paper from its liquid demise just as Boswell entered and gave a grumble of vexation. Edward waved the man off when he begrudgingly proceeded to actually tidy up the mess.

Two Times the Mischief

Edward stared at the gossip rag's headline, summoning up the will to re-reread the article.

The Bon Ton Tattler:

"*Two very pretty debutantes were spotted walking, unchaperoned, with one Lord "R" last eve. After Lord "R" was seen leaving the townhouse of Lord "W".*

Let us state the hour was late and the two lovely ladies were dressed as young lads and dripping wet. Let us also state there was no rain last night.

If we are waiting for the best scandal of the upcoming season, we best train our eyes on not one, but two, new beauties. Gentlemen, keep on the lookout and you might find yourself as happy as Lord "R" must have been last night.

Lord "D" better watch it, for it appears he'll have competition. Assuming he still has designs after he reads this tidbit.

The only thing more shocking to this writer is the absence of Lord "W", who was not spotted anywhere on the scene last night. Might our resident cad be settling down?

Keep your eyes set on tomorrow's paper for more on these interesting and scandalous developments from your local Bon Ton Tattler."

Edward was having a hard time managing his emotions, which were coming in strange sequences. First, anger, followed by blind rage. Not to be out done by murderous intent bringing up the rear.

On second consideration, now that he categorized them, they all closely resembled the same emotion: maddening, irrational, possessive fury. What was it about this damn woman? Did she really have no one looking out for her better good?

Was the Duchess Vandicamp that inept? Because it certainly did not take a mastermind to figure out *exactly who* this was about. Anyone who had read yesterday's column would put two and two together. Lord "D" was clearly the man with competition. Thus making 'the new redheaded debutante' one of the two ladies dressed as men from last night.

And...Lord *R*, seen leaving Lord *W*'s townhouse. Edward knew, all too well, there was no other Lord "W" that the *Bon Ton Tattler* was fonder of writing about than himself, Lord Wellington. Henry, who everyone likewise knew as Lord R, had left Edward's townhouse late the previous evening. In plenty of time for some duplicitous writer to gobble up the tale and get it to press before the bon ton woke to their favorite gossip paper. *Bloody hell!*

"Boswell!" he bellowed, and the china on the table actually shook.

His dignified, and much too sardonic, butler reappeared. "Yes, my lord? How might I best serve such a truly noble and deserving master? Again," Boswell asked, not appearing rattled at all that Edward was, at present, nearer to resembling a grizzly bear than a peer of the realm.

"Fetch me Lord Rockafetch. At once!"

Boswell bobbed his head and ambled toward the door, as if he might actually follow through with an order. A first. But alas, he swung back before his heel was completely across the threshold, cleared his throat, and schooled his features to just the precise level of irritating.

Edward closed his eyes and waited. He was in no mood to sack the man. Again, this week.

"Where, pray tell, would I find Lord Rockafetch? At his townhouse? Then, once located, should I mention that he is being fetched, as if he might be a lady's lap dog? Or perhaps I am all together wrong in understanding and we have acquired a dog that you have honored by naming it after your dear friend?"

Edward opened his eyes and glared at his butler. It was entirely too early for this.

"Although," Boswell continued. "I daresay Lord Rockafetch might not think it such a compliment. Either scenario, really. Nevertheless, where should I go about looking for said pup?"

Edward glanced longingly toward the liquor cabinet, wondering if it were too early to pour the brandy. "Boswell, you know exactly where Lord Rockafetch resides. Send word for him to come here, posthaste."

"But of course, Your Magnificent Lordship."

"Go. Now!"

"Yes, my lord." He heard Boswell turn and start his exit.

Finally.

"When you return, you are fired," Edward added.

Boswell continued out the door, not hesitating in his laborious pace. "Yes, of course, my just and deserving master."

Morgan slipped from beneath the sheets. Smiling, she sat on the edge of her bed and replayed the previous evening in her head. A laugh tumbled over her lips, startling her. She clamped her hand over her mouth when another one threatened, lest she wake the still-sleeping house.

What on earth? Her hand went to her forehead. No fever. She laughed at that, too. Perhaps she was going insane. Or perhaps this was how scoundrels were made. One daring adventure and they were addicted, from that moment forth, to the thrill of being *wicked.* That notion, of her and Eloise becoming cads, made her giggle anew.

Get a hold of yourself, Morgan Sinclair. She scolded her blithesome reflection staring back from her vanity mirror. She should be terrified at the very real possibility that the man that had discovered them might be downstairs, right now, convincing her aunt to send her to a nunnery.

Instead, she was experiencing some sort of strange high after their scandalous swim in the lake. Perhaps her caution thrown to the wind was due in part to the sworn secrecy from the man that found them out last night. If Morgan had not believed him, she would be having a completely different morning. But, for reasons unknown, she *did* believe him.

Now she wished she had gotten his name. By his clothing and demeanor, Morgan could tell he was financially well off. And, he certainly was attractive, with his easy smile and his laughing eyes. He seemed to find their stunt amusing. Possibly even impressive.

He had remained a gentleman and escorted them despite their adamant refusals, back to their houses without even a scolding. He then patiently waited for them to go, whispering frantically to each other up the lane that linked their two residences.

He did not carry on his way until they were safely inside. Morgan knew because she rushed to her bedroom window and watched him, his tall, confident figure strolling under the burning street lanterns that illuminated the cobblestones.

Having had little time to interrogate Eloise on their brief walk up their lane unchaperoned, Morgan had fallen asleep not having the slightest clue who their mystery gentleman might be. All she knew was that Eloise, who seemed to know everyone, was at a complete loss herself.

Mayhap he was just passing through London. That wiped the giddy smile right off her face. Morgan hand not considered that she might see him again.

Her heart began to beat like a trapped bird. The idea of having to encounter the man who had caught her naked as her name day in a lake was mortifying. Surely, she would perish on the spot if they crossed paths again. Morgan would rather be sentenced to the gallows than to endure the shame she would experience if he ever told a soul about her and Eloise's midnight swim.

She would just have to trust him. Besides, there was little she could do about it now. What was done, was done.

Morgan glanced at the grandfather clock on the other side of her bedroom. There was no time to call on Eloise to discuss a possible exit strategy from polite society if he went back on his word. Surely a band of gypsies would welcome them into the fold. On that grim thought, she stood, stepped into her slippers, and rang for her maid. She had a pianoforte lesson to get ready for.

Exactly one hour later, she met Lord De Montrey. It was another productive lesson, but somewhere toward the end of it they got off topic, straying into an entirely different subject—swordplay. The baron showed her the concealed rapier housed in his walking stick. Morgan had heard of the popular accessory and could not resist asking him if he wouldn't mind showing her a few fencing moves with the thin blade.

After a brief nod from Bertrice, the three made their way to the garden. Her chaperone found a shady spot to resume her knitting and Morgan found herself having a grand time.

"What if someone should come at me like this?" She jabbed at Lord De Montrey's right side with her practice sword, a stick.

The baron spun with catlike grace, caught her by the waist, and disarmed her. He held her firmly, but gently against his side. "I would do that."

His breathing had altered slightly, and she was suddenly aware of her predicament, but strangely, she did not feel nervous or uncomfortable in his arms. Instead, she simply felt...*nothing.*

Oh, this was a grand sign! If she could be so lucky as to land a husband that did not make her tremble. That would bode well for her. An agreeable business arrangement of a marriage was just the thing she needed.

No butterflies, no danger, no abuse... Simply everyone doing their job when their job was called upon. Like most societal marriages. She was just about to venture a glance up at the baron when a familiar, but absolutely savage-sounding voice pierced the silence.

"Lord De Montrey, are you sure that is a lesson you should be having during your allotted pianoforte time slot?" Lord Wellington demanded.

Lord De Montrey turned slowly toward, but the earl but did not release his hold on Morgan's waist. "Ah, Lord Wellington, how good of you to inquire. The lady has mastered what I have asked of her for the day and has now requested I show her how one should engage in swordplay." He made a purposeful show of removing his arm from around her midsection.

The action did something to the earl, for every muscle in his body appeared to grow taunt, the loose areas of his custom suit filling out, becoming a stricter fitting ensemble. *And his hands...*Morgan's eyes were drawn to them as if he were holding a gun. White-knuckled, they flexed around the handle of his own cane.

She felt her stare widen. He had his own concealed blade. His fingers flexed over the ivory handle and curled around it again. One he very much wanted to use.

The clean, crisp sound of the baron sheathing his weapon brought her eyes up from the earl's cane. "I find it interesting that you should care what I, and the lady, choose to do with our allotted time." The baron, seemingly unaware of how close he'd just come to bloodshed, added cavalierly.

When Lord Wellington took an abrupt step forward. De Montrey flinched. Maybe the baron *was* aware. Regardless, Morgan noted, if he were merely making a show of not caring, all pretense was undone with that one reaction.

The earl looked down his nose. "Your time is up."

Lord De Montrey, likely eager to escape his close proximity to the earl—as anyone with common sense would be—turned to Morgan and bowed over her hand, placing a chaste kiss on it. "Until tomorrow, Miss Sinclair."

"Until then," she replied, likewise anxious for the two men to be separated.

Before the baron could get out of earshot, the earl spoke again, loudly. "Morgan, would you care to join me for a ride after our lesson?"

The baron faltered and nearly stumbled. Morgan was utterly shocked and trapped. She could not refuse him, but that did not stop her feeling bad for the baron. Why did he have to ask her in front of her suitor? And why use her Christian name when she had never given him permission?

She looked up at the earl grinning smugly down at her, and every one of those questions were answered. *Because he is rotten...* The blasted man knew he had her trapped between a rock and a hard place. That was exactly what he wanted. He intended to give a direct cut to the baron, and since he had not been able to actually fight him, this was the next best weapon...wounding the man's pride.

"That would be lovely," she answered smoothly, trying to keep her opinions, and her voice, neutral.

Whatever was going on between these two men had nothing to do with her. Of that she was certain. They clearly had a past, and she was now the unwitting, and most accessible participant, in their rivalry.

"In your carriage?" she asked, willfully obtuse.

The baron continued, his way out of the garden, albeit slowly.

"No, on horseback," the earl replied.

Ah, an out! Morgan seized it. "I am afraid I do not have a horse here and the duchess only keeps the carriage steeds since she is past the age for riding."

"Not a complication. I had my steward bring an extra for you." He smiled, obviously pleased at the emotional thrashing he was delivering the baron, who had assumed the exiting pace of a crippled geriatric.

Morgan could not keep her brows from knitting together in frustration. She would not applaud him for baiting the baron so. The earl did not have any interest in her, and she did not want him to scare the only man with promise away.

"That was most gracious, my lord," she said through clenched teeth.

"Good. Shall we get started inside with your lesson?"

The baron rounded the garden's edge.

"That was not very gentlemanly," Morgan scolded, her voice barely audible.

"He is not acting in your best interest," the earl said flatly.

"Please elaborate, what are my best interests?"

The earl took a step closer to her and bent his head down, casting her in shadow. His breath was warm and seductive as it whispered across her skin. "He is taking too many chances with your body and reputation, my dear."

Morgan felt the blush rising. She would not retreat. But *heaven help her,* her pulse was about to burst from her veins. *This was decidedly bad.* It was as if her body was on its own mission to destroy any calm and collected façade she was desperate to present.

Her palms grew clammy. This was the *exact* opposite feeling she had experienced with the baron. Yet...she was not afraid as she would be with Roderick. She was just out of sorts. If he would just take a step backward.

Morgan marshaled a calming breath. "I feel it is not your concern, my lord. Now, I believe we have a lesson?" She turned to go.

He reached out and grasped her arm, turning her back to face him. Tiny fires lit over every inch of skin that his hand covered.

"I have decided to make it my concern." His voice brooked no argument.

"So that you can best Lord De Montrey in whatever game you two have going?" she sniped.

His eyes frosted into ice chips. "I assure you; this is not a game."

"Then, why?"

The question was over her lips before she could stop it. Surely, it was not wise to challenge this man. Yet, here she stood arguing with him like some sort of old married couple. "What exactly is the *concern* you have with me?"

His blue eyes bore holes into hers, as if he could mentally place the answer directly into her head. "I have... No. Earthly. Idea."

Morgan watched in puzzlement as the brutally honest admission settled around them. His reply spoke volumes; a complexity of chapters filling a book neither of them had read.

For a long moment, no one said anything, both of them rendered speechless. Speechless, until Morgan let out a laugh. A laugh that transformed quickly into a full-on cackle. It was everything a well-bred lady should *not* do, but she could no more put a stop to her fit than she could blot out the sun.

The earl's deadpan stare morphed into a sly grin, a flicker of gentle laughter dancing in his eyes. "Miss Sinclair, are you laughing at me?"

Morgan covered her mouth and nodded. It did no good. The laughter continued.

Lord Wellington's smile grew wider still until laughter broke free of his lungs. They both stood there, smack dab in the middle of the garden, chortling like two crazy people as the humor of the situation overtook them, their intertwining mirth just as sincere as the earl's forthright answer.

Lord help her. His joy—*that laugh.* It was as splendid as she had expected. And precisely as Morgan had feared, she was drawn to the honey-poured melody like a dizzy little bee.

Edward had gone from wanting to insist guardianship over the impressionable young debutante to wanting to press something altogether different upon her—his body. All in the space of a few seconds. Somehow, both desires brought about an undeniable yearning.

And here she was, laughing at him. Edward took in every inch of her as she continued her amusement, completely unaware of his simmering inclination. He had to smile as he watched her polished little temper roll to the ground in a fit of consuming giggles. It felt good, liberating, to let all previous pretenses go.

She had played her cards close to her chest. As guarded with him as he had been with her. Had she done it for the same reasons? The fear of falling prey to a baser desire?

Edward knew for certain that he had. Only, his cravings were accelerating at a rate that scared the hell out of him. The past few days had been filled with nothing but thoughts of her. And he had responded to those thoughts and emotions by acting as if she carried the plague around in her reticule, ready to douse him with it.

He had been so afraid of what giving into those temptations

might mean. Deep down, he knew they signified something more than mere physical pleasure. It meant that he felt for Morgan Sinclair what he had not felt for another. *That she was intended for him.*

Now that he had faced off with the part of himself that sought to deny those feelings, all he wanted to do was embrace them. He wanted to pursue her. He wanted to *win* her heart.

At that moment, a very real clarity hit him like a ton of bricks. *De Montrey would not have her.* Before Edward knew what he was doing, he cupped her jaw in his hands, drew her face to his and kissed her.

Her body froze, but her lips parted when his breath brushed against them. It felt like the most natural reaction in the world. He hoped to hell she had not been getting kissing lessons from other men. Her tongue circled his gently and he forgot that hideous thought.

His hand wound around the back of her neck and he laced his fingers through her loosely piled hair. When he deepened the kiss, she moaned. The sound was just about his undoing. He was sure he was about to drown in her light jasmine scent and the feel of her perfectly shaped body pressing against his.

Something struck him on the back of his head.

He whirled around to kill the man who had dared strike him, only to find himself confronted by a shoe-wielding lady's maid. The woman who had always acted as Miss Sinclair's chaperone was now staring him down as if she would enjoy nothing more than to flay him. Ah, how foolish of him to forget that she would, *of course*, be nearby.

He stared pointedly at the fuming chaperone who said nothing, just shook the shoe in his face as if challenging him to a duel. He held up his hands in surrender, trying his best to not laugh. After all, he had been at fault.

"I am very sorry, madam, it shan't happen again."

Miss Sinclair, from behind him, reassured her maid that everything was fine and that she would not allow the action to happen again. After the older woman fixed him with a warning shake of her shoe, she turned and headed back to her spot under the shade tree.

Edward laughed once she was out of earshot. "Does all of your staff act so boldly?"

He turned back to Morgan. She was staring at him, her eyes the color of spun gold, her pouty lips now a ruby red color from his kiss, and a pretty rose blush bathed her cheeks. *Heaven help him,* she was the most stunning woman he had ever seen.

"She has been in our employment since I was a small child and feels a deep sense of protection toward me," Morgan replied, her voice taking a huskier tone.

He rubbed the back of his head. "Indeed, she has a mean right hook. Maybe the Queen should have your maid instruct the royal guard in this new form of combat?"

Miss Sinclair continued to stare right into his soul with those burning eyes. "Shall we start our lesson, my lord?"

"Yes."

Edward motioned for her to pass and then followed her into the house, enjoying every second he was blessed with the view in front him. How he would survive holding her in his arms for dancing instruction, he was not sure. If she did not stop swishing those hips, he might not last long enough to find out.

As he struggled to calm himself, his eyes caught sight of some sort of movement in one of the upstairs windows. He looked closer, but saw only the curtain. It must have been swung by the breeze.

That, or he was so caught up in a lust-filled haze that he was imagining things. What the hell had he been thinking by kissing her? What if someone other than the maid had seen them? He would have to ask for her hand in marriage.

Most peculiarly, he mused, that notion did not scare him to death.

Morgan followed the Earl of Wellington out to the stables after their dance lesson. A dance lesson where she had learned absolutely nothing, except how not to salivate on her much too handsome dance instructor. *Her dancing master!*

Who had kissed her!

She was sure the world must have shifted on its axis. How else could one explain the day's events? First, she was arguing with the earl in her aunt's gardens, then *he had kissed her!*

Not just any kiss, either. The earl had kissed her with an intensity Morgan could have never dreamed possible. Desperate, raw, and passionate. Like a man deprived of water for days on end and then, finally, provided a ladle. To make matters even more shocking, she had kissed him back with a rivaling intensity. Feverish need stirred parts of her body and mind she did not know could, *or should*, be stirred.

As the soles of her shoes made crunching sounds across the rock path that led to the stables, the only thing Morgan was certain of was she wished she had not said yes to this ride. She had barely survived the lesson. What she needed to be doing right now was sitting in her room, locked away from polite society, until she could figure out how to rearrange herself in it. More importantly, how to handle it when it kissed her full on the mouth.

Polite society, *pish!* Morgan corrected her thinking. Edward Wellington was not polite. He was more in line with a hurricane. An unexpected and capricious force that pulverized everything in its path.

And that is exactly what a man like this would do to her reputation if word got out about that kiss. *Destroy it!* What she needed now was decidedly *not* more time in the path of a hurricane. She needed a storm shelter, a quiet place to hunker down and process her emotions regarding the hurricane that had just entered her life.

They reached the small stable and were greeted by a wide-eyed smiling groom who Morgan assumed was Lord Wellington's man. The lad was leading a beautiful bay stallion with a bright white blaze down its forehead and two large, intelligent eyes staring back at her. Morgan had never seen a more beautiful animal. Lord De Montrey's newly purchased steed did not hold a candle to this horse.

"He is incredible!" she said, in awe.

Lord Wellington stared straight ahead at the horse prancing toward them. "Yes, I quite think so, as well. His name is Elkinema."

"What breed is he?"

Morgan was sure she had never seen a horse such as this one before. The head was magnificently sculpted, a broad forehead dipping and tapering down to a delicate muzzle. The body of the beast was toned to perfection, its large powerful muscles flexing and constricting as it trotted toward them, his shiny coat gleaming in the sunlight. It was as if the stallion was aware of his own beauty, and proud of it. Morgan wished she possessed a fraction of the animal's confidence.

"He is an Arabian," the earl answered, a smile in his voice.

"I met a sheikh who was cultivating the breed in Egypt and immediately knew this horse was meant to be mine. But the man was unwilling to part with him. He knew he had a prize in this boy." His tone softened with pride. "However, after plying the man with enough liquor to kill an elephant, I was able to persuade him to sell."

Morgan had to laugh at the visual of the story. *Of course, he had.* She was just about to remark on his methods of persuasion when her aunt's groom walked out from the stable, leading the pretty dapple-gray mare from the auction. Morgan blinked, mouth agape with incredulity.

"What do you think?" the earl asked.

"That is the horse..." She strode purposefully toward the smaller mare. Reaching the animal's side and lifting her hand to its soft nose.

The inquisitive mare began to nuzzle her palm. Morgan smiled. This one might not be as impressive as the earl's or as dangerous as the baron's, but she was perfect in Morgan's eyes. She ran her hand down the horse's neck. Gravel crunched behind her, and a shadow fell over the mare's gray coat.

Morgan's hand stilled as a larger one laid across the top of hers.

Without a word, the earl turned her palm up and placed something small and round in it. "A peppermint." He smiled. "I daresay you will have her eternal love if you give her the candy."

Morgan moved the candy toward the horse's muzzle, keeping her hand low as she had been taught as a child. The clever mare had already zeroed in on the incoming treat, her lips reaching expectantly. Morgan opened her hand flat and laughed as the mare plucked it gingerly from her palm. "She is just splendid. I am so delighted you bought her."

"As I said at the auction, she is a very nice bit of horseflesh. I would have been a fool not to have snatched her up."

Morgan did not miss the emphasis he placed on the word fool. Opinionated and rivaling lords aside, she had also thought the mare would make someone very happy. She could not be more pleased that a man such as the earl would be giving the lovely steed a good home. He obviously took great care of, and had great concern for, his animals. Morgan liked him even more for it.

A fleeting suspicion ran like wild fire across her mind. Did he take such care and devotion with everything he held dear?

Probably not. If he did, he would not have garnered the reputation he had. She reminded herself that this man was rumored to care only for his own pleasure. Some people were just better with animals.

Although, he had shown considerable affection for his sister in the park. It was also common knowledge that the earl's entire family was very close. Likewise, he had a best friend and the two were rarely spotted apart.

All that gathered knowledge added up to the fact that the earl could care for others. However, he obviously drew a hard line in the sand as to who would be permitted into that lucrative circle of trust. Which might not make him selfish at all. He might simply be selective.

"Would you like to ride her?" The earl's question abruptly halted her ruminations.

Morgan looked up quickly. "Can I?"

"Any time you like." He smiled. "She is yours."

Her hand froze mid-stroke on the animal's neck. *What?* Morgan stared dumbly at him as he began adjusting the side strap on the bridle.

"Tommy," he addressed the groom. "You mustn't pull the strap so tight; imagine if you had to have a bit in your mouth, would you want it stretching back this hard?"

The stable boy looked mortified and shook his head. "No, my lord, it won't be that tight again, my lord," he stammered.

Morgan knew she was gawking like a dunce when he turned his attention back to her. She opened her mouth to speak, but words failed her. She really must stop this whole dying fish enactment she was adapting. Morgan closed her mouth and turned back to the animal.

"I am sorry, my lord, I think I misunderstood you," she said softly.

"The bit, it should not be drawn in too tight. Always double-check your saddle and bridle before you ride, for your own protection and that of your horse." He had leaned in and lowered his voice, obviously not wishing to embarrass her aunt's young groom.

The unexpected courtesy nearly knocked the wind out her. She had never known a lord to care about his servants' feelings. Why, her stepfather would probably have had the poor boy flogged.

Lord Wellington continued in a conspiratorial whisper. "Especially if you have not personally trained the staff to your expectations." He winked.

Everything Morgan thought she knew about the world flipped upside down with that wink. As a matter of fact, the only two things she was sure of now was that the Earl of Wellington was not what people painted him to be. *Not entirely.* The second certainty was that it was perfectly clear why every woman in Christendom wanted this man. He was charming beyond measure. *When he wanted to be.*

"Point taken." She took a calming breath before rephrasing the question. "However, I was asking about what you said before that."

She turned her focus back to the gray mare, unable to look him in the eyes. She was surprised how timid her voice sounded to her own ears.

The earl stepped close, his warmth flooding the space between them, and put one finger gently under her chin, tipping her profile to face him. "Yes." He smiled down at her. "I bought her for you."

Edward watched as three different emotions rolled across Miss Sinclair's face: first shock, followed by joy, then finally, concern. "I daresay it would appear most improper to accept such a gift, my lord."

"And I daresay, I have already behaved most improperly with you, Miss Sinclair." He leaned in, unable to stop himself. "Actions of which I have no regrets."

She dropped her gaze to the ground, but not in time. He could see the blush race up her neck. All she had achieved was to gift him a glorious view of her ample bosom. Heaven help him, but they were perfect. He wanted to test their weight in his palms. Push them up to his mouth. Taste her rose colored...

"Do you not agree, my lord?"

When she looked up, Edward had to quickly avert his eyes, leveling them on a stone cherub shooting water from its mouth in the middle of a bubbling fountain. He feigned contemplative interest in the water feature as his mind scrambled backward, a desperate attempt to recall what the first part of her question pertained to.

"Why do you suppose your aunt has a water fountain beside her stables?" was the only response he could think of. *Avoidance.* It had been his best friend on more than one occasion.

Miss Sinclair chuckled softly. "I suppose she wishes the horses to have the same tranquil sounds as the birds in the garden." She deliberated, gaze upon the ornate structure alongside him for a heartbeat.

"Now." She fixed her sights on him. "About the mare?"

"It is all taken care of." He looked back at her, hoping that would cover whatever he had missed.

It did not apparently, for she arched a brow the way women did when they had a man cornered. "How?"

Damn it to hell!

"I must apologize." Edward prepared his face for the slap that was about to come. "I did not hear your question for I was rendered stupid staring at your breasts."

For a moment, she said, and did, nothing. She simply looked at him, assessing. Likely considering if he might have been kicked in the head multiple times, by multiple horses, as a small child.

"Are you always so blunt, Lord Wellington?" she finally replied.

"I am afraid it is a trait I have possessed since youth. I am sorry if it offends you, but I have never mastered the art of lying."

"Am I to believe then, that you did not just tell me that because you are a horse's ass?"

He was ill-prepared for such a vivid characterization. "I am many things, but on this topic..." Edward felt himself grin. "I was not trying for that particular descriptive."

"Well then, I suggest we move on," she stated pragmatically. "Now that I know of your rogue tongue ailments, I can better prepare myself for them in the future." A smile threatened one edge of her mouth. "At least you are honest."

"To a fault."

"I am relieved to know you have them. Other than just being an insufferable cad." She turned back to the mare. "Care to help me up?"

Edward watched her for a moment, speechless. He had never heard such words from a woman before. Not from one that was not hurling an inanimate object at his head, anyway.

She looked over her shoulder at him. "I think I can get used to this honesty bit." She winked.

Of all the interesting revelations that had just occurred in their conversation over the last five minutes, that wink was the most telling. Edward was not even sure she knew she had done it. It was as if he had just been allowed to glimpse a side of Morgan Sinclair that had never before been seen.

Not that calling someone a horse's ass was likely anything that had crossed her lips before. But the wink was personal. And, *utterly adorable*. He took a step toward her.

"Now please, pray tell how accepting this gift will not cause scandal?" she asked, facing her saddle.

Edward placed his hands around her waist. It was so small. The young lady really did have curves in all the right places. *Like an hourglass.*

"I spoke with your aunt; she has agreed to tell anyone who should ask that she requested me to pick out the animal for you as a gift. From herself."

He silently applauded himself for having not gotten distracted by her body and lifted her up into the saddle, instantly regretting the action when his stitches stretched under his jacket. He was not quick enough at hiding his pained expression.

"Oh, are you all right?" She was looking down at him, worriedly. "I should have asked the groom."

Edward chuckled and cast his eyes to the spindly groom, who could be no older than twelve. "I assure you." He took a step back as his own groom approached. "I am more than capable for the job."

He thanked the lad and pulled up on to Elkinema, fighting to not put any undue pressure on his bad arm. "My arm was injured the other day, and it is not yet healed."

"Oh, no. How did you hurt it?" she asked, as he circled the stallion around, lining the two horses up with one another.

"*I* did not hurt it. Someone else hurt it when they shot me."

"Good God!"

"You really must stop using such language, Miss Sinclair." He smirked.

He could feel her eyes on him. "How were you shot?"

"With a pistol."

"Well, obviously, but why were you shot?"

He faced her, noting the way concern pinched her brows. "I am not clear on that. It happened when I was picnicking with my sister."

"Oh my! Who would do such a thing?"

Somehow, the notion that she cared touched him in the strangest of places...his heart. Or at least, he thought that was how that particular organ was referred to. "Not entirely clear on that one either. However, I would rather like it if this did not get out. I would appreciate it if you would not mention it to anyone."

"Of course," she said reassuringly.

They began to walk toward the park's east side entrance, with Miss Sinclair's shoe-wielding chaperone in the carriage not far behind.

"I bet you will be glad when you are married and no longer in need of a chaperone." He changed the subject now that they were starting to pass other people.

She sighed. "You have no idea... And thank you ever so much for the horse; she is the most splendid gift I have ever received."

He fully faced her, stupefied. Had she really just said the mare was the best gift she had ever received? The lady was from a good home. Surely, she had been given only the finest. At least, that was what he would do if he ever had a daughter. Hell, Greyland had been presented the world on a platter by their father. It was what fathers were supposed to do for their little girls.

"Surely you jest?" he queried. "I would have guessed you were rather doted on."

"My father was very loving, but he was not one to place value on the finer things, and we did not have a lot."

"How about your stepfather? I know he has extravagant taste. Why," he said, pausing to make a show of consulting his memory, "I remember him betting an ungodly amount on a race just last year. Good thing his mount won."

The silence was abrupt. Edward cut his gaze over to her. Her back had gone rigid, her fixed gaze locked straight on the trail, her lovely face unreadable.

"He has a son he likes to spoil," she finally said. "I merely came with the wife."

Though she delivered the words smoothly, their arrangement left an irrefutable impression. Those two sentences...Edward felt them like a punch to the gut. It was no secret that fathers wanted male heirs. Edward's family was the rare exception, but Miss Sinclair's brief summary hinted that there was more to it than that. It felt cold.

They rode in silence while Edward tried to process what he had just heard, his mind circling back on everything he thought he knew, searching for clues he might have missed. Her mother seemed reserved. He had not seen the earl in town as of late. Edward had assumed he was away on business.

A butterfly landed on Miss Sinclair's sleeve. She gave it a wan smile. It rode there, its yellow wings fluttering gently against the cool light blue fabric of her day dress. A dress Edward had seen her in three times now...

The bloody bastard!

The realization came crashing down on him. The earl was treating Miss Sinclair like unwanted property. He was not seeing to her needs at all. Her stepfather was likely hoping to discard of her sooner than later. And the jackass could not even see fit to outfit her properly for her deuced debut! *Why*, Edward's anger continued to mount, *the man's whores had more dresses than his own daughter!*

"He is a damned fool!" he snarled into the wind.

Morgan stared, shocked into wordless wonder at the fuming lord riding by her side. She immediately regretted the indiscretion of her words. She should have just nodded and changed the subject.

These men, her stepfather and Lord Wellington, were both peers of the realm. They would, of course, come in contact with each other.

What if the earl made mention of her conversational slip? All her well-laid plans could be over in the blink of an eye. Her stepfather had the power to lock her away for the rest of her life if he got word she was dishonoring his name.

Morgan closed her eyes. She had been so careless. So foolish. She needed to correct this. Quickly.

"I am sorry, my lord. I seem to have given you the wrong impression," she lamented. "My stepfather provides greatly for his family. I was being ungrateful."

He drew his stallion up short. "Ungrateful?" The word shot out of his mouth, more accusation than question.

Morgan pulled back gently on her reins and circled her mare back to face him. "I overstepped my boundaries. I would hate for word to get back to my—"

"Do not do that." He scowled. "Do not fear your secrets with me. And never diminish your worth in front of me."

"My worth?" Morgan blinked, unsure if she should be offended or honored. "My worth is only the sum of what my stepfather deems it. I am merely protecting that value." She decided on practical.

The earl muttered something unintelligible and spurred Elkinema forward. "That should not be the case," he stated as he passed.

Morgan, utterly uncertain how to proceed, turned her horse and followed at a distance. He was mad. *Very mad.* And she was not entirely sure why. There were no startling revelations in her statement. Any man of the bon ton would favor a blood heir over an inherited daughter. Secondly, there was nothing drastic in her wishing to amend her words.

*Still...*She watched the back of the earl as he rode in front of her, his jacket stretched tight across his broad shoulders. She was surprised the thread could hold the seams together. A blind man would be able to discern the earl's mood. His energy was palpable, rolling off him like fog through a valley.

"Sorry," he said finally, not turning to face her but slowing his steed's pace. "I was not raised to think that way. I fear I still have a rather hard time accepting the archaic beliefs of some men."

Morgan drew her mare alongside his stallion. They rode side by side in silence. She was not sure what to say. *Archaic beliefs of some men.* He might as well proclaim himself a unicorn. How was it even possible? That a man of his rank would be not only opposed the expectations outlined by society, but be adamantly angered by it?

Considering the earl was a man rumored to take his pleasure in consuming women, he was the last man she would have expected to find championing them for equal rights. *Was he?* Did his words and reactions honestly reflect that? She wanted to ask him, but she feared that would lead further into dangerous waters. She was already swimming in over her head.

The earl was so passionate, so straightforward. So...*opinionated.* Morgan feared she was on the cusp of something dangerous. She should change the subject, start talking about dresses and bonnets. Something utterly droll.

Why then, did she not? Why was she riding alongside the man, allowing him to brood over life's little injustices? More importantly, why did she want to know more about how his mind worked?

She swallowed hard as the next realization hit. Why did she ache to find out if the opinions in his head aligned with those of his heart? Did he have a heart that truly felt a woman should not diminish her worth? He most certainly had a mouth that would tell her just that.

She shook her head, trying to dislodge the wayward thoughts. This man, Edward Wellington, was about as beneficial to her plans, as gunpowder was to a spark. She was supposed to escape Roderick by finding a nice man who would protect her through marriage. Morgan had never allowed herself to consider a love match. There was no such thing for her.

With time, she was sure she would grow to care for her future husband. But she had no foolish ideas of being swept off her feet by blinding romance. The Earl of Wellington, with his soul-consuming kisses, dashing good looks, and progressive thinking, was wreaking havoc on all this.

The man had even bought her a blasted horse! Had he literally walked out of a fairytale novel? Morgan needed to put some distance between them before she did something stupid. However, she was pretty sure kissing him in broad daylight, then accepting a thousand-pound, fur-covered gift would qualify nicely as addle-brained. *Stupid, stupid, stupid.*

Just as she was about to suggest that they turn back, a carriage crested the hill. Morgan looked to Lord Wellington. He was squinting, trying to make out the family crest engraved on the side of the shiny black phaeton.

"This is going to be Lady Printmose," he concluded as the carriage ambled toward them. "Have you been acquainted yet?"

"No, but I am to attend her ball."

"Well, it seems you will have the honor today." He nodded as the phaeton rolled to a stop.

Lady Printmose, a woman close to Morgan's mother's age, sat perched across from a pretty brunette in a beautiful green day dress that fit her as if she had been melted down and poured into it. There was no modest way to describe it. Her breasts were huge.

"Lady Printmose, Miss Rosewood." The earl smiled. "Might I have the pleasure of introducing you to Miss Sinclair, Lady Vandicamp's niece?"

Both women looked at her now. Morgan was not sure what she had expected from the gentlewomen of the bon ton, but what she was receiving was calculated observation. There was zero warmth in either set of eyes.

She decided to make up for the frosty reception by being overly cheerful. "It is so nice to meet you." Morgan smiled brightly, looking to each of them. "I am looking forward to attending your ball next week, Lady Printmose."

"A pleasure, Miss Sinclair," Lady Printmose replied dryly. "My niece, Miss Rosewood, will also be in attendance."

Morgan beamed from the older woman to the younger Miss Rosewood, who looked to be close to her own age. "It will be lovely to have some familiar faces. So nice to meet you, Miss Rosewood."

The younger woman nodded dismally before looking expectantly to Lord Wellington. "You will be there, will you not, Edward?" She smiled radiantly up at him.

Lady Printmose cast a quick, scolding glance at her niece, but the pretty brunette did not seem to notice. She was too focused on the earl, *Edward,* and her efforts to lean provocatively forward, gifting him the best view down her cleavage. Morgan recalled what the earl had said earlier, in blunt honesty, about her own neckline and wondered if he would be able to respond to the question.

"I would not miss it for the world," he said evenly, looking Miss Rosewood directly in the eyes.

A little flag rose and waved victoriously in Morgan's mind. *Take that, harlot.*

Yes, Morgan morbidly realized, she was jealous. And no, this would most certainly *not* do.

VI

*L*ady Printmose's ball was in an hour. *One hour.* Morgan fought to keep down the cucumber sandwich she had picked at during high tea. That had been two hours ago. Still, every time she thought about the lengthy list she needed to remember, in order to present herself as the perfect debutante, her stomach twisted anew.

She staved off another bout of nausea and tried to execute the last pattern in the waltz. She simply needed to keep her mind on the task. Right, left, pivot, pivot, pivot, over-sway.

Oh, blast it, was it an over-sway or a same-foot lunge? Why had the man gone and kissed her beforehand, leaving her head spinning to the point of distraction and unable to concentrate on their lesson. Was this what Eloise had had trouble with, too? Morgan wished she had been more sympathetic to the *cons* of having a handsome dance master now.

She sighed. She had not seen Lord Wellington since their ride in the park. The day he had kissed her, given her a horse, and then promptly up and lost interest. She should not be surprised. Morgan had been warned about him.

Edward Wellington was a rake, and rakes were not known to maintain interest in silly young ladies. They had reputations to uphold, after all. What she was surprised by was how much it hurt. Morgan thought she had glimpsed another side to him that day in the park. But perhaps she had been wrong.

She imagined she would see him at the ball tonight. She would act like nothing was amiss. *Even if it was.* Because the truth of it was she had felt his absence over the last week like a void...something important missing in an otherwise pleasant routine.

Her mornings were quiet with her mother and aunt at the breakfast table. Morgan took her afternoon tea with Eloise still, and her music lessons with the baron fell right on time. Everything was as it should be, except for that missing hour... The hour she had gotten used to sharing with Lord Wellington and his devil-take-all attitude. The lost hour in her day that she had filled in with self-practice, alone in the ballroom, with only her thoughts.

Morgan plopped down on her bed, abandoning all efforts to recall the dance pattern, and stared at the ceiling. She needed to wrangle in her forlorn reasoning. The earl was a conundrum that she could not afford to waste energy on.

Not when she had a task at hand to focus on, making the best possible entrance into society tonight. Her head rolled to the side, observing the interlacing designs of the burgundy wallpaper. Her thoughts felt as twisted as the fabric.

At least, Lord De Montrey was consistent. He had sent flowers every day and had continued her musical instructions without missing a single one. His intentions were clear. Morgan was not sure why she was not happier. He was a kind man, attractive, and financially sound.

He had only once been put off—when he had seen the dapple-gray mare in her aunt's stable. Morgan had played it off, just as the earl had told her, and the baron seemed somewhat mollified.

Lord De Montrey was quite perfect for her plan, really. Then why did she have such reservations? Maybe it was the stark differences between him and the earl.

Morgan had thought the baron might try to steal a kiss on one of their lessons, but he had remained always the gentleman. She really did need to stop comparing the two men. Lord De Montrey was vastly different from her unpredictable, say anything, earl.

Morgan caught herself, *her earl?* Wonderful. Even her subconscious was becoming possessive. She really must put a halt to this. It was most unproductive. She had an astute plan that allowed no idle time for childish daydreams. A soft knock came at her door, saving her from herself.

"Come in," she called.

Bertrice opened the door and hurried in with a large white box.

"Is that?" Morgan sat up, eager.

"Yes, miss, and it is not light." Her maid laid the box atop Morgan's bed and lifted the lid.

Both women let out a gasp.

"It is exquisite!" Bertrice exclaimed as she carefully lifted the ball gown from the silk-lined box.

Every debutante had to wear a shade of white or cream for their first appearance in society. Even though the season would not officially start until the spring, the duchess had insisted Morgan adhere to the rule since this was her first formal debut. Everyone knew better than to argue.

The modiste, masterful indeed, had assessed that Morgan's hair color and golden skin tone would best be served in a champagne color gown. Everyone agreed. All the subsequent fittings, five, had gone smoothly and Morgan had been quite pleased with the creation she had last tried on at Madame LeMore's shop.

However, this was not that dress. The dress Morgan had been fitted for was to have a simple, nothing exceptional, square-cut neckline. This gown's neckline was shockingly lower than what she had asked for and scooped off the shoulders. Why, the cut would be scandalous on a small-chested girl; Morgan's ample bosom would barely be contained.

She studied the rest of the gown, trying to find what of it *was* as discussed. The gossamer sleeves were as planned, stitched tight at the shoulders, then cascading freely to fall loose at her elbows. The gold thread, delicately interwoven throughout the champagne material of the gown's skirt, was as promised and simply gorgeous, catching the light just enough to make it shimmer. And it looked to be the correct length, Morgan noted. She supposed that was saying something.

But the bodice... It was to have started just below the bust. An older fashion, yet, still respected as being discreet, but the modiste had given her a snug fitting one, trimmed with gold lace and nipped in tightly at the waist. It would require a corset. A corset that would only further highlight her hourglass figure.

This would have the exact opposite effect from the one she had been hoping for. Morgan had told her aunt and Madame LeMore she did not wish to flaunt her curves; she had been specific in her insistence that the skirt must start below the bust, diminishing her measurements. *This...*allowing the waistline to start at the waist would highlight just how vast-ranging her bust to-waist-to-hip ratio actually was.

Why, it would leave absolutely nothing to the imagination. It would be as if she were wearing no clothing at all. Morgan wanted to cry.

"Blast it!"

Bertrice admonished her with a quick wagging finger. "Let us get you into it before jumping to conclusions." She suggested, reading Morgan's mind. "It is quite fashionable."

She turned and allowed her maid to begin undoing her day dress. "It will show too much, Bertrice. What man will want to associate with a woman who dresses so...wantonly?"

She huffed and kicked out of the rest of her gown before turning to step into the ball gown. Bertrice's lips twitched, as if she fought back a smile. "What?" Morgan asked.

"I believe your aunt's intentions with this dress were based on a different belief."

Morgan lifted her mass of hair and Bertrice laced the stays on the back of the scandalous ball gown. "My desire is to find a good man to marry. Not to be seen as a temptress."

"My dear." Bertrice turned her around. "A man wants to be tempted. And any man lucky enough to claim your hand would no doubt consider himself the luckiest man alive. Why, if more women possessed your wits and charm, I daresay there would be far less— well, let us just say that your future husband's eyes shall never look at another."

Her maid stepped back. "Now, look at yourself child and remember this; the physical body is only a small part of what tempts a man."

Morgan turned back to the large mirror standing by the chest of drawers and stopped in place. The image looking back at her was not what she had expected. The woman reflected in the mirror was truly beautiful. The dress fit like a glove but, somehow, did not look wanton at all. In fact, she appeared both elegant and alluring. She did not feel that the dress displayed her like a trollop, but rather, a confident young lady.

A slow crawl of confidence began to spread through her mind. Could she do this? Could she cast aside all the doubts Roderick had sowed into her mind and put her best foot forward? Could she *not* be ashamed of her body?

Instead, could she embrace it? Bertrice, fiddling around at the hem of her dress, brought Morgan back to the present. She looked down to see what her maid was consumed with at her feet.

"This dress will be the talk of the bon ton, Miss." Bertrice began gathering up one side of Morgan's many skirts, then duck-waddled around her and began hemming up the other.

Morgan stood in awe, noting for the first time what made the garment so heavy. The underskirt was gold lace, delicately beaded with white seed-pearls. The effect was magical. It made the bottom of the dress come alive, as if a treasure chest has been unearthed at her ankles.

"Turn," Bertrice ordered, sitting back on her knees.

Morgan obliged, spinning in place. The colors caught the light and lifted the many layers of material, drowning the room in joyful rich hues. This dress would *indeed* get her noticed tonight.

Perhaps her aunt, mother, maid, best friend, and dressmaker had all known what they were talking about. Morgan beamed, on the verge of a new set of tears. She felt like a princess in this gown, straight out of a fairytale.

Oh, blast it to Hades. She was damn sure going to enjoy this feeling! She might not ever get the chance to experience it again. If only for tonight, Morgan vowed, she was going to adore herself.

Edward felt the pressure in the room shift the moment Miss Sinclair entered through the lush fern and palm-filled hall. Henry was standing in front of him, facing the entry. Edward read every damned thought in his friend's head when the earl looked back over his shoulder at him. He knew every man in attendance was suffering from the same affliction, speechlessness.

"Henry?"

"Yes?" he replied, his attention turned back to the entrance, his gaze fixed on the staircase, which Miss Sinclair was now descending.

"Must you stare so?"

"Yes."

"I realize she is pretty, but surely she is feeling rather intimidated under the extreme scrutiny she is receiving." Edward ventured a glance around the room. Sure enough, more than a few mouths had gone slack. "Lord Hunten just took an elbow to the gut from his wife. I insist you look away."

"She does not seem to mind the attention. In fact, I believe she just kissed Lord Kinsworth on the mouth."

"What!"

Edward whirled around and found his target smiling warmly, surrounded by at least seven men. He could only see her face, *and indeed,* she did not seem fazed in the least. Thank God, Lord

Kinsworth was not one of the men salivating at her feet. Edward rounded on Henry, who was smiling with unbridled satisfaction.

"My, my, I do not believe it." Henry teased.

"Don't." Edward cautioned. "I am merely concerned for her."

"Ah, yes, merely concerned?" Henry mocked. "That makes complete sense. But tell me, how it is that you have managed to repress your more... shall we say, *libertine* nature?"

Edward lifted his chin, dignified. "I have rather strong willpower when I choose."

"Since when?"

"Since now!"

Edward was fighting to keep his voice at a conversational level. Much as he had fought the relentless pull of his fist toward Lord Rockafetch's mouth earlier that week when Henry confessed to having escorted Morgan home from her rendezvous with the lake.

God's teeth, but she must have been a sight to behold emerging from that water. And Henry had seen her first. *First...*

Did he just imply, in his own meanderings, that *he* would be partaking in that pleasure? *What on earth!* Henry's gaze moved to the dance floor, pulling Edward from his distracted state.

"Well, I daresay other men will fail where you have so gloriously succeeded."

Edward followed his friend's line of sight across the room. Miss Sinclair was being escorted into the first set of the night, a waltz, by Lord De Montrey. The man was beaming with his accomplishment as he puffed out his chest and pulled her possessively into his arms.

Edward saw red. *Literally saw red.* He glanced down at his palm and realized he had drawn blood with his fingernails from the pressure caused by his clenched fist.

Henry, who never missed a beat, removed a swatch of cloth from his inner jacket pocket and handed it over. Edward nodded his thanks. They were best chaps for a reason. Henry might bait him in jest, but he always had the good sense to know when Edward had had enough.

"I believe a drink is in order." Henry turned toward the bar.

"I will join you in a moment." Edward tossed the bloody handkerchief onto a serving boy's empty tray as he walked by.

"You know where to find me."

The two parted as Henry headed for the bar and Edward drifted closer to the edge of the ballroom, as if pulled by a mystical force. Why did he need to see this? Why did his feet keep marching him closer to the grim scene unfolding on the dance floor? This was *exactly* what he had told himself he would *not* do!

Edward finally managed to get an unobstructed look at her. *That gown.* It was perfect on her. He swallowed hard. She was the most exquisite woman he had ever seen!

Why in God's good name had her aunt and mother allowed her out of the house in that dress? She would have ten proposals come tomorrow. He tasted bile in his mouth at the thought of whose name would no doubt be at the top of that list.

He suddenly wanted to rush onto the dance floor, snatch her away from the smug baron and kiss her so passionately that all of England would know who she belonged with. He started to move on that notion when a firm hand landed on his shoulder. He turned sharply, ready to confront whoever dared touch him.

"I am going to insist, just this once, that you do not run off half-cocked," Henry advised. "This would be an ideal time to pretend you were someone else. And think before reacting. Maybe ask yourself; what would Perkin do?"

Edward stared at his friend, processing the surprisingly logical suggestion. How did the man manage that? The ability to know what Edward was about to do, oftentimes before he himself knew?

Regardless—Edward put aside the puzzlement over his friend's mind-reading abilities—it had worked. He exhaled and applied the sage advice. This would be the ideal time to exercise what his older brother might do.

"You are right."

"What was that?"

"Oh, bugger off, Henry."

Edward chuckled and took the glass of sherry his friend held out. He really should not be surprised. He and Henry were both cast from a similar cloth; second sons. And, as said 'spares' they had both vowed, early in their friendship, to make no apologies for the circumstances of being born after the heirs. Nor would they be bothered by envious gossip concerning their new titles, or the unorthodox fashion by which they had come about them. Murder, no matter how deserved, tended to set tongues wagging, after all.

"Mayhap, I spoke out of turn." Henry turned back to the dance floor, interrupting Edward's trip down memory lane. "That impulsive side of yours might come in handy this time?"

Edward lifted the back of his hand and pressed it to the earl's brow. "No fever," he proclaimed.

Henry swatted it away. "It must be another affliction." He narrowed his eyes. "Or perhaps I am simply growing tired of being your voice of reason?"

"Oh, do not dare stop giving your steadfast opinions." Edward shook the ice loose in his glass. "Even if I usually fail to take it, I assure you, I do lock it away for rainy days when I am in need of something to bore me." He tipped back the last swallow of sherry.

At that moment, a large pink hair configuration appeared in front of them. The two men gazed down to find Duchess Vandicamp beneath the oversized turban. Smiling like a cat with a canary stuffed in its mouth, she produced a dance card and proceeded to write Edward's name on it, and then added Henry's. Edward looked at his friend mystified. Henry only shrugged.

"Are you honoring us with a dance later, Lady Vandicamp?" Henry inquired, smiling.

"Oh, no, Lord Rockafetch." She laughed, and the headdress bounced about as she continued to scribe. "This is for Miss Sinclair." The duchess peeked out from under the listing turban, smile broadening. "I am securing all the best bachelors for my niece tonight." She winked.

Edward was not sure if the sudden sensation of his jaw unhinging was due to the sheer assumptive boldness of directing a man's dance card, or from hearing that the duchess considered *him* to be one of the bon ton's *best* bachelors. Before he could object, she continued.

"You are most certainly on that list, dear boy." She patted his arm almost sympathetically. "As a matter of fact, you are up first."

Lady Vandicamp wrapped her arm around Edward's and began pulling him toward the dance floor. Despite his muttered protest, the duchess marched him right up to Miss Sinclair and Lord De Montrey. Only when they were standing beside the couple did Lady Vandicamp release Edward to take hold of her niece, practically prying her from baron's dance frame.

Miss Sinclair was thrust into Edward's arms before anyone of them had time to draw a breath. "Oh lovely." The duchess clapped her hands twice, as if it would hasten the process. "Another waltz."

There was absolutely nothing to indicate the next song. Edward cast a glance around the room, wondering if he had gone deaf. Couples were lining up, but no one had started to move. He was just opening his mouth to comment...*on anything*...when the first low strings of a violin weaved into the crowd.

Having no viable out, he lifted his arms and shifted his weight, preparing them for the first movement. Surveying his position among the other dancers he couldn't help but notice that Lady Vandicamp looked pleased with herself. De Montrey looked as if he was trying to set Edward on fire with his eyes.

Miss Sinclair simply looked gorgeous. Her innocent owl-shaped eyes blinked up at him from beneath the thick curtain of her lashes. *Morgan Sinclair...* The woman who had consumed his dreams for the past week was in his arms, once again.

By Jove, she felt good there. The warmth of her. Her familiar scent of jasmine...

He closed his eyes. *Count, damn it.* Edward forced his mind to respond to the melody drifting in. The next waltz. But one had just played. This was the second; *most unusual.* The second waltz played... that *only* Lady Vandicamp had heard...

Edward opened his eyes. The duchess stood by the edge of the dance floor, satisfaction practically rolling off her like scent off a skunk. She had orchestrated this whole stunt!

Why though? Morgan all but had the baron on bended knee. He was the much safer choice. Everyone could agree with that.

"Hmm?"

Edward looked down, to the source of the sound.

"Whose bosom has you so entranced tonight, Lord Wellington?" Miss Sinclair smiled, her gold eyes shining, conspiratorially.

He began to move to the beat, if only for fear of getting trampled. "I daresay I have not had time to get so marvelously distracted."

She huffed. "I expected more from you tonight."

Edward felt his lips pull into a smile. "And whose bosom do you think I should survey first?"

"Mine, of course."

He ran into Lord Herst.

After a quick apology, they resumed their dance.

"Please do not talk that way, else we will end up on the floor." he admonished, unable to sound serious.

"Well, that is not very romantic."

"I meant falling to it. As in a crash. A painful, non-romantic, embarrassing, not-at-all sensual, flub." He chuckled and glanced down.

Her smile was pure delight. *She was messing with him.*

"Why Miss Sinclair, if I did not know better, I would think you were inciting mischief?"

"I know it is such an unusual word for you." She smirked. "Try sounding it out. M.I.S.C.H.I.E.F."

The child in him rose to the playful goading. If she wanted to test him, he would test her right back. He whisked her into a series of pivots, then followed them up with an advanced pattern he knew they had not studied. It worked; she pressed her lips together, determined, and closed her eyes. Doing just as he had instructed her on their first lesson.

She moved through the next sequence of patterns as if she had danced them a thousand times. Encouraged by her follow, Edward continued to swing and sway, diving and suspending their movements to the music, matching the tempo's insatiable hunger with his own unspoken desires. He spun her in three tight turns and lunged forward, taking both their weight nearly to the ground in a dramatic and finalizing dip.

He stared down at his bewitching partner, her breaths now coming in rapid succession, fueled by the dance's exertion. Unable to let go despite the music's end, Edward held her in the suspended position, his large body hovering over her more delicate one. Someone, somewhere, started clapping. Morgan's eyes fluttered open, panic flashing in her golden orbs.

Edward smiled down at her. "You were poetry, Miss Sinclair."

Gently, he lifted her back to her feet. The room had gone as silent as a tomb around them. They were the only ones left on the floor. Not even the musicians dared interrupt the silence that hung in the dance's finale.

Edward took Miss Sinclair's arm and escorted her off the floor. Lace fans flipped open and rose to mouths around them like a Roman stadium wave. He ignored them.

When they reached the edge of the dance floor, Edward did not stop. In addition, he did not politely deposit Miss Sinclair back with her aunt and mother. Instead, he marched on, her hand encapsulated in his, past the quizzical and gossiping onlookers, through the veranda doors and out onto the balcony.

Lord Wellington released his hold on her when they reached the wide stone balustrade of the terrace. Morgan stood speechless as he turned, leaned over the edge, and braced both hands on the railing.

He dropped his head between his shoulders after a long moment and sighed.

"I am afraid I am destined to bring scandal to you, my dear." He stared out into the dark of the garden.

Morgan watched his resplendent profile. His honey-blond hair seemed to beckon the moon to its strands so the light could play in the thick, golden waves. His aristocratic nose and forehead were straight, as if carved of stone. His jaw and cheekbones were sharp and strong.

Morgan found herself wanting to taste him there, just underneath his jawline, where the hard angles met the soft skin of his long neck. She wondered if he would flinch if she did so now.

"I fear that I find myself a willing participant in said scandal." Her words sounded strange, her tone raspy, a hungry growl to it.

He turned his head slowly to her, hesitation in his eyes. "If we are being honest, I need to make an amendment to a pledge I made with myself. Before our first meeting."

"That would be?" Morgan found herself stepping closer to him, her legs moving on their own accord.

Without so much as a blink, he focused on her. "I believe I would like to call on you tomorrow." He paused, looking to be considering his words carefully. "Not as your teacher. But, as an admirer."

Morgan swallowed. The desire to touch him was too strong. He took a step toward her, as if moved by the same impulse. She reached out and gently allowed the tips of her fingers to trace the pristine tailoring of his jacket. He loomed over her, his hooded eyes conveying more than words, challenging her to retreat. She did not.

Instead, she dragged in a shaky breath. "I would very much..."

"How charming, my dear sister has a smitten beau." Roderick's venomous words split the air.

Morgan felt her spine go ramrod straight. She stood, paralyzed in place, cold dread crawling over her skin. Her fingers retreated, back down to her sides. They were shaking.

She heard footsteps echoing off the stone, descending on her.

Still, she could not move. Her eyes stayed locked on the earl's neatly tied cravat.

"Morgan?" the earl asked directly, his voice pitched low, but not so low that Roderick would not be able to hear.

He blatantly used her Christian name, same as he had done last week in the garden with Lord De Montrey. Only this time, it sounded different. It gave her strength. In that one word he was giving her a weapon. *Himself.*

She slowly turned toward her stepbrother. Roderick smiled tightly, barely contained fury radiating off him in waves.

"I am so glad I found you when I did, else you might have succeeded in using your charms to lure this poor man to his doom." Her stepbrother's smile twisted in on itself, growing ugly.

"Who are you?" Lord Wellington asked icily.

Roderick's eyes darted up and over Morgan's head to challenge the man standing behind her. "I am this young woman's guardian." He snorted derisively. "Who the hell are you?"

"A man who does not take kindly to the words you are hurling about," the earl ground out as he gently nudged Morgan aside and stepped forward.

She could see Roderick bristle at the challenge. Without warning, he reached out and snatched her arm, pulling her hard to him.

She smashed into his chest as he hissed into her ear. "Be a good girl and get inside. Before I am forced to teach you a lesson. In public."

The earl's voice boomed, reverberating around them. "Touch one hair on her person again, and I will meet you on a field at dawn."

Morgan whipped her head around. *No!* A whole new fear seized her. Roderick never missed. It was one of the few things he was good at.

Her eyes latched onto Lord Wellington's, begging him to back down. She could see by his stance—shoulders squared, and feet braced apart—that he had no intention of doing so. His expression was one that welcomed the idea of his challenge.

"I will go in." She looked back, frantically. "Please," she pleaded to Roderick. "Let us go in before we cause a stir."

"Get your things and tell your aunt I am taking you home," he snapped.

Morgan knew her horror was painted across her face. She tried to keep her voice even. "Surely, I can ride back with the Duchess..."

"No!" Roderick bared his teeth. "You are leaving with me. Father would be most upset if he knew I allowed you to behave so wantonly. Why, you disgrace the good name we allowed you to borrow!"

Her stepbrother leaned in so close she could feel his breath on her forehead. She closed her eyes. "It is time you learned your place."

Morgan had no time to react as she was shoved away with enough force to send her tumbling into a nearby potted plant. She heard herself scream, but was not sure if it was from the jolt of being pushed, or from the sound of bodies colliding behind her. She quickly righted herself and spun.

Both men were locked in battle, rolling across the terrace, fists flying. The ballroom doors burst open, and half the guests poured outside. A lady shrieked. A man was shouting. The terrace became a blur of black tailored suits.

Morgan searched the chaos, desperate to locate *Edward*. Someone was dragging her stepbrother upright. There, amidst a flurry of flailing arms, was the earl. He looked murderous, his blond hair falling lose into his face as he was restrained by four men. Roderick was cursing like a rabid dog, clearly unaware that he had been losing the scuffle and should probably shut up now.

"What on earth is going on?" The duchess's voice rang out, rising above the confusion.

"Lady Vandicamp," the earl snarled. "I wish to pay court to your niece."

The crowd collectively inhaled, leaving the statement to hang in the dead silence of the crisp autumn night.

Roderick lunged forward, breaking the quiet like shattering glass. "Absolutely not!" He sounded near hysterics, his accusatory hand reaching out, one long manicured finger shaking, like a man in the onset of an apoplectic fit. "Why, I just caught the brute pawing at her!" He spat the words, obviously not realizing his accusation's potential ramifications.

"Let me rephrase." The earl's gaze sharpened, his voice galvanized. "I have compromised the lady. I would like her hand in marriage."

Morgan heard a multitude of gasps, just before her vision began to grow fuzzy around the edges. Was that Eloise near the doors? With the stranger who had caught them skinny dipping? Did the earl just propose to someone? *Was this how one's debut into London society typically went?*

Morgan's head grew heavy; she reached for the railing. *Roderick was going to kill her.* Her world went black.

Edward, aided by everyone's distraction at Morgan fainting, was able to dislodge himself from the men who had been restraining him. He rushed toward her, pushing bodies out of his path.

"Out of my damn way!" He shoved a man to the right, elbowed another in the ribs to his left. "She needs air, damn it!"

The sea of onlookers parted. He saw Henry gathering Miss Sinclair up and starting to rise. Edward reached his side and took over, carefully allowing Henry to transfer her into his arms. She was out cold.

He heard her stepbrother bellowing. Thankfully, someone had seen to holding the idiot back. Though Edward very much wanted to kill the man, he needed to make sure Morgan was safe first.

A young lady, whom Edward had been introduced to earlier but whose name he could not recall, was shouting at people to clear a path. Surprisingly, the diminutive blonde was quite the commander, issuing directions and warnings. Edward could feel every eye in attendance on them as they made their way into the house. He heard several voices offering assistance.

"Water, smelling salts, a doctor, wine," the blonde ordered ahead of him.

He stared down at the lifeless beauty in his arms. There appeared to be no blood, none that was gushing, but he would have to look her over more carefully once he put her down. By God, *if she was hurt badly...* Heaven help her foolhardy stepbrother.

Lady Printmose could be heard moving into the fray and taking over for the younger woman, ushering them into a quiet parlor. Edward entered and looked up at his surroundings for the first time since he had taken possession of Lady Sinclair. Assessing the room, he walked swiftly over to a damask-covered sofa and gently laid her down.

Lady Vandicamp was close behind, rushing to Morgan's side. The occupancy of the room swelled as De Montrey marched in, followed by Henry, and lastly, three servants with baskets of provisions.

"Is she alright?" asked the blonde lady who had been leading the way, her voice sounding not nearly as confident now.

"What is the meaning of this, Wellington?" the baron demanded, clearly more concerned with the loss of his marriage prospect than with the woman herself.

"She will be fine," the duchess announced, taking a wet cloth offered by a servant and applying it to Miss Sinclair's brow. "The poor dear just had a nasty swoon. Can you blame her? A proposal on the heels of a public brawl, after being ruined at her first ball?" She gave Edward a pointed look.

Edward felt a new anger building inside him as his hand flew out from his side to point angrily, in the general direction of the door. "Did you know how that posturing little shit treats her?"

Lady Vandicamp turned to the others. "Out, all of you." She looked at Edward squarely. "You will stay; you are her intended, after all," she added hotly.

Once the door was shut, Lady Vandicamp turned back to him. "I will have to discuss your proposal with her mother and stepfather, of course." She removed a blanket and covered her niece, who was starting to stir. "Making an enemy of her brother may not bode well for you."

"That man is no normal stepbrother!"

Edward turned and paced to a brandy decanter located on a side bar. "He threatened her! He is perverse, and I demand to know what you know about this family!"

"This stays between us." Lady Vandicamp stood and moved cautiously to his side.

"Her stepfather beats my sister." She spoke quickly and in hushed tones. "I need to help get Morgan away from him before he turns his fists on her. I know nothing about the relationship between the siblings, but based on Roderick's outburst out there..."

The duchess wrung her hands worriedly and glanced over her shoulder at her niece. "I too, now have deeper concerns."

Edward ran a hand through his hair. He would kill the sick bastard if he had to. Did this explain her shyness the first time they had been alone? Had Miss Sinclair been scared of him?

She had most certainly been terrified of her stepbrother, practically turning to stone when she had heard his sardonic voice. And it had nothing to do with being caught standing too close to a known cad. She had been terrified of Roderick.

That thought, that singular notion, that the bastard outside might have given Morgan reason in the past to react like a beaten dog in his presence now, was too much to process. *He would kill him!* Edward turned back to the sofa. Miss Sinclair was starting to push herself upright.

He moved to go to her, but the duchess stepped into his path, pressing a flat hand firmly to his chest. "No one can know of our suspicions."

"Of course," Edward answered tightly.

"Where am I?" Morgan muttered.

"My dear, you fainted." The duchess turned and walked briskly to her niece's side.

Edward could see the moment realization lit in her eyes. It looked a lot like dread. He moved to the opposite side of Lady Vandicamp and took Miss Sinclair's hand.

"Everything will be fine. Just leave it all to me." He tried to smile, to reassure her, but it withered on his lips when her breath hitched, and tears welled up in her eyes.

Before he knew what he was about, he swept her into his arms and held her tightly while she sobbed. He would *definitely* be killing the damned man!

Morgan became dismally aware that she was likely ruining the earl's expensive dress shirt with her blubbering right around the time a knock came at the parlor doors. The duchess rose and walked over to it, opening it only enough to see who it was. Her aunt stepped back and allowed Eloise and Lady Printmose to enter.

Eloise ran to Morgan's side. "Are you faring all right?" she worriedly asked.

The earl adjusted their positions so that she was less on his lap, and more situated on the settee. Morgan bashfully looked down, to where her hands were clasped together tightly atop the fabric of her skirt.

This was all just a dream.

Had she just been sitting in the Earl of Wellington's lap, sobbing like a child, while he stroked her hair and whispered all the right words to ease away her fear? *It had to be a dream.* Regardless, Morgan needed to push it aside like a dream and find a way to recover from the unrecoverable. *Ruination!*

She took a heavy breath and looked up into her friend's eyes. "I guess that question has more than a few answers." She exhaled a ragged chuckle.

Eloise took the seat to Morgan's right and reached for her hands, prying them apart she took one firmly in her own. Her dear friend looked as haggard as Morgan felt. As if she had just been the one publicly shamed.

"When I saw you fall..." Eloise squeezed Morgan's hand. "The look on your stepbrother's face! And then, when the earl announced —" She broke off, as if suddenly realizing the man in question sat just on the other side of Morgan.

Morgan squeezed her hand back. "I know." She assured. "It was all a grave misunderstanding. I will take ownership of the situation and free Lord Wellington of any misguided sense of chivalry."

"You will do no such thing," the earl said flatly. "I have offered for you, and I do not intend to cry off."

Morgan jerked her head in his direction. "I will not marry a man who does not wish to be married."

"You do not have a choice," he said sternly enough for her not to doubt him. "I will travel to meet with your stepfather tomorrow and make the arrangements."

He stood. "We shall be married by the week's end."

The earl turned and walked to the door, leaving no space for argument. He paused briefly to speak in a hushed voice with the two older ladies before quitting the room. Morgan slowly rotated her attention back to Eloise, who wore an expression of unbridled awe.

"Oh, my," her friend said.

"He is a fool if he thinks I will allow Roderick's childish temper-tantrum to force our hands," Morgan said, resolved.

"Your brother did not seem pleased over the outcome."

"He was not." Morgan stood and swiped a mutinous tear off her cheek. "That would mean he would no longer have me to torment."

As soon as the words left her lips, she froze. Not because she was making vocal the secret that had orbited around her for the past year. Roderick had already blown any family normality out of the water with his spectacle on the terrace.

No, what was most startling about her statement was the revelation that the earl was offering her exactly what she had wanted. A husband. Someone to take her away from her stepbrother and the life she had been living. If the earl would have her, especially after tonight, she might just have to make it work.

Her reasoning circled back to Lord De Montrey. He would no doubt be hurt but, surely, he would not want spoiled goods. Even if the accusation had been one sided. Men always believed men. And Lord Wellington had outright confessed. Hell, the dratted man had almost been eager to state it.

That gave Morgan a new cause for pause. Why had he been so quick to condemn himself? He was a much higher peer of the realm than Roderick. Lord Wellington could have just denied everything, yet he had arranged their engagement instead. *Why?*

Morgan rubbed her temple. Her mind was running all over the place, chasing thoughts like a child with a butterfly net. She turned quickly back to Eloise as another one landed just out of reach.

"Was the man you were standing with on the terrace—before I immortalized my name in the hall of shame—the same man who found us out the other night at the lake?"

Her friend blushed deeply and nodded. "He will not tell."

Morgan sighed and sat back down beside her best friend. "Well." She smiled weakly. "We wanted more adventure out of life."

Lord De Montrey stormed out of the manor. How dare Wellington take what was meant to be his? The rogue had been granted more than his fair share of English pride. Must the bastard have a hand in everything?

De Montrey sneered into wind, his breath crystallizing in the chilled night air. Come to think of it, the whole damn family was rather skilled at stealing things that did not belong to them. He hesitated, looking down the long line of carriages in search of his own. The party was far from over, so no drivers had lined up yet.

He cursed and continued down the drive, directionless. Six more carriages back he finally glimpsed his own driver asleep in his seat. *God damn, Wellington!* The degenerate probably had better staff to boot.

He swore anew and kicked the gravel, taking mild satisfaction when it ricocheted off someone's shiny new phaeton. Something jetted out at him, and he skidded to a stop to avoid running into it. His eyes focused on the baroque designed wolf-head handle of the walking stick that blocked his path, a scant inch away from his nose.

De Montrey turned, his vision tracking the long-polished cane back to where it had manifested from. "Have a care, sir!" He glared into the black window of the carriage.

"Get inside!" An eerily familiar voice directed. "Your debt is due."

VII

*E*dward stared out the window of the rolling carriage, revisiting all the milliseconds that had added up, linked together like tiny soldiers of fate over the past twenty-four hours. Fractions of seconds where he could have made different choices. Minutes that had changed the course of multiple lives.

Hours that led up to him now, on a bumpy country road, traveling back to town after having to ask a man for his daughter's hand in marriage. All because of one uncontrollable impulse. *An impulse he did not regret in the least...*

After having left the Printmose ball the previous evening, Edward had gone straight to his father's townhouse and told him everything that had transpired. Better the duke hear it from his own lips. Plus, Edward knew he would need his help. His own name carried a fair share of weight, but his father's could outright sink a ship.

By the time Edward had completed the story, the sun was starting to rise and they were on their way to the Earl of Vistmont's hunting lodge in the country.

The arrogant older man had greeted them with as much warmth as Edward had expected. Absolutely none. Which was why he had dragged along his father. The other earl might hear Edward out, but the chances that he would entertain his request were slim. Richard Kingston, advisor to the Queen, on the other hand... No man dared turn down his father.

Once they had been admitted into the small hunting cabin, Richard had simply lined up the facts: Edward desired Miss Sinclair's hand. And the joining of the families would be beneficial to the earl's dwindling pocketbook.

Lord Vistmont, unable to deny his compulsion for the tracks and his ineptitude at winning, had considered the offerings with as much possible denial as a man in his situation could. It was common knowledge among the bon ton that the earl's bank accounts were paltry. Aligning himself with the Kingston's would be an advantageous move.

Having the stain on his good name—that came from Edward compromising his *dear* daughter—was far too insulting, the earl explained. All the time looking down the bridge of his nose, disdainfully. The ruining of the girl was a slight that could only be corrected with coin. Or, in this case, the lack there of. There would be no dowry.

Edward ground his teeth together so hard, he wondered if a few had cracked. His father's quickly raised hand halted him from voicing exactly what he thought of the smug bastard, and his feigned love for his *dear* daughter. The Duke, aware that his son was a scant breath shy of killing his future father-in-law, agreed under the circumstances the dowry could be waived.

Edward did not care about the traditional bridal offering in the least. He had more than enough income and could provide ten times over what the Earl of Vistmont did for Miss Sinclair. *Two fucking dresses!*

Nevertheless, Edward thought Miss Sinclair might have a care in the matter. Since it was quite likely that her dowry would have been passed down from her biological father, not the abusive earl. Now, the only material wealth she possessed would be left in the slimy hands of her stepfather and stepbrother. They deserved nothing!

While Edward mulled over various ways he would like to see the earl and his whelp meet their demise, papers were drawn up and he and his father were sent on their way back to London before the noon sun had even begun to warm the sky.

"You know that whatever her dowry would have amounted to, it was not worth the fight. He would have only doubled down and just refused you." His father spoke judiciously, seated opposite Edward in the rocking carriage. "And is that not the reason for this trip? To save Miss Sinclair from her tormentors."

Edward had not spoken more than two words since exiting Vistmont's hunting lodge. He knew his father had been more than patient, allowing him to brood in insufferable silence. Apparently, that allotted time of loathsome introspection was at an end.

"Yes. Saving." Edward continued to stare out the window. "That is what she needs."

"Indeed." Richard concurred, dangerously agreeable.

The wheels rolled on, beating a familiar cadence in the absence of conversation.

"Oh, come on!" Edward rotated in his seat, to take his father head on. "Out with it. I know you have your opinions."

The graceful line of the Duke's mouth tightened a bit, but he did not say anything. Instead, he swiveled his head and stared off into the distance, amused at nothing in particular.

"Father?"

Richard turned his gaze back to him. "Son?"

Edward felt a muscle hop in his neck. The man was not going to make this easy. "Listen, I know this is not what you had in mind when you suggested I take a wife."

Richard folded his long fingers together in his lap. "Is it not?"

Edward threw his weight back into his seat, exasperated. "Can we not do this?" He waved a hand "This...evasive dialogue."

A gleam lit in his father's eyes. "What would you like me to say, Edward?"

"Damn if I know." Edward let his hand fall to his knee, loudly. "Tell me, what a tragic mistake this is. Remind me how much better

Perkin would have handled the situation. Give me advice on what to do next."

His father studied him, his expression unreadable. "You were never an easy child," Richard finally said. "You were headstrong, impulsive, willful to a fault, and a dreadful student. You were unpredictable and easily roused. There were days that I thought you had been born simply to test me."

His father paused. "But you were always consistent. You never let others impress upon you their will. You have always taken your own road. Albeit a path you do not always give considerable thought to." He smiled gently. "But a direction in which very few men can say they have earnestly traveled."

Edward waited, sure there was at least a few more considerable faults he could handle hearing. He had asked for this after all.

"The path of integrity," his father said without preamble. "There is not another man alive that I can say that about."

The Duke stared at him, his gray eyes, both hard and soft at the same time. "You will never make a truly *wrong* move, my boy. Not when you have that sort of grace on your side."

Edward was speechless. His father was not a man to hand out praise, nor was he a man to sugarcoat his words. Richard Kingston was an upstanding pillar of the community, generous friend, devoted father, diligent businessman, and a sound advisor.

But above all, he was a man of honor. Hearing his father say what he had... Edward cut his gaze to the seat cushions.

"You are correct," Richard continued. "This is not at all how I envisioned your future. I could have better predicted the fall of Rome." He chuckled. "But I would not have it any other way than how events lined up for you on that balcony last night."

Edward scoffed. "Embarrassingly?"

He could feel his father's gaze on his downcast face. Edward looked up slowly.

"Gallant." The Duke's eyes grew glassy. "You have never made me more proud."

"Well," Edward said, deflecting his rising emotions. "You have always had a healthy sense of humor."

They both laughed at that.

"Now." Richard leaned forward. "Tell me more about my new daughter. She is certainly a beauty."

"You will approve." Edward nodded, smiling as he considered Morgan for a few beats of the carriage's rhythmic rolling. "She is rather..." He met his father's inquisitive eyes again when he landed on the right description. "Consuming."

"Ah, so you cannot get her out of your head?" His father sat back and crossed his arms.

"That is putting it mildly." Edward sighed. "She is quite the enigma. Stunning beyond measure, fun-loving and inquisitive. Yet, she also has a rather astute and reserved side. And, she has no difficulty putting me in my place. Something I am not entirely sure I admire." He grinned.

"She sounds like your perfect match," the Duke said after a moment. "You need someone with spirit. Someone who will challenge you, but also steady you. This young lady appears to do both. I cannot wait to formally welcome her into the family. I only wish Perkin and Greyland could make it. But on short notice, and with your brother away right now..."

Edward knew there was more to his brother's last-minute trip to France than his father was letting on, and that worried him. He was just about to press the subject when their driver started shouting frantically. Edward craned his head toward the window just as the rig lurched to the side and then jerked back abruptly. Both he and his father were sent crashing into the right side of the carriage as it tipped precariously and then slammed back down to the ground.

Edward and his father stared, braced against their seats, assessing one another. "Is anything broken?" Richard asked.

Edward shook his head, his eyes going to a trickle of blood on his father's forehead.

"I am fine." The Duke waved him off. "Check your driver."

Edward scrambled out to find Hornsby rounding the rig. "My

Lord," the driver huffed. "'Twas a runaway carriage." He pointed down the lane.

Edward whirled, just in time to see a speeding black carriage effortlessly round the sharp bend in the road. The only identifiable markings he could catch before the rig disappeared looked to be an embossed crest on the door: hounds on the hunt.

His father alighted from the door, a handkerchief pressed to his hairline, doubt evident in his voice. "A runaway carriage, huh?"

"One that managed that turn." Edward scowled in the direction of the road's curve. "Without any effort at all." He turned and marched to the front of the rig to check the horses.

They were wide-eyed from the fright but seemingly hale. Edward cooed soothing praise as he ran his hands over their legs, checking for swelling, from hock to hoof. Other than a scrape on the front left fetlock of the bay gelding, they were unscathed.

He returned to where his father and Hornsby stood, analyzing the carriage. "How is your head?"

His father brought down the cloth. He had a nasty cut but nothing fatal. "It will be fine. But I daresay, we will not be making it back to town today." He inclined his head toward one of the back wheels.

The driver looked up from his hunched inspection and confirmed the problem. "It's cracked, my lord. There is a village just a ways up the road."

Edward nodded wordlessly and moved to unharness the horses. Within a few minutes, they were walking toward the town. Edward recalled a tavern and lodge called the Wild Hare; they could stable the horses and wait there for the wheel to be repaired. He decided now was a good time to tell his father about the *other* attempt made on his life this past week. The one that did *not* involve him getting shot or run off the road.

"Someone wants me dead." Perhaps not the lengthiest story, but the most direct.

His father looked over at him as they walked.

"A few days ago, prior to a ride, I gave Elkinema's saddle a once over," Edward elaborated. "The girth strap had been slit and loosely stitched back up." He could see his father's brows rise out of his peripheral as they continued down the dirt road. "Stitched back together well enough that it would likely go unnoticed by the groom, which it did, but would break the moment the horse was moved into a canter."

"Are you sure the groom did not know?" Richard asked.

"The boy is green, but loyal."

They walked on in silence. "You should have told me sooner." His father finally stated.

"There was nothing you could have done about it, and I still do not know who it is."

"There is *always* something I can do!" Richard snapped, causing Edward to stop short. His father seldom lost his temper. "You take too much on by yourself, Edward."

"I am a grown man, Father. Fully capable of managing my own life's assassination attempts."

The Duke whirled on him. "This is not a joke, damn it!"

Edward bristled. "I am well aware."

His father motioned Hornsby on with a curt nod of his head. The driver, clearly relieved to be dismissed from the two feuding lords, led the horses on ahead.

"Are you?" His father countered. "Are you aware that there is more to your life than just you?"

"Yes, well, I am not a man born to selflessness."

"Cultivate it!" The Duke turned on his heels and strode away.

VIII

*T*he smith was out sick, so they were forced to stay the night at the Wild Hare where Edward's father stubbornly chose to ignore him, retiring to his rented room above the tavern. Edward walked to the end of town and back to kill some time, drank two pints of sour ale, took an early supper of chewy meat-pie and stale bread with the pub's only other patron, Hornsby, and then retired to bed.

The next morning, while he and his father were taking breakfast, Hornsby returned to the tavern and relayed that the wheel was still not ready.

Richard peered over his newspaper, spectacles tipped low on his nose. "The barmaid said a farmer at the end of town had a mare for sale," he stated before flipping the paper back into place. "I will wait here with Hornsby if you want to get on the road."

Edward paid their remaining tab and set off down the muddy one-lane road. Truth be told, he *was* in a hurry to get back. For reasons other than boredom.

He was anxious to check on Morgan and let her know of her stepfather's acceptance. Edward could only hope that she would not break into tears when she heard the news. But honestly, it was a coin toss. Half his brain reassured him that he was doing the right thing.

The other half gnawed at him that part of this rash decision was *exactly* what his father had shouted at him for being. *Selfish...*

Edward admonished his self-doubt and kicked a clot of dirt in the middle of the road. He needed to focus on the path ahead. In less than an hour, provided the horse he was about to purchase did not go lame, he would be riding up to his townhouse in the city. He would then wash up quickly and head straight to Lady Vandicamp's residence.

Miss Sinclair... "Morgan," he said, testing the sound of her name on his tongue. Intrigued by the ebullience the word induced, he tried it again. "Morgan..."

He wanted to sound the name out on her bare flesh, and feel the gooseflesh rise against his lips when he did. Edward closed his eyes. *Damn it to hell,* he was in over his head. This was *exactly* why he had stayed away this past week, coming up with a litany of excuses as to why he must cancel dance lessons. To save her, *from himself!*

Because, truth be told, saddled somewhere between excitement and fear echoed a humming and constant desire to make her *his*. Abstinence had been his only friend. And then he had gone and lost that at Lady Printmose's ball. All thinly veiled control collapsed like a glass house being hit by a boulder.

How he had wanted to smash in the face of every smitten young buck there. Why, he had only lasted one dance before openly manhandling her through that waltz. Then to top it off, he had hauled her onto the open terrace, like a lion dragging a gazelle back to his den in the underbrush. *Savagery!*

It was no wonder her stepbrother had been so enraged. Any man would take insult with a lady of their family being pawed over. He would have killed Alexander if he had behaved as such with Greyland.

Edward felt his knuckles curl in on his palms. *Except...*there was more to that man's behavior than just *brotherly* concern. There was something twisted and depraved. The way Morgan had reacted to his voice the other night... It had been as if the cold hand of death itself had wound around her throat.

What had her stepbrother done to her? The various answer's chilled Edward to the bone. He'd had little time to contemplate his new role in all of this, having rashly asked for her hand when he saw the perverse desire in her stepbrother's eyes. Roderick's possessive nature toward her was tangible. Right there, laid out mockingly for all to see the control the bastard wielded over her.

Nay. Edward had not been given a choice but to step in to save her from that monster. Now he would keep his word and marry her, then he would take her away to one of his estates in the country. Maybe Crestmont. He had heard it was lovely.

Yes, Crestmont. He remembered his father going on about its beauty and prosperous land during one of his rants about how his middle child should 'claim his property and run it like a good landlord instead of relying on his man of affairs to oversee it'. Crestmont would be perfect for Morgan.

Edward would see her set up there, make her comfortable, and then he would return to London and oversee the new ships coming in. She would be happy there. She would have a high-ranking title and, most importantly, she would be free of her hideous step relatives.

Edward would let her have her freedom, then with time, if she desired, he would give her a child. The thought renewed the stirring down below. Yes, this plan would work. He was sure of it. How hard could having a beautiful wife be, after all?

Morgan strolled down the path through The Queen's public gardens with her arm linked loosely over Lord Rockafetch's. Eloise, Morgan was aware, clung rather tightly to his other side as they rounded a bend.

The orange tree section, in all its magnificent splendor, had not yet been touched by the cooler weather. Although the fruit was long gone, the leaves still held tightly to the branches, as if defying Mother Nature's request for them to let go. Morgan watched as one stubborn leaf fought to hold on as a rather unexpected breeze whipped by.

A soft murmur at her side reminded Morgan she was still in the presence of others and completely missed the question Lord Rockafetch just asked. "I am sorry." She looked up at him and smiled. "Absentmindedness."

"I daresay, I do not believe you capable of aimless thought. I am sure your mind was very much focused on something," he said with an engaging grin. "Care to share?"

"Yes, please share," Eloise piped up.

"I was just admiring nature's quiet little rebellion." She pointed to the tree with the mischievous leaf. "Seems not even that leaf wants to obey winter's warning."

"Oh, Morgan!" Eloise trilled. "I love that analogy."

"A very unique observation," Lord Rockafetch said, after an appreciable pause.

Uncomfortable with the attention, Morgan's cheeks filled with warmth. "I suppose I simply enjoy looking for the small details in life."

"A refreshing trait," the earl stated.

"Thank you, my lord."

"Henry," he corrected.

"Henry," Morgan acquiesced, smiling.

"This is why I claimed her as my best friend. Before anyone else could." Eloise beamed from around his chest at Morgan.

"And all this time I thought it was for my aunt's lemon cakes." Morgan grinned. "Thank you. Both of you, for thinking so highly of me."

"Can I join in with this intelligent group?"

Morgan turned abruptly, along with Lord Rockafetch and Eloise, to see Lord Wellington walking briskly toward them. "Of people who think highly of you, Miss Sinclair," the earl added, coming to a stop before her and bending low to kiss her hand.

The sensation, left behind by his lingering kiss, caused a strange reaction in Morgan's body. All her nerves seemed to vibrate atop her skin and a heat pooled deep in her stomach. It was as if he incited an involuntary physical reaction within her body every time they came in contact.

How did he do that? And, where had the blasted man been? He was supposed to have returned the previous day.

Afraid of running into Roderick after the ball, Morgan had sheltered in place at her aunt's manor. She had spent the last forty-eight hours on pins and needles, scared every time Perry entered the room to announce a visitor. Not that her stepbrother would do anyone the courtesy of entering a home respectably via the front door.

The monster had already made one attempt to confront her, showing up at the townhouse at four in the morning the night of the ball, completely inebriated and shouting for her to come out. Perry and two other footmen had to forcefully remove the drunken imbecile. Only after they threatened to call the night bobbies did her stepbrother concede and leave the property.

Fearing exactly how far Roderick might go to seek her out, she had vowed to stay hidden until the earl returned. The plan had been going swimmingly until that morning when Lord Rockafetch and Eloise showed up at the duchesses. Through abject pleading, Eloise, and rational logic by Lord Rockafetch, the two had managed to convince her that her evil step-relation would likely not be awake at the hour planned for venturing out. If he were awake, Lord Rockafetch pointed out, he would likely be nursing a headache in a dark parlor somewhere.

The day was beautiful and so her aunt had urged Morgan to go and take in what would likely be one of their last pleasant fall afternoons. Feeling admittedly safe in the earl's company, and never being one to turn down a request that came with such forlorn delivery (as her best friend was so accomplished at), Morgan had relented on her vow to wait for Lord Wellington's return.

After all, she was not entirely sure he would return. What if he had wised up and run for the hills? It was not like she could blame him.

Now standing before her was the ever-changing earl in all his masculine glory, appearing as if everything was right with the world. As if it was nothing to recover from being caught trying to smash in the face of another peer of the realm at a private house party, declare a surprise betrothal, then vanish for two days, only to magically reappear on a walking trail in the Queen's gardens, smiling.

Did everything in life really come so naturally to him? Was he just that accustomed to being unaffected? Or, was he simply accomplished at being the storm that wreaked havoc on other people's lives?

Only one thing was certain. *The man was insufferable!*

"Lord Wellington, this is Miss Woolworth. You may recall meeting her the other night. After you proposed marriage in front of half the bon ton," she added offhandedly.

Lord Wellington's fixed smile faltered a notch, but he inclined his head toward Eloise, nevertheless. "A delight to meet you again, under less stressful circumstances."

"We need to talk." Morgan cut off the pleasantries.

Henry and Eloise took the cue and walked on ahead without comment. Bertrice, who had been trailing them, looked unsure how to proceed. Lord Wellington nodded in the maid's direction, excusing her as if he were already in charge. Morgan watched with borderline abject horror as her loyal servant plodded on after Lord Rockafetch and Miss Woolworth.

She stared in disbelief at her intended.

"Sorry that I did not make it back yesterday as I had planned. Bit of a carriage problem." Lord Wellington said once they were alone.

She almost gaped at his aplomb.

"Let us walk." He swept his arm ahead of them to suggest they follow where the others had led. "Your friend is an unattached young lady, after all." He grinned. "Would not want more fuel for the gossip rags involving our dear friends."

"No, indeed not." She had to agree, despite the stubborn part of her that wanted to argue with whatever he said. "Best we keep the collateral damage to a minimum."

"About that," he said as they meandered down the tree line path. "I spoke to your stepfather about our union."

The earl suddenly paused, causing Morgan to as well, and peered into a particularly overgrown orange tree. "Well, look at that."

Morgan looked into the branches, half expecting to see a genie granting wishes to small woodland creatures. Because what else could be more astonishing than whatever words were about to follow up *"I spoke to your stepfather about our union."*

"A bird's nest," he said, identifying the only 'note-worthy' object nestled within the tree.

"An empty bird's nest!" Morgan flared at him. "You think that is of greater importance than whatever my stepfather's answer to your proposal was?"

She swung her gaze sharply back up to him, annoyed, and ready to expound further on said annoyance. What she was ill-prepared to find staring back at her was a look of earnest vulnerability as an unasked question swam around in those cobalt blue orbs.

"If he had agreed," the earl hedged, ignoring her vexation. "Would you have me as your husband?"

Morgan gawked at him, speechless. Was he actually concerned she might say no? As if she had a choice. *Yet, still...*he seemed genuinely concerned that she might find disfavor with him. Which would be laughable under any other circumstances. This was a man who could have any woman he wanted. He had the world at the tips of his fingers. *He* spun his own story.

Why would the Earl of Wellington be concerned with the feelings of someone like her? *Except...he was.* Something caught in her throat and she looked away, finding renewed interest in the abandoned robin's nest.

"Are you asking me to marry you, Lord Wellington?"

"Not until you answer me."

"Why?" Morgan looked back at him. "Why does it matter what I might want?"

"Because it does." He leaned into her, a towering mass of muscle and sinew blotting out the sun. "If I am going to pledge the rest of my life to one woman, I want to know that *I am* what she wants."

"Oh." She gaped up at him. The fluttering of her heart had started back up, beating a rhythmic tattoo against her ribcage. "What of your own desires?"

His large hand lifted, fingers extending to softly caress the side of her face. Despite the stirring touch, and her overwhelming desire to lean into it, she kept her gaze latched onto his. Everything mattered in these next few moments. *Everything.*

A ghost of a smile crossed to his lips. "I desire you, in all fashion of ways, Miss Sinclair. Starting with the desire to have you return my affections. Would you have me as your protector? Your lover? Your friend?"

He lowered his head with each question, until their eyes were level, and his words were a mere whisper on the breeze. "Do you want me, above anyone else?"

"I do." She spoke the words without thought, only feeling, as if her heart had commandeered her mind.

His full lips curled at the edges, producing a satisfied and sensuous appeal. His hand lowered from her face, traced a path down her arm and took hold of her hand. "Morgan Sinclair?"

He dropped in front of her, taking a knee on the dirt and smiling up at her.

"Will you marry me?"

Morgan nervously looked about, as if begging the universe to *speak now* or forever hold its peace. Turning back to find his eyes, she said quietly, "Yes."

He squeezed her hands lightly in his, smile widening. "There is still a ring I must procure, but I am going to try very hard to make you happy."

He pushed to his feet, reclaiming his full height. "Now, do pray tell?" The content expression on his handsome face faded and his tone took a reproachful edge. "Why are you addressing Lord Rockafetch by his Christian name?"

"Because he asked me to." Her answer came fast and clipped, defensive.

Which was everything that it should not be. As there was no reason for the earl to be skeptical. Henry was supposed to be his friend! Was he implying he could not trust him?

Morgan's mind grinded to a crashing halt. *Or* was he implying he could not trust *her*? His next words all but confirmed her fear.

"Ah, he asked you to," the earl said, a chill in the intonation.

"Yes!"

Lord Wellington's focus on her grew sharper. "If he asked you to turn cartwheels down a hill in front of the Queen, would you?"

She could feel her face contorting unpleasantly, from both his ridiculous implication and his odious tone. "Of course not! He is your friend. Surely, he is allowed to make such a request."

"Had it occurred to you when you accepted *his* proposal you have yet to even use *my* Christian name?"

"You never asked me," she bit back, feeling her spine tighten at the challenge.

She had never been blessed with the ability to stand down. Her father had said it was a trait that came ready-made in redheaded girls. Now the Earl of Wellington, her future husband, was about to understand that theory.

"Although, I admit..." She could no more stop the words about to pour forth from her mouth than he could stop his evident suspicions. "I did love the way it sounded when Miss Rosewood purred it."

Lord Wellington grew still; apparently, her barb had hit its mark. "She is an old friend," he volleyed back.

"Oh, trust me; I am all too aware what type of *old friend* that vapid beauty is!" Morgan was finding it increasingly difficult to keep the sarcasm from her voice. Why hide it? If they were airing their dirty laundry, she might as well add her own displeasures to the pile.

"I am sure she is most upset over your upcoming nuptials and looking for creative ways to lure you back." She folded her arms and narrowed her eyes. "I only wonder how long it shall take."

Despite her grand posturing, Morgan was wretchedly aware how her last words wobbled, unsteady on her tongue. He likely heard it, too. She turned and walked away, swiftly and completely directionless, through the garden, unwilling to see the pity in his eyes.

She had only gone a few steps when she heard the most astonishing sound coming from behind her. Laughter... *Was he laughing at her?*

She whirled in place and came face to chest with a solid wall of hard muscle hidden behind a single-breasted striped waistcoat. Her hands went up, landing firmly on the familiarly patterned vest in instinctive self-preservation.

Unfortunately, they stayed there, molding themselves to his chest, clearly governed by some *other* instinct. She huffed and pushed off him, spinning away. Lord Wellington chortled harder.

She turned slowly and glared him down. "Is this funny to you?"

He snorted by way of answer and shook his head. "I am sorry, but yes."

He was now so consumed by his mirth that his head rolled back, face toward the sky, sunbathing him in glorious light as reverbering guffaws poured out of his lungs like breaking waves, each bouncing off the clouds like rolling thunder. It was inappropriate in the extreme, yet utterly contagious. They were behaving like stubborn school children arguing over a ball.

Morgan chuckled. Then, before she knew it, her own breath rushed out in fits of uncontrollable giggles. They both doubled at the waist, eyes dancing as they pointed at one another periodically, unable to form words. It was... *Everything.*

Once she was able to drag enough air into her lungs to speak in coherent sentences, she straightened and smiled over at him. "Are you always so...unpredictable?"

"Most of the time." He tossed her a wry smirk and held out a hand. "Come here."

She obliged, taking his hand. He pulled her into his arms. It felt perfectly comfortable to be tucked into his embrace. Warm and safe. She relaxed into him as her heartbeat synchronized with his. He held her there, both of them silent except for their breathing, for an undefined amount of time.

"Call me Edward from now on," he finally said, caressing the back of her head as her cheek pressed against his chest. "And please, never again walk away from me. It is a disrespect I cannot abide."

His head bent lower as he softly chided into her hair. "You may always speak your mind; I welcome it, actually. But do not dishonor me by turning your back on me."

His thumb tilted her chin up so that her eyes met his. "Even if you are jealous of nothing." He grinned down at her. "Do we have an understanding?"

Morgan felt her head nod. She could argue the fact that it was *his* jealousy that had landed them both in this circling conversation, but it felt a moot point now. *Now* that he had opened to her and put some of her biggest fears to rest.

Besides, this was what a union was supposed to be, a series of linking moments that made up an entire life. The joys, the heartbreak, the highs, and the lows. They would all come with arguments, laughter, compromise, and if one was lucky enough, love.

"I will be good to you," he said, as if confirming the words for both their benefits.

"I believe you will."

The sound of advancing footsteps brought their conversation to an end. Edward released her and took a step back, looking over the top of her head at whoever was coming up the path. Morgan took a large calming breath and composed her emotions, which had run the gamut over the past ten minutes. She turned, ready to greet whoever was walking toward them.

Her sights immediately landed on Henry. Morgan smiled, happy to see a friendly face, and then she glanced at the newcomer walking alongside him. Before she had time to get a read on the man, she felt Edward's hand on her waist. He pulled her in closely to his side, which had gone as taut as sails full of wind on a ship.

She ventured a cavalier glace up at her intended. The look he wore could not be deciphered, but it was far from warm. The absence of Edward's jovial, accepting nature, told her everything she needed to know about the coming exchange. This interloper was not someone her fiancé cared for.

Morgan, smile still locked in place, looked back to Henry. He had clearly picked up on Edward's body language, too, and was adjusting his pace to nearly a crawl. *The ruse was up.* The only person who knew who this stranger was, was Edward. And he seemed, for now, reluctant to enlighten them as to the identity of the mystery man.

Morgan doffed her own hospitable decorum and took a good long look at the new addition. He was a well-dressed, large man of a similar age to Henry and Edward, wearing an eager smile. *Too eager.*

Edward watched as Davenport promenaded up, clearly pleased with himself for deceiving Henry. He wondered what lie the smug bastard had told him to get the personal escort.

"I feel I have misled you somewhat, Lord Rockafetch," Davenport confessed, canting his head toward Henry. "I only gave you my titled name." He guffawed, seemingly unfazed by the fact that no one else shared his mirth.

"Mr. Kingston here," Davenport said, focusing his sights on Edward, "knows me only by my family name."

Henry turned sharply, squaring off with the intruder and effectively blocking his path. "I do not appreciate my hospitality being taken for granted." He glowered down at the shorter man.

Edward knew his friend was seconds away from laying the righteous lord flat. "Do not waste your time, Henry," Edward said. "My old neighbor has always been fond of games." He stepped forward, pushing Morgan behind him.

Henry did not yield. "You will address my friend as Lord Wellington from now on."

Davenport inclined his head a notch. He clearly had not banked on Henry's reaction to being set up. Most lords would step back, not having 'a dog' in this proverbial fight.

Not the Earl of Rockafetch. Henry was the most loyal person Edward had ever met, and Heaven help the fool who mistook his natural kindness for weakness. Edward's best friend stepped to the side, begrudgingly.

"Ah, yes. Seems little Eddie has also made some adjustments to his standing. Forgive me for remembering..." Davenport moved around Henry and smiled at Edward. "A different time in our lives."

"I do not recall the Queen gifting anyone a title." Edward tilted his head and took another step forward. "Did someone die?"

His nemesis matched his step and smirked. "I inherited it when I married a bonny Irish widow after dear Bess passed away. I am now addressed as Laird McGee."

"I am sorry for your loss."

Davenport regarded him coolly. "Yes, I am sure you are." He leaned heavily on his walking stick and looked around, affecting interest in their surroundings. "You will not believe who my new neighbors are; I think you know them."

An odd numbness nestled down deep in Edward's bones. He did not do well with ambiguous threats. There were too many variables in whatever Davenport was about to divulge, too many unknowns. It was akin to playing a blind hand of cards and going all in.

"Please," he managed to keep his tone even. "Enlighten me."

Davenport waited, allowing the coming answer to mull about for an annoyingly long length of time before smiling broadly. "The McGreggors."

The previous numbness spread like a fanned flame through Edward's bloodstream. He saw light dancing off the damascened blade of Henry's rapier as he withdrew it an inch from his cane-sword. Edward could tell by the whites of his friend's knuckles that he was one word shy of fully unsheathing it. The McGreggor clan had done more than their fair share of damage to both their families. Even speaking their name was a bold-faced threat.

145

Judging by the gleam in Davenport's eyes, he damn well knew it, too. Edward felt Morgan uncurl his tightened fingers and place her hand in his. The silent show of support tempered his mounting anger, but only by a fraction.

Edward's gaze locked onto Henry's. The warning was enough to still Henry's hand. *Not now*, not in front of Morgan.

His mind raced to anchor onto a logical reason for Davenport tipping his hand. Was he merely being antagonistic? He had never been the brains of his family. Or was the information intended to serve as a warning? Could Davenport and the McGreggors have formed an alliance? Were they who had tried to kill him? If so, why would he be sharing this information now?

There was more to this. *There had to be.* Before he could think of another option, Morgan stepped forward, making her presence again known. Perhaps to remind them all that there was a witness in attendance. Edward reached out and pulled her protectively back to his side.

Davenport's searing gaze raked over her and the corner of his mouth twitched. "My, my. Who might this ravishing creature be?" he drawled.

"Do you not know?" Morgan answered in a completely neutral tone.

Davenport cocked a quizzical eyebrow and looked at Edward for the introduction. For the first time in his life, Edward weighed his response. He wanted to tell the pompous ass to bugger off, but a rational and nagging voice in his head was warning him to tread carefully with this one. *Why?*

He had survived his whole life off quick reactions and instinct. This sudden hesitation was a predicament so foreign he felt momentarily paralyzed by it. How on earth did his brother do it? *Always think before speaking.*

He smiled thinly back at Davenport. "This is Miss Sinclair." Edward brought her hand to his lips and placed a gentle kiss on her knuckles. "My fiancée."

"You have done well for yourself, Wellington." Davenport gave an imperceptible nod.

"Thank you." Edward moved to pass his longtime rival. "You must excuse us; we have a date that we cannot be late for."

Davenport stepped aside and inclined his head courteously. "Nice to meet you, Miss Sinclair." His hooded eyes fixed on Edward as they passed. "Until we meet again, Lord Wellington."

Edward offered nothing in response as he steered Morgan toward Henry. The message was clear enough. Davenport was on English soil, and apparently, he was here to stay. He knew who the Kingston's' enemies were and while it was unclear still what his motives were, it was crystal clear that he was not hoping to establish a friendship. Far from it. Nothing good would come from this man being here.

"Where is Miss Woolworth?" Edward ground out once they were out of earshot.

"She is by the large oak tree with Miss Sinclair's chaperone. Lady Printmose and her silly niece, Miss Rosewood, are with them," Henry replied through clenched teeth. "Davenport was walking with the other two women and was introduced as Laird McGee when they came upon us. Lady Printmose inquired as to if you were back from your trip to the country and I explained that you were and that you were just down the path. Davenport then proceeded to tell me that he was an old friend of your father's. When you did not emerge, like a fool I suggested we go to you."

Henry sighed.

"I had no idea, Edward."

Edward waved him off. "'Tis not your fault. I just need to get the ladies away from here, post haste."

"Will one of you please tell me what this is about?" Morgan, clearly done being left out, inquired.

"Nothing you need to worry about. But you are never to speak to that man again," Edward added sternly.

She opened her mouth, most likely to continue her questioning, but closed it when they rounded the corner, coming upon Eloise and the three other women.

"So pleased to see you, ladies." Edward spoke brusquely as they approached. "Unfortunately, I fear I discovered a matter that requires my immediate attention. I beg your pardon, but I must see Miss Woolworth and Miss Sinclair back to their residences."

He bowed. "Please forgive my rudeness." Then he turned to leave, Morgan still tucked neatly at his side.

"Did dear Laird McGee find you?" Miss Rosewood's high soprano voice cut through the air. "He was very much looking forward to the introduction."

Edward turned back reluctantly. Morgan had not been incorrect in her previous observations regarding Lady Rosewood. He did know her better than he should. She had warmed his bed for the better part of last season. Until her mindless chatter, and inability to keep their affair a secret, had finally driven him to introduce her to another willing lord. It had been a little over six months since then and the silly girl had made her way through the upper class quicker than the plague.

He forced a tight smile. "I did, thank you."

Miss Rosewood's eyes dropped to where Morgan's arm rested linked over Edward's coat sleeve. "I suppose congratulations are in order. On your upcoming nuptials," she added, her eyes fluttering back up to his.

As if Morgan was not even there, she continued. "I did not believe it true when I first learned of your fate. The great Edward Wellington leg-shackled at last." Miss Rosewood sighed, a wan smile on her face. "Alas, I suppose even the best lakes do eventually dry up."

Lady Printmose blanched, three shades paler than a corpse. Miss Woolworth's mouth formed an O shape, so large she could catch flies. Henry cleared his throat uncomfortably and Morgan's chaperone appeared to be trying to take off her shoe. If there was a columnist hiding in the bushes right now, Edward expected to hear them praise Jesus. Fiction novels could not be written more uniquely than how this day was unfolding for him.

All simultaneously occurring reactions aside, it was his soon-to-be bride's that was the most scandalous. Morgan jerked her arm free of his, spun as if to slap him. Then she did the unthinkable. She grasped him by his neck collar with both hands, yanked his head down and thrust her tongue into his mouth.

Shock was immediately replaced by a slow burn that started in his nether regions and spread, like molten lava, through every fiber of his being. His body responded without a moment's hesitation, arms circling her, pulling her closer, encasing her, completely oblivious to the audience surrounding them. Entranced and uncaring, his hands roved lower, feeling the curve of her spine as his palms fanned out over her hips to cup her.

Still pressed firmly against his body, Morgan pulled back just enough to break the kiss, grinning against his swollen lips. "The lake feels pretty full to me."

His fiancée then turned nonchalantly back toward the gaping crowd. "He just needed to meet someone that could make *leg-shackling* an appealing endeavor." She smiled, elaborately polite. "Now, do excuse us, we have wedding arrangements to discuss."

Morgan turned them both in the opposite direction and marched off. Edward followed her lead, pride beaming from his soul. He had chosen perfectly.

Morgan decided she was a little embarrassed by her behavior, or at least she knew she should be. Yet, as she sat there, staring at nothing outside the carriage window, she could not help but feel a small victorious grin develop in her cheeks. The look that had spilled all over Miss Rosewood's pretty little face was worth whatever new rumors would circulate from the very public cut. Morgan decided now was a good time to stop keeping a mental tally running in regard to '*the further ruination of her name*'. She was basically all set in the ruination department.

She felt eyes on her and turned her head from the window, dousing the lingering smile. Best not to seem too unremorseful. She peered into the eyes of the dashing man sitting across from her. The positively resplendent man who was to be her husband. How long had he been watching her?

He said nothing, but the lopsided smirk he wore spoke volumes. His eyes danced with a thrill obviously ignited by her shocking behavior. At least she had served as a distraction from the awkward meeting with his old and unnerving friend. That had to count for something after her public display of scandalous behavior in the park.

Most high society men would be appalled. Her stepfather would have had her shipped off to the asylum. But not the Earl of Wellington. He seemed rather amused by her antics. Possibly even, if the hardness in his trousers had been any indication, a little provoked by it. Heat rose in her cheeks, and she cast her eyes down.

After a few seconds of pretending to appear as if she were contemplating shoe design, Morgan ventured a glance back up. He was still watching her. Her eyes met his and stayed there.

Edward continued to hold her gaze from where he sat, negligently leaned back in his seat. She wondered what exactly he was thinking. She blushed anew. The silence was killing her.

It was just the four of them in the cab of the rolling carriage now. Bertrice rode up front with Lord Rockafetch's driver. Henry sat beside Edward, and Eloise huddled next to Morgan, all of them mute. The gentle rocking of the rig deafened the quiet interior with its progression down the lane. Another small bump in the road emphasized its awkward point again, this time more loudly. Morgan could take the quiet no longer.

"Oh, would someone start a conversation already?" She eyed each of her companions. "In fact, I will start one. What a lovely day we are having, do you all not agree?"

"It is rather nice." Eloise tried to play along. "Not too chilly yet."

Henry chuckled softly, which provoked a burst of laughter from her intended. Once Edward's baritone broke their attempt at polite normality, Henry joined him. Eloise giggled quietly, an obvious attempt to remain well-mannered, but even she could not maintain her decorum when Henry lurched forward and proclaimed, "Did you see the look on those two ninnies' faces?"

Morgan's own levity swept into the mix, joining with everyone else's gales of uncontrolled laughter. The rocking carriage now likely sounded like a carnival plodding along to anyone they passed. That made it all the funnier.

"I daresay this will make the first page of all the gossip rags tomorrow." Eloise gave an unladylike snort, and then quickly covered her mouth, which only made everyone else howl louder.

Still giggling, Morgan clutched her ribs and gasped for air. "Oh, my sides. Corsets were not made for this much merriment."

Edward reached out and grabbed her around the waist. Before she knew it, she was on the other side of the carriage in his arms, and Henry was readjusting himself in her vacated spot beside Eloise. *What just occurred?* The questioned flashed across Morgan's unprepared mind.

How did both men move so fast? It was if they had rehearsed and successfully executed this little trick in the past. Otherwise, they could simply read each other that well.

Eloise seemed to be contemplating the same question as she stared up at the handsome Earl of Rockafetch, now seated at her side. Lord Rockafetch grinned, obviously enjoying the effect he had on Morgan's best friend.

Edward pressed Morgan to his chest and wrapped his arms around her waist, effectively capturing her attention back squarely on him. He held her there loosely, as if it were the most natural action in the entire world. As if there was absolutely *nothing* shocking about this show of affection. It was how Morgan imagined one might feel being married happily for years. Her limbs relaxed into her betrothed's hold. It simply felt...*good, honest, right...*

"I daresay," he breathed into her ear. Morgan could feel the curve of his smile against her neck. "That was the highlight of my week."

She twisted in his lap, enough to see his eyes. He stared intently down at her. Somewhere nearby, Henry and Eloise had engaged in their own conversation. Be it due to them being suddenly cut off or from something else, Morgan could not be bothered either way. Not when *her* handsome earl and his dangerous closeness were having such an effect on her nerves. Every inch of her skin seemed to cry out, aching with some previously forbidden sensation.

This was most improper, but she damn sure would not be the one to break the embrace. Besides, had she not just vowed to spare not a single care for what society thought proper? Indeed, she had.

Besides, this man's emotional hold over her was becoming stronger than even the physical one he held presently around her waist. So, there was really no turning back on said vow, even if she wanted to. Morgan allowed herself to reach up and hesitantly touch his chest.

His heart was beating rapidly. Her eyes swept his curiously. His deep liquid blue orbs had darkened dramatically, the same way they had the day he had kissed her in her aunt's garden. Laughter was not the driving force behind his quickened pulse now. She was.

Morgan placed a quick and chaste kiss on the edge of his mouth. "Mayhap I can arrange for every one of your weeks, from here on out, to be highlighted with mirth," she whispered, so only he could hear the raspy tone weaving through her voice.

He studied her closely. "Then I will be the luckiest man alive."

Right then and there, in a cramped carriage somewhere on Queens Street, Morgan realized the most scandalous part of it all...

She was falling in love with the Earl of Wellington.

IX

*M*organ watched the flames crackle and hiss in the fireplace of her bedroom. At any moment, Bertrice would be in to help her into her wedding dress. *Her wedding dress...*

She would be walking down the aisle later today! Which was something she should have better prepared herself for mentally, considering it had been exactly one week since her world was put completely out of order. But she had not. Instead, she had lived the last seven days in a haze, agreeing with what anyone said, smiling when smiling was expected, and going about her daily routines as if she were a marionette.

Now that it was *the* day of the impending nuptials, however... Something about the incessant ticking of the grandfather clock, droning on and on, brought the inescapable reality into vivid focus. Life as she knew it was about to be over. A new, unknown life was about to begin and she had not the slightest idea for how to manage it.

Morgan stared at the wedding dress hanging on her armoire door. It was her mother's from when she had married the first time. To everyone's surprise, Morgan's stepfather had responded quickly to his wife when she'd sent word that it be delivered post haste. The garment had arrived two days ago, which left little time for alterations, but Madam LeMore had done wonders.

The dress was beautiful, a timeless style that had weathered the past twenty-three years remarkably well. The notion her mother had wed her father in it gave Morgan hope for her future. Maybe she could make this marriage into something similar to the love her parents shared.

At least, that was what the romantic side of her was saying. Too bad the very practical side of her brain kept relentlessly placing reason upon reason why this was a disaster in the making. She was not a woman who liked surprises or changes. Even as a small child, she had hated it when something or someone was suddenly placed in her path.

A small laugh tumbled over her lips. Here she had considered herself quite the adventurer. At least, that was the story Morgan sold herself when she first arrived in London. She had even made good on her goals...sneaking out for a moonlight swim. And if she were counting her risks...well, there *was* getting married to a man she had known less than a month.

She was an utter failure at adventuring. Morgan flopped back into the down comforter of her bed. A true adventurer would be excited about this unforeseen turn in the road. A new challenge. An exciting chance. She sighed. She was entirely too pragmatic for that nonsense.

She decided to leave the risk-taking to her future husband and his best friend. They seemed to have the word 'carefree' down to an art form. So much so that one of them could stumble upon two naked women in a lake and think nothing of it. Morgan bolted upright.

The Earl of Rockafetch, best friend to the man she was about to marry, knew of her torrid secret. Had he seen her and Eloise naked? She assumed he only spotted them once they were submerged in the water. But what if he had seen everything leading up to that? Their mad, naked dash into the water... *Oh, dear heavenly Lord, no!*

Surely not. Morgan argued with her mounting fear. If he had, could he be trusted not to repeat the tale? What if he shared the story with her soon-to-be husband? What if the earl became enraged and cried off from the wedding? Why was this obvious concern just now presenting itself to her?

She stood up and began to pace. He would not cry off; he would *more* likely want to reenact the event. She felt herself blush as another thought joined in the dithery circle of her racing mind.

Tonight, was her wedding night and her future husband was a sizable man. Visions of his square back, broad chest, and impressive forearms leapt to mind. How many times had her eyes wandered down, when he was safely distracted and engaged in conversation, to marvel at the circumference of his calf muscles and how they stretched out the leather of his boots?

Enough to know the man was a solid wall of muscle. *What if everything on him was that large?* Morgan clutched the bedpost to steady her trembling hands. There would surely be pain involved with bedding this man. Could she manage it? An even more terrifying concern occurred before she could even fully process the last one.

Lord Wellington was a known rake who had most likely been with more women than he could count. What would he think of a virgin in his bed? Would she disappoint him? Would he seek out another bed if she did not satisfy his needs? Men did it all the time after all. Would she be able to abide it if he did?

It would not be a love match. Morgan knew in her heart of hearts she could never really love a man who would stray. She had been fully prepared for that exact marriage arrangement four weeks ago, when she arrived in London in her stepfather's beaten down carriage. All she had wanted then was someone to provide her with an escape. Any arrangement would have been better than the option of returning to Roderick's household.

So much had changed. Could she *not* love the Earl of Wellington if he was unfaithful? Did she even possess the ability to seize her heart back now?

She doubled over and sat on the bed, tears building and stinging the back of her eyelids. She needed to get hold of these turbulent emotions. Surely, it was normal to have such worries on one's wedding day. A knock at the door startled her.

"Come in," Morgan called, swiping away the dampness around her eyes.

The door slowly creaked open. "Miss Sinclair?" Perry's voice hedged from the doorway. "Might I have a word?"

She pasted on a ready smile before turning to face him. She would not let the young footman see her fears. The poor man had been worrying over her for the past week. No need to age him further.

She rose, motioning him to enter. "Of course, Perry."

He shyly stepped over the threshold and into her bedroom, carrying freshly cut flowers in his hand. "For you, my lady," he said, holding them out. "I thought you might like to carry them down the aisle?"

Morgan took the thoughtful gift. "These are beautiful."

She brought the bouquet up and inhaled the redolent roses and pincushion flowers. The gesture touched her deeply.

"Whatever will I do without you?" She smiled up at him.

"About that." He looked down at his boots. "I have asked the duchess if I might leave her employment. To go with you. She has agreed. Provided his lordship will take me on." He rushed out the words in nervous, clipped sentences. "You see. I have grown tired of the city. And would much prefer a quiet life in the country."

The country? Morgan latched onto those two words. Whatever else Perry was getting at, she pushed aside. Had she just learned where her future residence was to be from the footman? Was no one going to tell her? She assumed the earl would take her to his city residence after the wedding since the season was just underway.

Was this to be it then? Her biggest fears confirmed. He would cart her away to the country and stash her out there while he returned to his life here in the city? She turned quickly, shielding her crestfallen face under the pretense of looking for a vase.

"Do you object, Miss Sinclair?" Perry asked, hesitantly.

Yes, damn it! She objected very much. Just not to Perry's innocent inquiry. Morgan put her hands around the empty flower vase. Bertrice had dumped the garden wildflowers yesterday. She would just need some water.

She placed the bouquet into the vase and turned back to face Perry. "I would like that very much." Morgan tried to smile. "I will need as many familiar faces around me as I can get if I am to successfully manage a country manor."

Perry's face lit up like a Christmas tree. "Capital, my lady, just capital!" He turned, obviously eager to relay the news.

"Perry?" Morgan touched his arm, stilling him in his tracks. "You must remember that it will be his lordship who will be your employer now, not I." She withdrew her hand. "I would caution you to place yourself in his good graces at once."

She knew the young footman had become overly protective of her; perhaps due to their similar age, mayhap something else. Regardless of his reasons, she would hate for Perry to overstep his bounds and lose his place amongst the earl's household. She liked him very much. He was a kind soul who always managed to brighten her spirits. Plus, if she were to survive being a cast off wife, she would need all the uplifting people around her she could get.

Perry looked down to where Morgan's hand moved from his arm. "Yes, the earl will be my employer." He lifted his gaze, smiling tenderly. "But you will be my concern."

Morgan saw the adoration shining in his eyes. She hoped she was not making a mistake by accepting his offer to come with her. Only time would tell. Until then, she would enjoy having another friend.

She shooed him off with a smile. "Off now. I must get ready."

She turned back to face her dressing table as the door clicked quietly shut behind her. *Drat!* She had forgotten to request the water. Morgan started to call him back, but stopped.

There, on her nightstand was a glass of water, still half full from last night. She walked over, picked it up, and poured the remains into the vase. The flowers seemed immediately grateful. She sighed for them, and took a seat. Right as a cannon blast came through the wall.

Morgan shot up and whirled to the source of the explosion. Standing in the frame of her previously closed door was her worst nightmare. Roderick...

He stepped into her room, his posture the easy languor of someone well into their cups, but his eyes as wild as a crazed boar. Footsteps could be heard pounding up the back-servant's stairway, but they would not get there in time. Roderick closed the door and locked it.

"Do not scream or I will kill whoever ends up on the other side of that door." He slinked toward her, a dangerous smile nipping the corners of his mouth. "Tell them you accidentally closed it too hard. That you are all right."

A loud pounding rattled the door. "Miss Morgan, are you all right?" Perry called out, frantic.

Morgan cringed. He should not have used her Christian name. She could practically see the loathing rolling off her stepbrother like smoke off a cigar.

"Yes, I am hale," she lied, praying her tone was tepid. "The wind from the window must have caught it," she added, hoping Perry would recall how her room had been when he had exited; windows closed, a fire blazing to ward off the chill.

Silence from the hallway. "I will be just downstairs if you need anything, Miss Sinclair," Perry replied, formally.

He understood. But could he manage anything in time? Morgan backed toward the dressing table.

Roderick abruptly threw up his hand, halting her in her tracks. They both listened to the sound of retreating footsteps. With every one, Morgan felt hope slipping away.

"What do you want?" She nearly choked on the words, her voice sounding thin and helpless.

Roderick reached her in two long strides. "Do not play the fool." He grabbed hold of her wrist and yanked her forward. "Guess what I want."

Before Morgan could utter a response, he reached around behind her and gripped her bottom hard, his fingers digging deep into the muscles as he hauled her to his chest. She yelped and flailed against him, but he managed to seize both of her hands in a punishing hold.

"Did you really think you could get out of this family so easily?" He half groaned, half growled, into her ear.

"I am not your property!" she spat back and tried to knee him in the groin, but he was too close and her skirts were too encumbering. All she managed to do was anger him further.

"Yes, you are!" Roderick twisted her wrists so hard she thought they might snap. "Same as your pathetic mother belongs to my father."

Morgan cried out from the pain. He quickly muted the sound by covering her mouth with his own and thrusting his liquor-tinged tongue down her throat. She could not move, could not bite, could not kick, nor hit. All she could do was brace herself against the assault.

Smothering her with his kiss, he locked one arm around her back, securing her in place as he hitched up the material of her gown with his free hand. Raw panic raced over her, and she bucked and twisted. It was to no avail, but it did cause him to break the kiss.

"Stop fighting me," he hissed. "I am not going to take you here, you stupid whore."

The air rushed out of her lungs on a plea. "Please...let me go."

Roderick ran his free hand up the back of her thigh. Pushing the material of her pantalettes aside, he grabbed hold of her bare bottom with both hands. "Oh, not quite." He smirked.

"First, I want you to feel what I have in store for you." He pressed his engorged erection against her belly. "This effect you have on me is obscene." Her stepbrother moaned into her temple as he angrily needed her flesh with his groping fingers. "I hate you for it."

Morgan pressed her eyes shut as a tear rolled down her cheek. "Then let me go. Surely, if I am married and far away—"

"No!" He silenced her. "I *will* have you! A wanton whore like you must be dealt with," he snarled. "I will own you. Body and soul. You will come willingly to me, and I will not be gentle. You will not enjoy it."

Roderick suddenly released her. "Open your eyes."

Morgan took a deep shuddering breath and slowly did as he told her. His eyes bore into hers, blazing with loathing and lust.

"Why?" She managed to get the word out. Hearing it released into the air gave her a small amount of courage. "Why would I willingly do anything for you?"

She prepared herself for his physical response, but her stepbrother only smirked odiously at her. "Because I will do unspeakable things to the people you hold dear should you choose to be non-compliant. I will start with your dear mother. Then maybe that pretty little friend of yours." His grin grew into a snarl. "God forbid you have a child that is not mine."

He took a welcomed step backward. "Wellington might have your body first, but it will be me that you will not be able to stop thinking about."

Roderick pivoted and headed toward the door. "No one can save you, sweet sister. If the earl were to find out you were having an affair, especially one with your own kin, he would kill you himself."

Her stepbrother turned to face her when he reached the hallway. "I will come for you very soon. That should give your husband time to teach you how to please a man." He slanted her one last amused look. "Remember...our little secret. Too many people are relying on your good behavior." He disappeared down the hall.

Morgan collapsed to the floor, her barely contained tears breaking like a levee and flowing in rivulets down her cheeks. She thought she heard voices down the hall, but it was hard to discern over the pounding beat of her heart inside her chest and in her temples. She stared at the plush rug beneath her knees.

Her tears were landing and collecting in a pool on her skirt. The effect caused the light blue fabric to grow darker in color and shimmer. It reminded her of the Earl of Wellington's eyes. *It was pretty*, she thought, letting her mind chart its own course back to normality. *Or insanity*. She was not entirely sure.

A collective gasp resonated somewhere near her doorway and then a sudden rush of movement brought something heavy skidding toward her. Perry's worried face came into focus. He was on the ground with her, coaxing her chin up with his hands. A second bystander stood over her, caressing her hair and cooing affirmations of safety meant to comfort. *Bertrice.*

Someone else was coming down the hall. Heavy, authoritarian tread pounded the hardwoods outside her room. Morgan started to panic anew. Was Roderick coming back? Had he decided to change his plan and take her now? Could Perry stop him?

She trembled with fear until a familiar voice filled the room, demanding answers to questions neither staff member could respond to. *Edward!* He was here. Everything would be alright.

Hot tears returned to her eyes and then strong, steady arms were around her, lifting her up as if she weighed nothing at all.

"Morgan, what did he do?" The earl's voice drifted around her.

"Send servants to every exit!" he directed the others, his voice vibrating out of his chest as he held her, cradled like a baby. "See if anyone saw which way he left. Now!" He barked out and everyone in the near vicinity scrambled into action.

The room grew silent again. Edward lowered her to the bed and sat beside her. "Morgan?" His tone softened and focused, with pinpoint accuracy, on her. "Morgan?"

She felt his hand on her face, but she could not meet his eyes. She feared the truth of her shame would be too evident. He tried again and she shook free of him, nearly tumbling backward in her attempts not to have him bear witness to the horrific images Roderick had placed in her mind. She turned away.

"Morgan, you must tell me, so I can call him out."

She whirled on him. "No! He is too mad." She shook her head. "He would not fight fair."

She looked back down, unable to withstand the rolling angst she found swimming in his sapphire eyes. "He just needs to calm down. The sooner we can rid the city, the better it will be."

For all of us, she told herself. She must protect those she loved.

And sitting beside her was the loss she would feel the most if Roderick did exact his revenge. She would find a way to handle this, but she would not risk any of their lives. She had to be stronger than the fear residing inside her.

"I have never run from any man, and I certainly do not intend on doing so now," Edward stated.

"That is not what I meant," she said. "I just think that..." Her mind raced for a plausible excuse. "That some time away would give us all space from our immediate emotions."

"Morgan, I just found you on the floor shaking like a willow branch. Due to that imbecile!" He growled and stabbed a finger toward her door. "He does not need *space* from his immediate emotions. He *needs* a bullet between the eyes."

"Please." Morgan mustered all the strength she had left and looked up, imploring him.

Worry and confusion had replaced the anger in his eyes. A part of her heart cracked, as if the organ itself was fighting against the struggle that everything must remain hidden. She could never tell anyone what transpired between her and Roderick. For her stepbrother was right; no one would believe her. And if they did, he would kill them.

"It is not for him that I ask. Can you please do this for me?" she begged. "Can you trust me to know what needs to be done? At least for now?"

He stared at her for a long time before responding, expression indecipherable. "I can try." The pads of his fingers caressed her face. "Just know that it goes against every instinct that resides within me to do so." His hand lowered. "I do this because you ask. Not for him."

"Thank you."

Morgan walled up her teetering emotions and stood slowly, testing that her legs would support her weight. Knowing her eyes would betray her words if she continued to face him, she walked over to her vanity, picked up a silver hair comb and sat down.

"Is it not bad luck to see the bride before the wedding?" She ran the brush through her hair, watching him in the mirror and hoping her attempt at normality was convincing.

"Under the circumstances..." He pushed to his feet and walked up behind her. Gently he reached down and removed the brush from her hand. "I believe the forces behind old wives tales will grant us immunity."

Morgan stared at his reflection in the mirror as he softly pulled the brush through her hair. The intimate gesture shocked her. She studied the handsome man behind her as he carefully parted each strand with his free hand, so as not to pull overly much when he smoothed the thick tresses. Seemingly lost in thought, he smiled as if recalling a distant memory.

When he spoke again, his voice carried a sort of melancholy sadness. "My mother used to let me comb her hair out. I found the process calming and would always marvel at how the strands shined like black silk in my hands. Perkin would make fun of me, of course, but the quiet moments I got to share with her made the teasing bearable. It was the one thing that belonged solely to her and me."

He continued to focus on her mass of wavy hair, lost to the remembrance. Morgan felt her heart expand deep in her chest. The thought of this strong, confident man as a small boy reaping so much innocent joy from such a mundane act...brushing his mother's hair. It was everything that was right about the world.

"Your hair is glorious, Morgan. Would you keep it down today? For me."

Morgan felt her breath hitch in her throat. She was going to cry anew, for totally different reasons. "Yes."

"I am to be your husband now." His gaze fixated on hers in the mirror. "I also hope, your friend. Please do not keep secrets from me. I want to be the one consistent thing in your life. The one you can rely on. To do that, I need you to place your trust in me."

He placed the brush back on the tabletop and turned her in the chair to face him. "I do not ask for all of this now. But in time, I would like to earn it from you."

Edward bent down to her eye level. "I will not never hurt you, Morgan Sinclair. Not intentionally."

Too overwhelmed by his earnest vow to respond, Morgan collapsed into his arms. He held her to him, gently stroking the back of her head with one hand. Could she learn to trust? How she wanted to unburden her fears on this man, tell him everything, and hope he did not judge her too harshly.

She could not. *Not yet.* For while it would unburden herself, it would cause him a great deal of pain. And if his temper was to be believed, which she now knew to be true, he would place himself in harm's way trying to defend her honor.

Morgan needed to shoulder this weight alone until Roderick grew tired of tormenting her, which she was sure would happen once she was far away and no longer within easy reach. She simply needed to retire with Edward to the country and in time, all would be forgotten. It had to be. The only other possible future was far too grim.

She breathed in the clean scent of Edward's freshly laundered shirt. The garment had a crisp sun-bleached hint to it, as if someone had hung it out to line dry. Morgan closed her eyes, her own memory taking her back in time to when her mother once exercised the same chores—hanging the wash up with pins in the open air while her father chopped wood.

Back when life was innocent, and they were happy. She nuzzled into the comforting scent. It blended nicely with the earl's more masculine smells of smoke and brandy. The scent of *him.*

Morgan opened her eyes, not ready to pull away from his warmth just yet, but curious. "Does your staff hang your laundry out to dry?"

"What an interesting observation." She heard the smile in his voice. "They do. Upon my instructions."

She sat up. "You do not have them serviced outside of the house when you are in the city?"

She was no expert on bon ton living, but she knew her aunt had their laundry done elsewhere in town. Every Tuesday, a footman would load it up and disappear down the lane, only to return with freshly washed and pressed garments the next day. She had assumed that all elite society did the same.

"I prefer to have them air dried. I suppose it is another carryover from my childhood." He smiled wistfully. "My mother insisted that a drop of bleach be added to the wash and that it be hung out on warm days. There is something about the smell of the sunshine..."

His voice trailed off, as if he might have said too much. Morgan did not push him further. Instead, she folded herself back into his arms and allowed time to pass. They sat for several minutes, both their pasts collecting silently, an echo of mirrored joys and losses.

Morgan lifted her hand and placed it under her chin against his chest. "How old were you when she died?"

"Seven." He took a deep breath. "She was the one person who truly understood me."

"I am sure she would be very proud to see the man you have become."

"She would have loved me no matter what I became. I was her favorite." He smirked, the mood instantly becoming lighter.

"Perkin was three years older, you see, and stayed shackled to my father's side, always proving to be the type of firstborn any father would be proud of. He would have gotten even more praise if our little sister was not always tagging along, hanging from Father's arms, or standing on his feet." Edward chuckled at the memory. "Which was most entertaining when Father was trying to entertain dignitaries."

Morgan grinned. "Your sister sounds like she stole many a show from her big brothers."

"Indeed, she did," he agreed, nodding. "My sister has never been one to miss an opportunity to shine. Neither of my siblings' have."

"Well, I have not met your brother, but it seems to me that your entire family has tremendous talent for captivating the general public." She nudged him in the ribs. "You *are* the *notorious* Earl of Wellington after all."

"Oh, just wait until you meet my brother." He winked. "You may leave me for him."

"Stop that!" Morgan swatted his arm playfully. "I think I prefer the self-deprecating one best."

Edward smiled. "I am glad my unique skill set has come in useful for something."

They both laughed. It felt good. Maybe they could make this rushed relationship work. He seemed to genuinely want to care for her, and she was already falling head over heels for him. Morgan watched the way his eyes crinkled at the edges as he laughed. She wanted that mirth encapsulated, sealed up, and suspended in time so that nothing could ever mar it. For when he smiled...the man was a gravitational force.

And here she was, caught up and willingly pulled toward him, the sea to the moon. Could she be blamed? Surely it was too much to ask anyone to forsake.

Plus, *line-dried clothes...*

"Now, here is the issue with virgins..." Henry prattled on. Edward wondered if he might be more nervous about Edward's upcoming marriage bed duties than he himself was. "You have to go very slow."

Edward stared blankly across the carriage at his friend. The man might as well be declaring a desire to give up his title and lands to farm turnips in Russia.

"Henry, I daresay, I am not a virgin; you need not draw blood from my ears any longer."

Henry narrowed his eyes pointedly at him. "Oh, for heaven's sake, I know that! It is the girl I am concerned for."

Edward hoisted up straighter in his seat, growing irritated now. "She is not your concern. However, I am beginning to wonder what sort of Neanderthal you think I am."

"For the love of everything good and holy! I know you have never been with a virgin." Henry paused, as if considering a better argument. "I have. I merely wished to enlighten you as to how different the experience is, so that you might...take care."

His best friend let out a long-suffering sigh. Edward was used to those; he had been on the receiving end his whole life.

He sat back indolently and closed his eyes. "Contrary to popular belief, I am capable of being gentle. But please..." He rolled his wrist. "Give me the 'how to remain a gentleman while fucking a virgin' speech if it brings you peace of mind."

Henry actually inhaled a hiss threw his teeth. Edward opened one eye. His longtime friend, a man he had fought beside, gambled beside, and whored beside was now puffed up like some sort of old ninny, ready to flog him where he sat.

"Oh bother, Henry." He reopened both eyes. "You know I am simply being cavalier to have a go at you. I have full intentions of making the consummation duties as *polite* as possible. Even if that means forsaking my own pleasure."

He considered the plausibility of his words before nodding confidently. "I am sure I am capable. I will certainly be as mindful of her needs as I can."

Henry visibly relaxed. "May I suggest a glass of brandy beforehand and a drop of this in both your glasses?" He pulled a small vial from his pocket. "I obtained it from a friend."

When Edward arched a brow, his friend shrugged. He took the bottle. "Surely you are not suggesting I drug my new bride to lay with her? I daresay, I am becoming mildly insulted."

"It will not drug either of you," Henry said. "It will merely relax the muscles so that the experience can be better...enjoyed." He offered a wry smile. "Furthermore, it will keep your libido in check. So that you do not accidentally forget your gentlemanly ways."

He wanted to cuff his friend on the ears, but his father had just stepped up alongside the carriage door. Edward pocketed the liquid. With one last ruffled look to Henry, he opened the door.

"They are ready inside," Richard stated.

He stepped out of the carriage and followed his father into the cathedral. *Relax the muscles...* Who needed such a thing? He was more than capable of controlling himself with her. Foolish Henry, *what the hell did he know of marriage?*

Morgan was having a difficult time recalling much after she alighted from the carriage and walked through the back door of the church. It was as if the ceremony had been but a passing dream. She did remember there had been an enormous turnout. Likely due to the salacious circumstances of their joining.

They had exchanged their wedding vows and then Edward had kissed her briefly to thunderous applause. After that, they were shut in a carriage together and whisked away. *A passing dream.*

Perry, Bertrice, and her husband's most unusual butler, Boswell, brought up the rear in a second carriage. Five lives, all brought together by happenstance, would now be forced to coexist and adapt. It was anyone's guess how this would all play out.

Morgan felt her brows knitting together. Poor Perry was already facing an uphill battle with the Earl of Wellington. She had seen clearly the look of doubt on Edward's face when the eager young footman had bowed after the wedding, placed a hand over his heart, and declared *he* would watch over Lady Sinclair with the devotion of a lion.

To Edward's surprising credit, he did not sack the man on the spot. Instead, he simply reminded his new hire that *Lady Sinclair* was now to be addressed as Lady Wellington. Dear, foolish Perry would have to devote himself equally to his new master if he wanted to stay employed for longer than a fortnight.

As for her groom. Morgan watched him where he sat across from her, gaze cast out the window. He had been on edge and gruff in their preparations for departure, snapping at the staff more than a few times to hurry up. At first, she assumed he was mourning the loss of his single status, but as the carriage meandered through the city streets, Morgan began to question that. However, once they were out of the town center his behavior changed markedly and he notably relaxed.

"Your father seemed happy today," she ventured.

"He seemed relieved." Edward began untying his cravat. "One down, one more to go."

Morgan watched as the immaculate cloth loosened enough to reveal the long column of her husband's tan neck. The sun streaming through the window made art of him, calling attention to where the silk lay against the skin. Just as Morgan was becoming transfixed, he sighed, his Adam's apple rising and falling. Her mouth went dry and she had the strongest urge reach over, take the cravat, twist the silk in her hands, and pull him to her.

His gaze swung to her, and she had to find an excuse to cover her mouth with her hand. *Yawning!* Yes, a yawn was appropriate on a long journey. Drooling was not.

What kind of wanton hussy was she turning into? Mortified, she turned and looked out the window. "Where are we going, exactly?" She focused on another subject.

Morgan heard him chuckle, but she dared not look back. She would not confirm his suspicions. "I have an estate about a three-hour ride from my sister and Lord Ravenswood's castle."

She turned quickly from her feigned interest in a farmer with his drag hoe, working a field. "A castle?"

"Theirs. Not mine—er, ours," he corrected. "Although I have heard Crestmont is a close rival."

"You have never seen it?" Morgan asked, astonished.

"No, but I have had servants sent ahead to warn the staff of our arrival. I am sure all will be in place when we get there." He paused. "Have you any ideas on how to run a large house?"

She got the impression that the question was not merely a curiosity, but a hope. "I helped run the house I grew up in, but it was just a small country house. I did not oversee any of the buying and selling, or train any of the staff."

She looked back at him curiously. "Have you?"

He outright laughed. "No, I do not have a clue where to start."

She was momentarily taken aback. Surely, he jested; he knew about everything. But when his laughter quieted into a pensive snicker, she knew he was serious. *He had doubt!* Doubt in himself! This confident, worldly lord was unsure.

The thought propelled Morgan into action and her hand shot out to pat his thigh, encouraging him to meet her gaze. "We will figure it out together then."

They would! Maybe they could teach each other something after all? The notion of not being the sole student in this pairing, but instead, being a contributing force, a partner, emboldened her. A sudden protectiveness fanned to life.

Morgan moved to his side and looked up into his eyes. "The first thing you need to know is that I will always support your decisions. I will do your bidding and never work against your interest. I will be your strength whenever you need it."

He placed an arm around her and pulled her close. She relaxed into him, feeling both appreciated and protected. It was as if she belonged here, nestled under his arm.

She closed her eyes. Perhaps this was how all true love stories started out. Upside down and inside out, yet wholly meant to be.

Edward knew the instant Morgan fell asleep on his chest. Her breathing slowed and her weight grew heavier in slumber, completely vulnerable. He watched her for a long time before allowing himself to stroke the soft waves of her hair. One by one, he removed the pins until it cascaded free of the tiny flowers, her maid had woven through it. She had worn it loose, as he had requested, with the exception of the few well-placed roses.

He replayed her last vow in his head. *I will be your strength whenever you need it.* Could she have any idea what those words meant to him? Could she even begin to conceive how they might be tested?

Yet, here she slept, earnestly trusting in him. Trusting in *them*. He allowed his eyes to close, loving the feel of her body pressed against his.

Before he knew it, he was awaking from his own blissful slumber. He guessed, from the sun peeking through the branches, that they had traveled quite far and should be getting close now. A faint whiff of sea salt-laden air played in the breeze and brought back fond memories. He was much more at ease now they were far out of the city. Too many people wanted to see harm befall him and his new bride.

His new bride. He looked down at her sleeping, feeling her body warm against his. She had wrapped her arms around his middle and curled her legs up on the cushioned seat. Her head now rested on his lap, the mop of red hair fanning out like a fiery halo around her face.

Good God, she was beautiful, he mused. His pulse began to quicken with a more primal desire, but before it could manifest bodily, his mind aggressively chased it away. What would their coupling be like for her?

He had never been with an innocent. Henry was right on that account. What if he hurt her? He did not think he could knowingly inflict pain on the beauty nestled in his arms. He could certainly not conduct *business as usual* on his end if he thought she were suffering.

Edward let his head roll back. Damn, why had he not been more of a debaucher and stolen at least one young lady's virtue? Then he would at least know what amount of discomfort the act created. More than a score of willing young debutantes had wanted him to do just that, but even he had limits when it came to his hedonistic pleasures. Maybe he would lace both their drinks tonight, after all.

Just as he was fingering the small vial in his vest pocket and contemplating using it, the carriage rounded a turn. His breath caught. They were off the main drive now and on what was presumably his land. The dirt lane stretched out in front of them, parting a rambling meadow filled with wildflowers.

It was, without question, one of the prettiest plots of land he had ever seen. He shifted as gently as he could to crane his neck out the window for a better view. Morgan stirred and lifted her head sleepily.

"Are we getting close?" she asked.

"I believe we have just arrived."

She bolted upright and peered out the opposite window. "Oh my, this is all yours?"

"Ours," he corrected, smiling. "This is all ours."

X

Richard's eyes scanned the front letter addressed to him in the bold elegant hand of his eldest son, Perkin. As he read it again, tiny hairs on the back of his arms began to stand on end. Davenport's name was on the list of suspected investors attached to the second missive. But another name troubled Richard more.

Dear Father,

As you are reading this, I hope your mind is at ease with the knowledge that Thomas, Dalton and myself are all hale. We made port three days ago and have uncovered a number of people we believe to be involved. I have sent a letter to our Queen with the list. However, I wanted to get this in your hands as well, for a few of these men sit rather close to you in Parliament. One of the names will not surprise you, I am sure. Attached are my findings.

Your loving son,

Perkin

Richard flipped to the attached list of names, confirming what he had already seen. Sure enough, there were quite a few recognizable names. Edward's childhood enemy, Davenport, was not the one that worried him most. That one, as Perkin predicted, he had expected. It was another scribed name that was responsible for the chill in his veins. *Ratcliff.*

Richard had first heard that name when it came time for Edward to receive his title as the Earl of Wellington. The Queen granted it to Richard's second son after the late Earl of Wellington passed, leaving behind no known heirs. John Ratcliff was a distant cousin of the late earl. When Ratcliff learned Edward would be gaining the title over his own claim, he became incensed, demanding it go to him.

Nevertheless, the Queen's wishes reigned supreme, and the title went to Edward. Ratcliff was furious. The Queen, still young and eager to appease her people, felt he should be mollified with something, so she had gifted him a title of his own.

Ratcliff became a baron, and all was good until he had the misfortune of getting pinned under a rig during a carriage race. The newly established lord perished at the crash, leaving his title to pass down to his younger brother. *Martin Ratcliff?*

Richard froze on the name, realization sinking in like a rock thrown into a deep pool. *Martin Ratcliff, Baron De Montrey.* Was that not the name Richard had overheard the duchess discussing with her sister that day in the parlor? Richard had been so eager to get away from his eavesdropping position outside the door and mortified by the realization that Lady Vistmont's husband was abusing her, that he had fled at the first opportunity.

His mind reeled backward in time, grappling for confirmation that De Montrey was indeed the name of the man who had been set on courting Miss Sinclair, his new daughter-in-law. How could he have not put two and two together if it were? He had to be mistaken. *But if he was not...*

Could Martin Ratcliff, Baron De Montrey, have been the one behind the attempts on Edward's life, harboring disdain over Edward's advancement from what his family thought was their rightful claim? If so, he would surely be angry now that Edward had stolen his intended.

Richard folded the missive as he moved purposefully toward the door, one goal in mind. He must warn Edward. He was just placing his hat on when a quick moving footman burst through the front doors.

Ocman reached out and caught the man by the jacket collar, halting his speedy advancement before he could plow over the master of the house. "Have a care, man," the ever-vigilant butler warned.

The young footman started to fidget about. "I...I...I'm sorry, my lord, but there is a fire at the dock." His voice shook. Whether it was from his sprint to the house or his collision with the family's sizable African butler, Richard couldn't be sure. "They say to come get you, for it be makin' its way to the Lady Mystic."

Richard's blood turned to ice. That cargo was loaded down with nearly twelve thousand pounds of goods. The ship was worth twice that.

Richard moved quickly to a sideboard table and penned a quick note of warning to Edward, then he thrust it into the nervous footman's hands. "You and Ocman take this to Crestmont. Make sure it is delivered directly to my son."

Richard turned to Ocman. "I will be there as soon as I have dealt with the fire. Go now, and..." He paused at the look of intense concentration in the larger man's dark eyes. "Stay close to him and his new wife."

His longtime employee and friend looked him in the eyes. "You know I will."

With that he was out the door and already blending with the night, the frazzled footman fast on his heels.

Morgan felt Edward stiffen beside her at the exact same moment she did. An ominous black cloud was on the prowl; its thick fingers of suffocating smoke twisted through the sky. Upward toward the heavens it advanced, a demon hell-bent on war.

Something was dreadfully wrong. Morgan had seen that type of smoke before and knew the fire that caused it was much too large to be a controlled blaze. This was not some farmer burning off summer crops. Edward seemed to realize the same thing. He gently, but insistently, moved her over in the seat.

Craning his head out the window, he shouted for the driver to speed up. With a jolt, the rig began racing down the lane. Panic churned in her stomach, but she had little time to entertain it. The violent lurch of the carriage sent her reeling backward and scrambling to regain her balance, lest she be tossed on the floor.

Once securely pressed into the back of the seat, she tried to get a better look, but Edward's large torso was filling the window. She inched herself across the carriage and peered out the opposite window. *Nothing!* That side of the horizon was clear. *It had to be the estate!*

Morgan reached for Edward's arm braced against the door of the carriage. His tendons felt like solid rods ready to snap off under the skin. She withdrew her hand apprehensively, afraid of putting any added pressure on him.

The carriage careened to a stop, but the realization had already seeped in through the cracks around the windows. *Fire.*

Edward threw open the door and bounded out, just as Perry dashed by the window to her left. The door slammed shut.

Frantic shouts, muffled by the velvet-covered walls of the rig, erupted from somewhere beyond Morgan's encasement. The stark difference between her interior environment and what was occurring outside gave the distinct impression of being trapped in a tomb.

She could not sit idly by and do nothing. That was not in her nature. She shoved open the carriage door and leapt out.

Edward quickly met up with who he assumed to be his estate's butler. "My lord!"

The man, dripping wet and covered in soot, rushed to reach him and executed an impressive bow. He pulled himself up tall, affected the best dignified look anyone could possibly muster when coated from head to toe in ashes and dirt. "We have put everything to order."

"To order!" Edward barked. "I am missing half a house."

Boswell came puttering up at that exact moment, assessed the other man as if he were a spot of hardened food left on a plate after it had been scrubbed, and scoffed, "And who might this be?"

"I am Truman," the younger man addressed Edward solely. "Crestmont's butler," he added for Boswell's benefit. "Someone has been sabotaging the staff's hard work the past week in our preparations for your arrival. But we managed to get it under con..."

Edward knew the second his new butler's eyes beheld Morgan, for an unmistakable male appreciation reflected in them. "I, er, that is to say, we—"

"Get on with it, man!" he interrupted with a snap of his fingers. "Have you the blaze contained?"

"Entirely unprofessional," Boswell huffed.

The man quickly regained his focus. "My apologies, my lord. Yes, we have isolated the remaining fire and will have it extinguished in no time."

Edward waved off any further idle chit-chat. "What happened here?"

"A letter with threats of the fire came last night, and after a week of destruction, half the staff packed up and left. The rest of us thought we had secured the perimeter well enough to keep out any would-be culprits, but someone managed to get into the house. They lit the fire in the main study. We were able to get it under control and block it from continuing to the rest of the manor. It is contained, but—"

Edward didn't wait for the rest. He had already begun taking off his jacket as he ran toward the house. His new butler rushed to keep up. Pushing up his sleeves, Edward began issuing commands as he grabbed the first pail of water.

"We need more water!" He pointed to the fastest-looking footmen. "You three! Get to the river and start bringing up more buckets."

His new footman, the love-struck Perry, was already making himself useful, draping wet blankets across the remaining wood paneling that separated the study from the rest of the house. The fire had burned the room nearly clear off from the rest of the house, but Truman's assessment of the situation was off. The lethal flames were still threatening to lick their way into the remaining hallway.

Edward grabbed a shovel and started heaving dirt onto the red embers. Out of the corner of his eye, he spied a puff of white dash by. He turned his head in time to see his new wife rip the lace sleeves from her wedding dress and grab a bucket of water.

At that very moment, a hot ember chose to leap up into his eye. He cursed and wiped away the vicious, stinging ash. He blinked and tried to focus, his anger swelling to a new level.

"Morgan!" Though he yelled, she did not hear him. Or rather, she chose not to hear him.

"My Lord, do you wish the lady to be putting out the fire?" Perry asked, hesitantly.

Edward groaned. "Of course not." He moved to retrieve her.

XI

*M*organ rubbed her aching toes as she sat on the hillside overlooking the manor. Edward was by the front of house, running a hand through his hair as he talked to the estate's butler, Truman. All the while his city butler, Boswell, glared on from the side of the house, clearly still upset Truman existed.

The scene between the three would have been comical had she not been too tired to laugh. Only *her* endearing husband would have forgotten he need not have two rival butlers. She felt herself sigh.

The fire was out. *Thank God.* The staff, and townspeople who had rushed to help, were now assessing the damage insofar as what could be salvaged, and what could not. A few men were already wheeling out debris. It had been a gallant effort on everyone's part. They had lost one room, not the entire house.

Edward, for all his efforts, had been unsuccessful in stopping her from helping. She had lifted, doused, and dug right alongside the others. She glanced down at her dress. So much for the pristine white silk that had been expertly knife pleated and embroidered with sequins, lace, flowers and ribbons.

Her bigger concern was for Edward. She had heard the word

sabotage from some of the staff. Her mind had flown to the only person she could imagine doing such a thing. *Roderick!*

She heard her name and looked up. "Miss Sinclair...I mean, Lady Wellington." Perry corrected himself.

The angelic-faced footman had surely proven his worth to his new master. Edward would not be able to overlook how quickly the young man had leapt into action.

"The earl wishes me to take you to the hunting cabin, where you will be staying for the evening while the manor is cleaned and made ready with repairs."

She glanced up at the setting sun. It was getting late; not much more could be done at night.

She allowed Perry to take her hand and help her to her feet. "Will Lord Wellington not be joining us?"

"He said to tell you he had a few more loose ends to tie up and that he would be joining you later."

"Oh, I see." She held onto Perry's arm as he walked her down the sloped hillside where her husband had all but demanded she stay put an hour ago.

"Food is being brought from the village and the cabin is being made ready for you," Perry explained.

"Where will you, Boswell, and Bertrice stay?"

"There is a servant quarters there as well. Bertrice, Boswell, Truman, and I, will reside there until the estate is occupant ready." Perry smiled. "I wonder how long it will take Boswell to try to kill Truman."

"Perry!" Morgan chuckled. "What an awful thing to say," she mockingly scolded, despite his rather valid point.

When they reached the carriage, he helped her inside.

Closing the door, Morgan looked back toward the house. Edward was still deep in conversation. He seemed to sense her eyes on him, though, for he looked right at her and smiled. Even though his expression was tight, and obviously not filled with mirth, she felt his smile as if it were a ray of morning sunlight. She drank it in.

The hunting cabin located on the east side of the property was a far cry from a lodge. It was as big as a modest townhouse in the city. Perry, Boswell, and Bertrice got right to work unpacking, while the local village storekeeper's boy laid out their evening meal and stored the rest of their supplies. Morgan thanked the lad and went to set the table.

Bertrice noticed and hurried over. "Let me do that. You must be exhausted."

"I am fine. I need to keep busy."

"Well, at least let me help you get out of this dress and into more comfortable attire, my lady."

She followed Bertrice to the master bedroom and allowed her to undo the buttons on the back of the dress. The weight of it coming off was such a relief. Every muscle in her body seemed to exhale.

"Perry is preparing a bath in the room next door," Bertrice explained with a bit of a blush. "It is a special night, after all."

The day's previous tension came flooding back with a vengeance. Dear heavenly Lord, *tonight was her wedding night.* She had not thought about that aspect since this morning. She took a calming breath.

"All will be fine, my dear." Bertrice effectively read her mind. "I will have a tray of food brought up while you bathe."

She tried to coerce her lips into what she hoped was a convincing smile. She really must take notes on how her new husband did it so well. Calm under pressure, and whatnot.

Bertrice assured her she was just on the far side of the house if Morgan needed anything, then she quit the room. Morgan finished undressing down to her shift, and made her way to the room next door. She rapped on it to make sure Perry was done and gone.

When no reply came, she entered and smiled at the sight of the steaming tub. This would do nicely. Her aching limbs were already beginning to relax in anticipation of the soothing water.

She padded over to the tub's edge, the steam from which was already filling the room. Morgan pulled her shift over her head and tossed it to the ground before stepping into the hot bath and slipping into the water. *Heaven.*

She was just starting to recline when the unmistakable scraping sound of a chair being dragged across hardwoods reverberated right behind her. She froze in place. Then she screamed.

Edward had barely closed the front door when the blood-curdling scream filled the cabin. He flew up the stairs, taking them two at a time, his heart pounding and fear lancing his mind like a cleanly driven arrow. *Morgan!*

Once at the top of the stairs, his thinking caught up to his pulse.

Only one scream, and then dead silence. That notion drained the life from his very soul.

He ran down the hall, nearly colliding with a door when it flew open. A half-falling, half-flailing, Perry came scrambling out backward. Edward was on him in a blink, murder his only focusing thought.

He grabbed the man by the throat, hauled him to his feet, then lifted him off the ground. The footman thrashed about in his attempt to find solid ground beneath his feet. Clutching at Edward's hands, he gasped as his face turned purple.

"Where is my wife?" Edward ground out.

"Edward, stop!"

Edward's head snapped around at the sound of the familiar voice. Morgan was standing in the doorway Perry had just exited, dripping wet and naked as her name day except for a towel. His grip tightened on Perry's throat.

His bride rushed forward. Edward brought his free arm up so fast and so straight she had to awkwardly stop to avoid running into his unyielding flat palm. She stopped dead in her tracks, unbridled fear in her eyes.

Fear of him, herself, or for her beloved footman's well-being? Edward was not sure what distressed her, so he squeezed Perry's neck tighter just to be sure. The footman's struggle's halted and he went limp against the wall. Edward let him drop like a sack of wheat.

"Edward, no!" Morgan cried out.

He was having a hard time compartmentalizing his warring emotions. He was livid. His new wife looked about ready to faint. His footman already had. And no one was talking.

He fought for understanding of all that he was seeing. If Perry had attacked her, why did she care what happened to him? Edward saw red! *Unless...*

"Is he?" She swayed where she stood.

"He is breathing." He raked over her with his gaze. "You better start explaining quickly, or he will not be."

"It is not what it looks like, Edward." She grasped for his arm.

"You have to the count of ten to tell me what it *should* look like," he said. "One."

"I was just beginning my bath."

"Two..."

"I thought I was alone."

"Three."

"Please stop doing that, I cannot—"

"Four, five..." He moved toward her.

"Perry was in the room, and I did not realize."

Edward stopped mid-stride and turned back to his intended victim, who lay on the plush carpet.

"Edward, no!" She placed a pleading hand on his arm. "He had fallen asleep. I think I woke him when I got in the water."

He turned slowly back to her. "Six, seven, eight, nine."

He looked to where her hand rested on his sleeve. "Did he touch you?"

She began to shake where she stood, tears welling up in her gold eyes. "No. He was just as shocked as I was. I screamed on instinct, and he panicked and ran for the door. In his haste to depart, he tripped and fell out into the hallway."

She begged understanding with her eyes. "He did nothing more than make a mistake by falling asleep in the wrong room. It has been a long day for everyone."

Edward could take no more. Before she could finish the sentence, he pulled her to him. Between the tears and the logical explanation, it all made since.

He felt like a complete arse. He had overreacted, which was *always* his first reaction. That would *have* to change! If he was going to have a shot in hell at this husband role, he had better get a tighter rein on his emotions. *Quickly!*

She wrapped her arms around him and sobbed into his shirt. "I am so sorry. I should not have screamed. I should have looked about the room more closely. I should have..."

"Shh, stop." He wrapped his arms around her tightly and held her close. "It is not your fault. I assumed the worst."

He took a deep breath and pushed her gently away. "I will see to Perry now. Please do not worry, I only made him black out; he will be fine."

Perry started to stir behind them.

"Go back in," Edward urged. "I will join you once I get him to his quarters and make sure that he has everything he needs. Starting with an apology."

Morgan felt the urge to protest, to insist she be allowed to help with Perry, but she bit back that impulse. Now was not the time for continued support of the footman her husband had just nearly killed under suspicions of manhandling his wife.

No, something told her silence was best. Her husband was weathering his own emotional storm right now and did not need any more push back. She did as he suggested and turned, closing the door behind her.

She heard Edward lifting Perry, and the footman's rush of muffled groveling as their voices faded down the hall. She wanted to cry. So many emotions were coursing through her in the day's aftermath, but the strongest one was still fear. Fear that the movement from the chair, which had started the downward spiraling of events, had been Roderick. Coming to make good on his threats.

Morgan shuddered. She wanted to crawl into bed and hide, but the tub was still steaming, and she still needed a bath. Drawing on courage, Morgan set aside the towel and stepped back into the warm water.

She washed quickly and climbed out just as she heard the adjoining room's door open. Instincts stilled her mid step. A light rap fell on her door.

"Do you need anything?" Edward asked, his deep voice soft.

How quickly that voice had changed, she noted.

"I am good." Morgan donned a dressing robe. "I am just finishing up. I will be right out after I comb out my hair."

"Don't."

"I am sorry, *do not* what?" Anxiety danced on her every nerve.

There was a moment of silence from behind the door, a space where time and thought were held captive. She saw the massive door give slightly, as if being pressed upon, and heard an exhaled breath. Morgan could tell her husband must be leaning against it.

A sudden realization seized her, and she moved quickly across the room, picking up the brush from the vanity. She reached the door and turned the handle slowly. As she had expected, he stood just on the other side.

Taking in the longing in his eyes, she held out the brush. "Will you?"

Edward stood speechless as she handed him the silver brush. She knew what he had not been able to put into words. She understood he needed to comfort her, as much as he needed the comfort himself.

Morgan gracefully glided past him to the dressing table and sat down. He followed and pulled up a chair behind her, lowered himself onto it, and looked at her reflection in the mirror. Her skin was pink from the heat of the bath; her eyes were soft when she looked back at him, kind and absent of judgment.

He had been so worried he might have scarred her for life, but the strength radiating off her now was proving he had *once again* misjudged her. She was made of much stronger stuff.

Edward reached up and traced the back of his hand down her cheek. She bent her head into the touch and softly kissed his knuckles. *God*, she was beautiful... He gathered her thick mane of auburn hair in his hand and took his time brushing it out, savoring the way she closed her eyes.

When he was done, Edward set aside the brush on the table and pushed the glossy waves to the side, exposing the thin column of her neck. He kissed right behind her ear, and she sighed. Encouraged, he trailed the kiss down to her collarbone, coaxing away the robe enough to reach the sensitive skin beneath. When he glanced back to their reflection in the mirror, her eyes were aglow with a look he knew well. She wanted him as much as he wanted her.

He slowly slid his hand down and between the layers of her robe, skimming a finger over one taut nipple. She shuddered when he took the whole breast firmly in his hand. He bent forward, watching her watch him.

She turned her head to the side, and he claimed her mouth, kissing her deeply. He brought his free hand around to cup her other breast, enjoying the weight of both in his palms. She gasped when he completely undid the garment and slid his hands between her thighs, parting them slowly. She closed her eyes.

"Look," he commanded.

Morgan did as instructed and watched, eyelids hooded with passion, as he moved his fingers between her glossy curls. She laid her head back on his shoulder and her body arched when he reached the sensitive nub and began his skilled torment on the silky flesh. Already slick with desire, she circled her hips as he divided the folds and slipped one finger inside. Slowly, he inserted a second. Her breathing caught and she clutched at his other arm.

Her body's natural response, the way her voice grew raspy when she said, *please*, and the intoxicating view in the mirror were nearly his undoing. His cock was as hard as stone and tortured beyond anything he had ever experienced. *But,* Edward reminded himself, he would take his time. Even if he did nothing more than bring her to climax.

He was leading, but he was also following. Taking cues from her body's reaction as to how much she was willing to do this night. He would not rush her. Even if it killed him.

Her body began to shake. Just as she was about to completely lose herself to him, she looked up at their reflection. Staring right into his eyes, his new bride said the best three words Edward had ever heard.

"Take me, now."

Faster than he had ever moved in his life, he scooped her up and carried her to the bed. He was out of his shirt in seconds and removing his trousers when Morgan inhaled sharply. He looked up, suddenly remembering she had never seen a naked man.

Her eyes were huge, but they were not fixed on the part of his body he expected might bring shock. Instead, they were anchored to his chest. He stilled. How could he have forgotten? The branded reminder that his barbaric past was real.

"I am sorry. I should have prepared you for the ghastly sight." He grabbed his shirt and began putting it back on.

"Stop!"

He slowly turned his head to her, expecting to see disgust. He didn't. In place of revulsion was something akin to understanding. A strange sympathy that did not make him feel ashamed.

"How could anyone find a scar ghastly?" She stared, unbelieving. "On second thought. Do not answer that. I care not for the opinions of others before me that might have placed such a stupid notion in your head."

He stood, utterly bewildered by her words. "You do not find them unsightly? I could leave my shirt on."

"Don't you dare threaten me on our wedding night, Edward Kingston." She propped herself up on one elbow, hooked a come-hither finger and smirked. "I want to see all of you. Up close and personal."

He had never been able to fathom the sensations that led up to a swoon, but he was pretty sure Morgan Kingston had him close. He tossed the shirt to the ground and prowled toward her. What on earth had he done to have gotten so lucky?

Climbing onto the bed, he took possession of her mouth as he parted her thighs with his legs. Testing the entrance of her womanhood, he nudged inside a fraction. Sweet pain coiled around his tightened balls as he fought for the control required to not bury himself deep inside her in one demanding thrust.

He took a deep breath. She was like a fire burning for his needed warmth. *She was his!* They were about to be bonded for life. He kissed her again.

Her arms came up and hooked his shoulders encouragingly. He looked down and into her eyes. Holding her gaze, he slowly pressed into her, pausing only when he reached the last thin barrier. She closed her eyes.

"Open your eyes," he coaxed.

She complied and he thrust deep, and stilled immediately. "Are you alright?"

When she nodded, he resumed as gently as possible. After a few strokes, her body relaxed. She clung to him, her hips joining his in movement. Matching his set pace, she kept her eyes glued to his. Completely trusting in his lead.

He grew bolder, his body driving him and demanding he fulfill its primal need...to lose himself in her. Unable to be harnessed any longer, he heard a tortured groan escape his lungs the same moment she called out his name. All his self-control shattered. He thrust into her with a passion unlike any he had known before.

She was his wife now; he need not take precautions. He felt her body tighten around his cock. He drove harder as she began to shake. She lifted her hips and circled his back with her legs, granting him greater access. As he buried himself deeper inside her velvety heat, Morgan moved her arms down his back and grabbed his ass with both hands, nails digging forcefully into the muscle.

The bold sensation of her needy grip on his straining and tight cheeks sent him spiraling over the edge. The force of his orgasm pumping deep inside her was blinding. He gave one final thrust and felt the warmth of his seed fill her womb as her body continued to spasm and milk him like a fist.

His! She was his.

Morgan could not draw enough air into her lungs. It felt as if she had been on the edge of a high cliff, and someone had pushed her off. She landed just fine, but the adrenaline from the fall still coursed through her body.

She was not sure what to compare it to. She knew only that she had never, in her wildest dreams, thought anything could feel this satisfying. Morgan looked up into Edward's eyes as he rolled over beside her, pulling her into his arms.

He smiled before drawing her in tight to his chest and resting his chin on the top of her head. He smelled divine. The rapid drumming of his pulse synced with hers. She felt safe and happy and, for the first time in her life, where she was supposed to be.

Morgan felt his chest vibrate low and realized he had spoken. She looked up. "Hmm?"

He grinned, and she wanted him all over again. "Are you hungry?" He chuckled.

She looked to the tray on the side dresser, right where Bertrice said it would be. Morgan gasped. When had her maid delivered their meal? She wondered how much Bertrice knew of what had happened earlier.

Edward must have read her mind for he intercepted her thoughts precisely. "I brought it up once I saw to Perry," he said.

"Oh."

Still smiling, he rolled to the side of the bed and stood. Morgan was gifted with a backside viewing of what looked like a Greek God's sculpted rear. She shook her head. That perfect male body had just been on top of her, *inside her,* and had done things to her she had never thought possible.

She could feel the blush race up her throat when he glanced back. *Oh, the rogue!* He knew what effect he was having, too. By that smile, he was enjoying every moment of it.

She tried to compose herself, but the attempt was for naught when he sauntered back with a plate and a still very much erect manhood. She blinked. Did they not deflate afterward?

"Are you always like that?" She blatantly gawked. They were well past bashfulness.

He followed the path of her gaze downward and laughed. "No, not unless I am thinking of you."

"Well." She felt her lips curving up. "Does that mean you might be in the mood for a second go?"

He set his plate down by the bed. "Absolutely!"

XII

*T*ruman was just handing Serenade's reins to Morgan when a carriage bearing the York family crest came tearing up the tree-lined lane to the estate. Morgan had been overseeing the removal of ruined furniture all morning. Edward had been neck deep in papers, going over architectural designs for the expansion of the estate. Designs he had randomly decided sometime during the night needed to be completed on the house post haste.

"No better excuse than a fire to make some much needed changes," he had said when they left the cabin that morning. Morgan was not sure she agreed, but the absolute joy radiating from the man had been contagious and she had gotten swept up in the imaginations of a new, grander ballroom.

The vision of the carriage kicking up a cloud of dust in its wake sobered her daydreams quickly. Something was not right. She dismounted and headed over to Edward, who was watching the approaching rig with a similar perturbation. He felt it, too.

The team of exquisite matching bays came to a halt just a few feet from them and the door flew open before the driver had a chance to jump down and assist. A huge African man stepped out, followed by a nervous-looking footman.

She recognized the bigger man immediately as her new father-in-law's giant butler, Ocman. Morgan stole a side glance at Edward. He had gone as still as a statue.

"What's happened?" he asked.

The man stopped right in front of them and held out a note. "Your father sent me to warn you of a matter he believes places you"—he paused to glance at Morgan—"and your lovely new bride in danger."

Edward ripped open the letter and began to scan the note.

"It seems as though he was correct," the dark man said, looking expressly toward the half-burned house.

"Where is Father now, Ocman?"

"He is dealing with another...fire," the stoic man replied, completely void of expression.

Morgan felt a cold dread sliding down her spine. "Roderick."

Edward spun to face her. "What?"

Morgan had not even realized she'd spoken the thought aloud. She looked up into his stormy blue eyes.

"My stepbrother means to torment me for the rest of my days."

Edward reached out and took both her arms, as if to steady her. "It is not your stepbrother's name on this list."

He searched her eyes.

"It is De Montrey's."

Edward paced the cabin study like a caged tiger. A cornered beast imprisoned by invisible bars that trapped him in a space he could not escape. He could not skirt this one, not with a new wife to look after and love. He paused, mid-stride. He *loved* Morgan Sinclair!

He loved Morgan *Kingston*, known to the public now as Lady Wellington, he corrected. The woman who had driven him to mind-numbing distraction since their first meeting. The woman for whom he had forsaken his plush, independent lifestyle. The woman who could set a fire ablaze in his loins with just a smile. The lady he could not fathom living without. Edward ran a hand through his hair.

A familiar rage began its steady tormenting crawl into his quickening pulse, a battle drum of warning that always came from deep within. His body's learned alert system for when he was about to lose control. He clenched his jaw. The feelings were growing stronger. Chanting, taunting... Daring him to snap. He tried to push them down, but they only grew louder, bolder.

He cursed, as mad at the emotions as he was with his own inability to rein them in. His pacing increased, as if he could outrun the mounting sensation. Why could he not be more like Perkin? Why was he doomed to walk the fine line between gentleman and beast?

Why! Panic and fear welled up, a flash flood slamming against a thinly barricaded dam. He yelled, rattling a painting above the fireplace. Someone called out and footsteps sounded from somewhere down the hall. *Damn it!*

He punched his fist through the window just before the doors burst open.

Concerned voices, like distant buzzing, filled the room. Edward glimpsed the look of sympathy on Ocman's face as he withdrew his hand from the shattered glass. He could only make out the tone of their worry; not the actual words, the pounding in his ears was still too strong. The pain was resounding.

He looked down at the blood and felt the first bit of peace begin to take root. *The calm after the storm.* The letting of blood was the only thing that quieted the demons that plagued him.

One particular voice cut through the throng of concerned utterances. Edward brought his eyes up to meet the look of sheer panic painted across Morgan's lovely face.

She rushed to him. "What happened?"

She yanked a sash from her waist and started absorbing the blood from his hand. He said nothing. How could he possibly explain?

"Edward!" she demanded. "What happened?"

Martin pushed through the crowd of partygoers in the ballroom. He needed time to clear his head. He turned left down the manor's impressive hall and entered the library. A quick scan of the room proved that it was void of occupants. He closed the double pocket doors and walked to the sidebar where a decanter of sherry sat.

After filling a glass, he downed it in one swallow and then refilled it. What the hell had he gotten himself involved in? Before he could entertain the idea, he heard the doors separate behind him. Martin swiveled in place.

"We still have a deal, De Montrey?" The intruder pulled the doors together.

Martin took in the man now standing before him. He hoped the chill that swept over his skin was not apparent from across the room. It was the same sick feeling he got every time he encountered the other lord.

He schooled his features. "I told you, I need more time to think. This is not what I signed up for."

The man moved farther into the room. "Need I remind you that what you *signed* up for was to help out however we saw fit? Time for contemplation is at a close." He had spoken smoothly, but Martin caught a hint of venom.

He bristled. "I have my limits. I am reaching them."

The cool demeanor slid off the other gentleman in an instant. "You should have stated those limits when you asked for help." He strode forward, closing the gap between them.

Martin pulled himself up taller. "Are you threatening me?"

The man guffawed. "Yes!" The word shot through the air like the crack of a bullwhip.

Martin tipped back the last of the liquor and made to move past. He had heard enough.

"I can break you as quickly as I made you!" the man hissed. "You do not think that carriage your brother was driving just wrecked on its own, do you?"

Martin stopped.

The man continued. "You wanted the title. We saw that you got it."

Martin turned slowly back to face his tormentor.

"You made the deal," the lord leered. "It is time to repay the favor owed."

"I never asked you to murder him!"

The man chuckled, derisively. "How else did you hope to obtain the title you take such great pleasure in waving about now?"

The anger Martin had felt became a bone-chilling realization. This loon was going to try to frame him.

"I never agreed to hurt anyone...physically." Despite his best efforts, he stammered over his words. "You only wanted me to play court to the girl. A tantalizing prospect, indeed."

The added lie rolled off his tongue with a practiced ease. He did not give two farthings about Morgan Sinclair. Martin only wanted her for appearance's sake.

When the wager had been made it seemed to be a win-win scenario. He would repay a debt owed and gain a wife to improve his social standing. He would then proceed doing the deed of getting her with child. Once that tedious aspect was over, he could focus on his new, and sure to be, prosperous dealings in the trade market. It had all been going exactly to plan. Until it hadn't. Martin used that annoyance to muster his final retort.

"My debt is paid."

The words barely left his mouth before the man grabbed him and pushed him into the wall. His face contorted with rage, coming up swiftly to meet Martin's. "It is not, you halfwit!" he spat. "You failed!"

Martin thrust the man off him. "It is not my fault Lord Wellington compromised the girl and was forced to ask for her hand."

He raked his hand down his jacket front in an attempt to smooth it. He was never clear on the motives behind the arrangement that he pursue Morgan Sinclair. Judging by the murderous look in the other man's eyes, there was much more to this story than he wanted to know.

He found himself asking the question, nevertheless. "Why did you want me to go after her in the first place?"

"That is none of your concern." The other lord seemed to sober at the question. He stepped back, his anger appearing to abate. "What *is* your concern is a broken arrangement. You still owe me a favor. And since you failed so miserably at the first one, I expect the next to be fulfilled *without* derailment." He turned and moved toward the door. "No matter what it entails."

Martin started to protest, but the man cut him off. "On second thought, I know exactly what I need."

He stilled and turned back slowly to face Martin. "I need you to retrieve a ledger from the palace."

"What?" Martin blurted out incredulously. "I have no access to the palace! Are you mad?"

The man smiled thinly. "The guard will change on the hour at midnight. Melbrooke's office is on the main floor, west wing. He has a ledger with gold script that reads *tangents* on it. It is in a desk drawer of his. Get it and bring it to me. You have three days."

The other lord strode briskly back to the double doors, slid them open, and slipped out into the hall before Martin could close his gaping mouth.

Morgan was beyond confused and her husband and his staff were of no help, whatsoever. After Bertrice had busted in and taken over doctoring Edward's hand, both he and Ocman had become as quiet as death. They shared a secret, and Morgan meant to uncover it.

After all, there was nothing quite as frightening as hearing one's husband bellow from another room in the manor, followed by the distinct sound of shattering glass. Then to find him staring blankly, standing in a pool of his own blood, and realizing he had done it to himself. Purposefully smashing a window with his fist in a fit of rage.

And no one said a damn thing! Not one single explanation had come forth. Instead, Edward had spent the rest of the day avoiding her. It was as if he had cocooned himself up. The lighthearted man from that morning had gone into hiding. Morgan had no reasoning for any of it.

During dinner, a note had arrived from Richard Kingston. It stated simply that the fire at the docks, which Ocman had informed them of, had been extinguished without much loss. The news seemed to lighten Edward's burdens somewhat. He remained polite throughout the rest of the meal, but the spark in his eyes was still absent. It was as though the day's earlier events had transformed her husband into a completely different person.

Only Ocman seemed to understand this dramatic shift in mood. The patient butler regarded Edward with something equivalent to understanding, as if he had weathered a storm similar to this with her husband in the past. The quiet and steady way the older man handled the situation was a testament to the two men's past together.

Ocman was looking after Edward's current state, not like a member of the staff, but as a friend. Or more over; a father. It spoke volumes. *Heartbreaking volumes.*

The two men disappeared into the study after dinner and did not emerge. Morgan took a book into the library, where she must have drifted to sleep, for she woke to strong arms lifting her gently from the sofa. She opened her eyes to see Edward smiling down at her; the first sign of honest good cheer in him since that morning.

She smiled back up at him but did not speak. If she had learned anything from observing Edward and Ocman all day, it had been that less could be more. She would be *more.*

He carried her to the bedroom and laid her on the bed. She rolled to one side so he could unbutton the back of her gown. She assisted in the removal of it only by wiggling her hips a little, enough for him to be able to pull it over them.

When she reached for her slippers, he intercepted her hand with his own and did that as well. He stripped her naked and then, he stripped her naked again with his intense gaze. She felt beautiful under his appreciative regard. He pulled the covers up and over her, tucking her in thoroughly with a playful smirk before undressing himself.

He crawled in beside her and pulled her to his chest. Comforting, steady, and assuring. Just as he had been with everything else. He was once again guiding her, teaching her how to love him. Possibly proving to himself that he was worthy of love.

That is exactly how she fell asleep. With her husband's powerful arms around her, asking nothing more of her than the silent acknowledgment of a deeper connection. A bond that did not need words or actions to be whole. This was love.

XII

$\mathcal{M}$organ crested the hill beside Edward, mounted atop Elkinema. They had made tremendous progress that morning regarding the new architecture designs. Edward apparently was enjoying the same realization.

His lips curled up into a smile as he looked out over the land. "Ah, Morgan, it is coming along nicely, is it not?"

Her heart swelled at his boyish excitement. The previous night had only made them stronger. She still wanted, and needed, to know what had upset him to the point of self-injury yesterday morning. Nevertheless, the ending result, a deeper bond, had cast aside any lingering doubts she had about her husband's investment in their marriage. He cared as deeply for her as she did him.

Morgan had fallen asleep and awoken curled in his arms. Only in the early morning light had he made love to her. *And what a teacher he was at that.* She felt a blush creeping up her neck as she remembered. The slightest touch from his skilled hands had unraveled her.

"Remembering something enjoyable?" Her husband smirked devilishly.

"Perhaps." She grinned back coyly.

"Good, I wish you *daily* enjoyment."

199

She giggled. "Daily? I do say, sir."

He laughed as he drew his hand to his brow, shielding his eyes from the beating sun. "Is that a new carriage?"

She turned her head back to the manor. "Yes." She tensed; could they withstand any more bad news right now? She squinted to make out the crest on the door. "It appears to bear a crest...a dragon and a rose?"

A smile broke across Edward's face. "It is Greyland and Alex." Giving no further elaboration, he kicked Elkinema into a canter.

Morgan pressed her heels gently against Serenade's sides and followed suit.

Edward leapt off the stallion and jogged up to the pair staring at his battered estate. Alex turned as Edward drew near, making Grey's petite form visible where she stood in front of her much-taller husband. As soon as his sister's gaze landed on Edward's, she broke into a full run and jumped right into his arms.

He spun her around before setting her back on her feet and kissing her forehead. "Grey, it is so good to see you. How is my niece and nephew?"

"Magnificent!" she exclaimed, beaming up at him before turning back to the house. "Oh, Edward." Her smile vanished. "It is awful, how could someone do such a thing?"

His sister's voice wavered, and she pinched her bottom lip between her teeth—another of his sister's signature traits when she was worried. "To you, and to father!"

About that time, having not catapulted off her horse as he had, Morgan approached. Greyland did a complete emotional about-face when she saw his new bride. She rushed to Morgan, dragging her forcefully into a tight hug. Edward heard Alex chuckle over his shoulder. No one could ever be fully prepared for his sister.

Edward saw the momentary surprise in Morgan's eyes at the overfamiliarity, but she shed it quickly, embracing Greyland back. As if it were a completely normal greeting. He wondered how long it would take his lovely wife to get used to his sister's unbound affections. By the recovery time just witnessed, she would fit right in with his unusual family.

"It is so wonderful to see you, Morgan," Grey gushed. "I am thrilled you are a part of our family. It was about time my notorious brother settled down. I cannot wait to introduce you to your new niece and nephew. They are back at home today, but the next time we visit, we will bring them."

She paused for quick breath. "Have you met my husband?"

Alex bowed. "Allow me to echo my wife's sentiments. Welcome." He smiled. "I see you are adapting gracefully into the indoctrination that is our *peculiar* family."

Grey swatted her husband's shoulder playfully. "We are *not* peculiar; we are fun!"

"That is one way of putting it." Edward could not help but laugh.

Alex glanced over Grey's head and caught Edward's eyes. "May we talk, brother?"

"Yes." He addressed his sister and Morgan. "Morgan, would you care to show my sister the drawing for the new design?"

"Of course." His new bride smiled and was immediately tucked into the fold of his sister's arm and marched toward the house.

Edward turned his attention back to his brother-in-law, just as his sister began to interrogate Morgan on the subject of children. He shook his head. "Lord, help her."

Alex shrugged. "What else would you expect?"

"Nothing less." He chuckled and wandered a few paces next to his brother-in-law, assuring they were well out of earshot before continuing. "I assume you have been informed of the attempts on Father's and my life? Not just the fires?"

"Yes, word reached us this very morning, hence"—he waved a

hand toward his retreating wife—"our being here before I could even have my morning coffee."

"I am sorry to bother you." Edward sighed, hating how many lives were being affected. "You should not have to raise two children under this sort of family stress."

"Stop that," Alex chided. "I joined this family, for all of its many blessings and strife, of my own free will."

"You know what I mean. You two have been through enough. I only wish this family of ours could cease to be so..." He searched for an appropriate word that did not rhyme with hated. "Interesting."

Alexander placed both hands behind his back as they walked. "We cannot change the minds of other men hell-bent on doing us harm."

He stopped and faced Edward, an old familiar glint in his eyes. "But we can quell the heartbeat."

Edward felt as if a weight had been lifted from his shoulders. Simply relaying to his brother-in-law all the bizarre occurrences that had transpired over the past few weeks had put his mind more at ease. Stringing it all together and sifting through various scenarios cast a bigger net over the events leading up to the fire at his estate and at the docks.

He told Alex everything he knew and everything that had happened, including Morgan's stepbrother and the strange obsession the blackguard had with her. The two talked at length for the better part of an hour while the ladies worked alongside the staff, setting right the untouched sections of the house. They would be able to move in by tomorrow.

Alex, reclined against the hillside in seeming contemplation of the sky, finally spoke. "I have an idea."

"Please, explain." Edward looked over at him.

"A ball."

"I am not sure how dancing the night away will fix anything, Alex."

Alex arched a brow and propped himself up on his elbow. "A means to draw them out." He flicked a blade of grass. "We have a better chance of getting one of them to talk if we can get them all under the same roof."

His brother-in-law looked down across Edward's estate. "We will hold the affair at Greenshire Castle. In one week."

"I will not bring the people who may want us dead to your house." Edward was shocked at the *normally* intelligent man's suggestion.

"Greenshire is perfect. So far, all threats have been made on you, Morgan, and Father. Plus, due to my standing in Parliament, I would have no reason not to invite them all. For political reasons, of course."

Alex and Edward continued to watch Grey and Morgan below, inside the hollowed-out window of the previous study. They were perched over the architectural drawings and talking with their hands as they laughed.

"The children will be safe in the nursery for the event, with armed guards surrounding their wing." Alex proceeded. "Lord Vistmont has need of my vote to pass a bill he wishes to see through. De Montrey is new to his title and eager to show it off. Davenport will come simply for the opportunity to piss you off."

"It is the Earl of Vistmont's son who made the threats against Morgan," Edward said, fixing his gaze on the two women inside the burnt-out space. Morgan had just tucked a stay strand of hair behind her ear and was motioning for a tray of scones to be placed on the table. His sister pushed the papers aside to make room. Edward's heart squeezed. "I will not willingly put her in the same room with him."

"You will have to." Alex faced him. "If the man is as obsessed as you say, and as volatile, then we need to find out how unhinged he can become. Lure him into his own trappings."

Edward felt ill at just the suggestion. There was no way he could occupy the same space with that man, and not kill him. Likewise, he would have to be dead himself to allow Morgan anywhere near the weasel.

"Alex, I cannot do this, this that you put forth."

"Would you rather risk both your lives by waiting for the man to strike next?" His brother-in-law's gaze swung back to the estate, making a point of the obvious. "Because it does not appear that whoever did this has any plans of heaving off."

As much as he did not want to admit it, Alex was right. Whoever was behind these attacks was just getting started. He inhaled deeply, then exhaled. "She will have to give her blessing first, and I will not leave her side."

"You will not be there, Edward." Alex gave him a steady look. "You will have to trust me to protect her."

XIV

*I*t was Morgan's second day in her new residence, Crestmont Manor. Greyland and Alexander stayed on, and Morgan could not be more relieved, considering how understaffed Edward's estate was. With Greyland's help, the two women had cleaned the remaining soot from every wall and started on the upstairs curtains. Morgan had gotten a great deal accomplished with the midnight-black, curly haired beauty helping her.

Edward, Greyland's husband Alexander, and the remaining male staff, with the help of a local mason, had begun work rebuilding the ruined walls of the study. In the evenings, Alex and Edward would hole up in the library and pour over design ideas. Her husband's absence, the hours of collaboration with the Duke of Ravenswood, would have been greatly felt were it not for his delightful sister.

Greyland, Grey—as Morgan had been instructed to call her—was a source of constant amusement. She had more energy than seven children, and her enthusiasm for absolutely everything was downright infectious. There was not an idle moment to be found with Greyland Hamilton about.

By contrast, Morgan had needed a bit longer to become adjusted to Alexander's presence. He was intensely handsome, just like her own husband, but in a darker and more dangerous fashion. It was as if Alexander Hamilton's natural disposition came with a clear warning, much like the talons on a hawk.

The Duke and his vivacious duchess were mirror opposites. Greyland was the very definition of light, whereas Alex was comparable to nightfall. At first, the Duke had intimidated Morgan to the point of discomfit. He had a presence that demanded respect and a keenness to his gaze that proved he did not miss anything. Even when the man was not looking directly at you, he still seemed to know your thoughts.

The one chink in the duke's armor was the head-over-heels-love he held for his petite wife. He showered the young beauty with affection. It was quite clear there was little the duchess wanted for that her devoted husband would not obtain. The love they shared was awe-inspiring.

The previous day, Morgan's aunt and father-in-law had arrived. Not seeing her mother in their entourage, Morgan became concerned. Her aunt quickly assured her that the countess was fine and was staying in London to meet with her husband. Morgan hated the idea, but she had no control over the situation. Later that day, her aunt pulled her aside and confided that she had a plan to separate the two, and that she just needed a bit longer to set things in order.

Richard Kingston was just as distinguished and pleasant as he had been on their wedding day. The walking definition of a high-born gentleman. She could see the family resemblance in her husband and wondered if the eldest, Perkin, had the same refined aristocratic qualities. According to Greyland, he had them in spades, same as Edward.

It was still hard to comprehend how little Morgan knew about her new family. She did know one thing for sure, she *adored* them. Morgan folded the pair of kid gloves she had been absentmindedly caressing and placed them on her dresser. She had thought to go riding, but Edward was deep in conversation with his master builder and forbade her to go alone.

After all that had transpired over the past two weeks, she absolutely agreed. She was wise enough to see how dangerous roaming about unaccompanied could be at the moment.

Morgan sighed. If only their problems could be solved soon. Sadly, she had the distinct feeling she would have to look over her shoulder for the rest of her life. Or at least, for the rest of Roderick's.

A knock on her and Edward's bedroom door pulled her from her woolgathering.

"May I come in?" Greyland's muffled voice asked from the other side of the heavy oak door.

"Of course." She hurried to the door, but it swung open on its own before she could get there.

"Sorry to bother you." Her sister-in-law sailed in. "I have a small headache and Edward said there was some medicine in one of your dresser drawers?"

"Yes, of course." Morgan frowned at her own ineptitude with what might be in her dresser drawers, or even where to begin looking. She turned and surveyed the room. *Where might a headache elixir be?* Her gaze landed decidedly on the nightstand across the room, and she walked purposefully to it. "I bet he has something in here."

"He said the house was not fully stocked yet with necessities. And until the staff is all back up to capacity, I daresay, we are all our own nursemaids," Greyland chirped behind her.

"I am sure I saw him place a small vial in here the other night." Morgan rummaged through the messy drawer. "I hope a valet is on his list of staff," she said with a light teasing tone.

Greyland giggled. "Edward has never been what one might call *tidy*."

Morgan held up the vial. "It is unmarked; do you think this could be what he is talking about?"

Greyland tilted her head and strode forward, squinting. "Looks like what we kept the medicine in at home." She took the vial and turned it in her hand. "Though he should have clearly marked it."

"If it tastes like the headache powder we had when I was growing up, then you will want a glass of wine to wash down the awful taste."

Greyland smiled, in perfect timing with another knock landing on the bedroom door. "I already took the liberties of having Truman bring us up two glasses."

"Why, Lady Grey, drinking wine before dinner?" Morgan grinned.

"We have an excuse. The medicine was quite ill tasting." She winked. "Oh, you came down with a headache, too."

Morgan laughed and followed her new friend, and accomplice in crime, to the chairs by the fireplace. Truman started to pour the wine, but Greyland stopped him and deposited the medicine into the two glasses with a small frown on her lips. "We both have nasty headaches, Truman."

Truman, to his credit, only looked slightly uncomfortable with the white lie as he poured the wine. Greyland shot him a winning smile, the likes of which probably won her everything she had ever desired. The smile did not fail to hit its mark. Truman's eyes softened and he beamed brilliantly back at her.

Incredible! Morgan really needed to start taking notes. Greyland's natural way of putting others as ease would be paramount in running her own household. Her sister-in-law seemed to know exactly how to handle people, and everyone seemed happier in her presence for it.

What a wonderful ability, Morgan marveled, as Truman took his leave. "How do you do that?"

Greyland stood, walked over to the door, and engaged the lock. "Do what?"

"Make everyone happy." She started to lift the glass to her mouth.

"Oh, do not drink that." Greyland stopped her. "Let me rinse it out first. I only put the medicine in there for appearance's sake. No reason you should have to tolerate the horrid taste." She made a face.

With a smile, Morgan tipped back the glass. It was a gallant show of unity, but the moment the liquid passed over her tongue she coughed and had to force herself to swallow. Choking, she swiped at her watering eyes.

After a disagreeable moment, Morgan drew in a ragged breath and forced a smile. "It is not so bad," she fibbed, eyeing the remainder of her drink skeptically. "I shall suffer along with you. If you tell me the secret to making others so appeased in your company."

Greyland tipped her glass back as well and grimaced. "All right, let us prove your theory correct, first." With that, she downed the entire glass and giggled. "Yes, I do believe it is best to get it over and done with."

Morgan polished off her own drink. "Good Lord, this stuff really is terrible."

Greyland laughed. "It truly is. Now, about your question. I do not *do* anything, other than look at everyone I meet with the assumption that they are a good human being." She waved her fingers in a whimsical circle through the air. "Some more than others, of course. But we cannot really look for the bad before the good, or we would make ourselves miserable. Would we not?"

Morgan felt her limbs growing relaxed from the wine. She leaned back. She had never considered that. Well, she had been optimistic when she was little, but after her mother married Lord Vistmont, her 'glass half full' philosophy had faded rather quickly.

In hindsight, she recognized she had grown fearful. Not only because of the situation in which Roderick had placed her, but toward everything. She had become *judgmental*!

The realization felt as horrible in her mind as the wine had tasted on her tongue. Morgan sat back up abruptly, ready to confess her treason to glasses everywhere that were 'half full,' and toppled right out of her chair.

As her butt hit the floor, she looked up and met Greyland's wide-eyed gaze. They stared at each other for a moment. Then they both broke into fits of uncontrollable laughter.

Grey made to reach for her in attempt to help her up, but slid right out of her chair. They both began to laugh so hard Morgan's eyes filled with tears. Grey was doubled over on the plush Oriental rug, her laughter mixed with hiccups as she fought to breathe.

"God's teeth!" Morgan managed to get out between gales of laughter. "That is some strong wine!"

"I cannot feel my arms." Grey snorted, then gasped, then laughed harder still.

Morgan thought she heard a knock at the door, but she couldn't move, much less form words any longer. *Drunk as little skunks they were.*

Edward was looking over the new drawing for the side study when, not one, but both of his butlers and Perry came rushing toward him. All three men wore slightly varied expressions of a similar reaction: controlled panic.

Jesus, what now?

"My lord!" Perry jumped in first, to the obvious irritation of both Boswell and Truman.

"What is wrong?"

"We have a slight problem," Truman said, panting.

"We have a *large* problem," Boswell corrected.

"It is the lady, my lord," Perry rushed ahead.

Edward headed straight for the house, moving so fast that only Perry could keep up. "Where is she? What is wrong?" he shouted.

"She is in the master suite," Perry answered, running at Edward's side. "They won't open the door."

Edward increased his pace. *They?* As in the only two woman that mattered in his life? Out of his peripheral, he saw Alex at the desk throw down his paper and leap from his chair.

He caught up to them before they reached the door. "What is wrong?" Alex demanded as they crossed the threshold together.

Edward snatched the pistol from the drawer of the sideboard. "I do not know."

Just as his foot landed on the first step, Perry called out behind him. "Both ladies are in there, sir."

Alex sailed past Edward before he could even fully register the words. He trailed after his brother-in-law, taking the steps two at a time. They reached the hallway and were at the door in a matter of seconds. When Alex tried the knob, it was locked.

"Morgan! Greyland!" he bellowed.

Nothing.

Perry met up with them. "Truman said he served them wine and left."

"Wine? In the middle of the day?" Alex rammed his shoulder into the door.

Edward lowered his shoulder and they both hit the wood at the same time. The door shook this time. They looked at each other, hauled back, and struck it again with all their weight.

The door burst open.

There, in the middle of the bedroom floor, lay his sister and his wife. *Good God,* they were dead!

He and Alex ran to them. Edward scooped Morgan into his arms, feeling for a pulse. He found one at the same moment Alex announced Greyland was breathing. Relief like none Edward had ever experienced flooded his senses. Morgan stirred in his arms and mumbled something.

He leaned in close. "Love, wake up."

"Headache," she responded dryly, though she did not open her eyes.

He gently shook her, but her head rolled back across his forearm. He looked at Alex, who was now grinning ear to ear.

"They are foxed."

Edward looked at his sister, lying in Alex's arms. Sure enough, there were little snores coming from her wine-stained lips. Truman rounded the corner, with Boswell right on his heels.

"How much did they drink?" Edward demanded. He was annoyed Alex found the situation amusing. Edward felt as if twelve years of his life had just been shaved off.

"I just filled the one glass for each," Truman answered, looking around for the bottle and locating it with his eyes. "It does not appear that they had more than that."

"That does not make sense," Alex interjected. "Greyland can outdrink most men."

Boswell stepped forward. "Might I suggest that his truly magnificent lordship consider sacking his less than proper, far inferior, second, and might I also add, less adequate butler?"

Truman huffed out, "I only did as I was asked. That is my job!"

"Serving the ladies wine before supper is most improper." Boswell added, looking down his nose.

Alex snorted. "Boswell, you obviously have never been asked to do anything by my wife."

Truman piped up once more. "Her Grace said she had a headache. That they both did. She put a few drops of that medicine into the glasses before I filled them."

All five men turned their collective gaze to the vial on the serving tray. Edward cursed, and all eyes rounded back to him.

"Out, everyone." He swung his arm. "Now!"

As soon as the room cleared, Alex asked the inevitable question. "Edward, what was in the bottle?"

"A muscle relaxer," he grumbled. *Damn Henry and his sensitivity toward virgins.*

"Dare I ask why you have need of such a thing?"

"Henry thought I might have need of it on my wedding night." Saying the words out loud was even worse than the way they had sounded in his head. "He wanted me to go...slow."

"Tell me you did not." Alex could barely contain his merriment now.

"No."

"Good, for I would never have let you live that down."

"I am well aware." Edward lifted Morgan and moved her carefully to the bed.

Alex, likewise, hoisted up his snoozing bundle. "Hang on to that relaxer. I imagine our shoulders will have need of it tonight." With that said, he chuckled and carried Grey out of the room.

Edward looked at Morgan and ran the tips of his fingers along the soft flesh of her cheek. She smiled in her sleep and leaned into his touch. The tiny gesture almost dropped him to the floor. She was so fragile, so innocent, so perfect.

The thought that she could have been harmed felt like cold steel against his throat. He crawled in next to her and inhaled the sweet scent of her hair. This was love, and it was *surely* going to kill him.

XV

*E*dward marched toward the stable, unable to find humor in the fiasco currently playing out in his parlor. He simply needed to go for a ride. *Yes,* a ride would do him good. Too many exploits as of late were rattling his nerves. Especially the one from yesterday.

After having his home set afire, finding his wife naked in the presence of another man, then to witness what he thought to be the murder of his new bride and sister, Edward rationalized that he'd had about all he could take in one week's time. Now, to make matters worse, everyone in his house was hell-bent on cheering him up. He would not have it.

He wanted his mood. To sulk when he damn well felt like it. Was that really too much to ask for? He thought not.

The stable boy must have seen him storming toward the barn, because the lad rushed to ready the stallion. Edward heard the doors behind him open and close and knew what was coming before any of them said a word. He should have known they would even make escaping difficult.

"We are all coming with you," Morgan proclaimed from the manor steps.

Edward threw his arms up in the air. "By all means."

He turned back to find his sister beside his wife, arms crossed, wearing a look of dogged determination. Behind them, looking like members of a mob, stood Lady Vandicamp, Alexander, his father, and Henry.

"Torture me further. After all, I am still breathing."

He saw the pleased smile form on Morgan's face just before he turned back to the wide-eyed groom, who had paused when he had heard the others approaching.

"Saddle seven," Edward growled.

"Oh, I shan't need one," Lady Vandicamp, who had arrived the day before yesterday with his father, called out. "I just came out to see your torment, dear boy."

The stable lad stopped and looked to Edward for confirmation. He held up six fingers and the boy made to run again.

"I will not be going either," his father's intoned merrily, to Edward's chagrin.

He stopped his advancement on the stables and faced them all again. There they stood, delighting in his abuse. "I am failing to see the humor."

"Oh, Edward." Morgan rushed forward. "Darling, we really must hear Greyland out. If she thinks seven children is an ideal number..." She paused, her lips compressing, trying hard not to laugh. "We should really consider her logic."

Everyone, unable to hold it together any longer, burst out laughing. Edward sealed his eyes shut even as he fought his own threatening mirth. His beautiful wife's summary of the previous conversation back in the house was pretty spot on.

It had all started with his tenacious sister and the ever-plotting Lady Vandicamp. Even Henry, his best friend, never one to miss an opportunity to poke fun at him, had joined in with *exact specifics* regarding how to go about achieving said goal.

Alex and Edward's own father had then offered their personal advice. *Their much too personal advice.* The conversation was only made worse when Lady Vandicamp insisted they name one of their future offspring Bertha, after her late mother.

How did they all end up at his house, anyway? *Oh yes*, the ball they were having in a week's time. The one to which they would invite all their enemies.

Recalling the plot set him back on edge. He was about to put everyone he loved in the same room with possible assassins. Somehow, they were all just dandy with that notion. How on earth had he become the practical one in his family?

He looked around at the people who loved him to the point of torment. They were trying to lighten his mood. They, too, were likely just as bewildered by his radical and mature new mindset as he was.

He took a calming breath. "I think you are all mad," he said expansively. "But I love you and know what you are trying to do."

"So, seven?" Morgan giggled.

He leaned down and kissed the bridge of her nose. "However many you desire, love."

He could not help it. He had fallen even more head over heels in love with her over the past week. He could not keep his hands off his new bride. In hindsight, fourteen might be a more realistic number.

He whispered in her ear, "We can try for the first one tonight."

He smiled when the blush spread like wildfire up her neck.

"I cannot wait, my lord." She grinned up at him.

Edward looked over her head to the others. "Do all of you really want to go for a ride with me?"

Henry, the newest arrival from early that morning, stepped forward. "I do."

"Anyone else?" Edward perused their faces, one by one.

He looked at Morgan who shook her head no. "I think you and Henry should use this opportunity to get away for a bit."

"Have I told you today how much I love you?"

"Yes. But never stop saying it."

"I shan't." He held up two fingers to the very confused groom, then he cradled Morgan's face in both his hands and kissed her softly. "Thank you."

Edward loosened Elkinema's reins and they galloped across the sprawling fields. The cool breeze in his face, chasing the wind with thundering grace over the rise and fall of the hillside as they kicked up dirt, exhilarated him. They came to a small brook and the stallion took it with little effort. He gently pulled the horse to a stop on the other side and glanced over at his best friend.

"That is exactly what I needed." He gave Henry a lopsided grin. "Now, maybe I won't kill you for your less than helpful advice on drugging my wife before our wedding night."

"Duly noted." Henry chortled. "It is a most agreeable day to stay among the living."

Both men drank in the quiet glen, lost to their own ponderings, at ease in the subtle stillness of the landscape.

"I never want to experience that feeling again," Edward confessed. "Thinking something terrible had happened to her."

"I can only imagine."

"I felt helpless." He looked over at Henry. "Now all I can think about is how easily she could be taken from me."

"I know." His friend's gaze was sympathetic. "Nonetheless, you know that nothing productive has ever come from worrying over the things we cannot control."

Edward faced the babbling brook. "It is a most peculiar turn of events, looking further down the road than simply the evening's festivities. I feel like a..." He shook his head. "I do not think I even know how to articulate the words."

"A responsible and proper gentleman?" Henry offered, grinning at him.

"Exactly!"

"I must confess, I never thought I would see the day myself."

Edward slipped off Elkinema and led him over to the creek. The horse lowered his head to drink.

"I love her, Henry," he said, patting the steed's neck. "More than I ever imagined I could. I knew I wanted her in a way I had never wanted another. But I never knew I could truly love someone so much that it physically hurt to think of my life without them in it."

Henry dismounted and joined Edward at the brook's edge. "You wound me." He looked sideways at him. "Here I thought I was the only one you felt that way about."

"You know what I mean."

Henry grew quiet. "Sadly, I do not."

"You will someday. When the right woman ensnares you." Edward turned to look at his best friend when he did not respond.

Henry stared straight ahead, at some unfixed point in the stream, his face marked with concern. "There is something I need to tell you. Something I could not say in the presence of others."

Edward tensed at the sudden change in tone. "Tell me what?"

Henry looked over at him. "I have kept an aspect of my life concealed from public record. Hidden from everyone. There is a part of my past that I have been too ashamed to share. Even with you." He averted his eyes. "It was my choice to make and my burden to carry. I have never spoken of it before today."

His friend exhaled slowly. "And the truth of it is I would not be telling you now if it were not for new information coming to light. Important intelligence that cannot truly be explained without me confessing all." He looked him in the eyes. "It is paramount that you know the whole of it."

"Henry, first of all, if one's past dictated their future, I would be sentenced to a death on the gallows."

Edward studied him closely, searching for answers, and began to grow more concerned with each passing second. The man standing before him was never one to sound despondent. Edward had his demons, but Henry was a virtual rock.

"Tell me, friend. I shall not judge you. The only anger I may harbor is you thinking I would."

The silence that followed seemed to stretch on forever. Edward tried to prepare himself for what would follow. He reached out and placed a hand on his best friend's shoulder.

He was nonplussed when Henry shrugged it away tensely and turned back toward his horse.

"What the hell, man." Edward exhaled. "It cannot be that bad!"

"I do not want or expect your pity."

"I never said you would get it." He bristled.

Henry reached into his duffel bag and paused. His back still turned. "You know I would do anything for you, right?"

He sounded so distant, a strange remorsefulness behind his words. Edward stepped closer, determined to be there for his friend no matter what he was about to say next. Henry turned and thrust a book into Edward's hands.

He stared at what appeared to be some sort of ledger. "I am sure you do not intend me to read all of this just to find out what you are going on about."

His words sounded clipped and impatient, even to his own ears. He was growing annoyed with this circling dance. They had always been blunt and brutally honest with one another.

"The short version reads like this." Henry squared up to him. "All those months my brother was searching for me, convinced I had killed our father, I was employed by the crown. As a mercenary for Lord Melbrooke."

"Melbrooke?" Edward chorused back, disbelieving. "A mercenary?"

Henry did not have a malicious bone in his body. It was as if he were talking to a complete stranger.

"Yes, all of which was done before I had even heard of your family. I was an outcast, my own brother believing the worst of me." Henry's voice trailed off and he looked back toward the water's edge.

"I did very bad things for him. Things I wish I could undo. Oftentimes, I was forced to entertain dignitaries by assuming different personas in order to obtain my information. On one occasion, I even had to kill lest my deception be discovered."

He paused, as if waiting for Edward to absorb the admission, then he looked at Edward again. "I severed all ties with Melbrooke after Greyland was kidnapped, but I kept a few connections that I had made along the way. In order to keep track of Melbrooke's dealings, and his seemingly nefarious motives toward your...*our* family."

Edward clutched the ledger tighter in his hands. His family never regained trust in Melbrooke despite the friendly face they put forth, for the sake of the Crown. Could it be that his best friend had found proof? Some fashion of evidence against the man? If he had, did that mean that their family had even more to worry about now?

He felt like he had swallowed a rock that was now sitting in his stomach. "Please tell me *this*"—he shook the ledger in his hand— "has nothing to do with my family, and that you have not wasted precious time in conveying what you know if it does?"

"Edward, I could not share this information in your parlor with everyone present."

"Why, damn it?" Edward bit out, "Why could you not have told me? Tell me what is in this document. Now!"

"Because of the means by which I obtained the information," Henry snapped. "I know you enjoying thinking the fucking world revolves around you, but I also have a reputation to protect!" Nostrils flaring, he said, "The ledger is a correspondence that states Davenport was brought here, hired by Melbrooke."

When Edward cursed, the horses snorted and sidestepped away from him. "I knew the bastard was not back here and taking up residence beside the McGreggors strictly by chance!"

He began to pace as a sickening new thought dawned on him. *His brother!* "Perkin is on a mission for Melbrooke as we speak, with Thomas and Dalton!"

"I do not know what Melbrooke is planning," Henry said. "I only know that there can be no good reason behind setting Davenport up, and wrangling him that title of laird. However, I *do* have it on excellent authority that Davenport has not left his estate In Ireland since he departed London last week. Hence, he could not have lit the fires himself, but that is not to say he did not hire someone to do it for him."

Henry answered the next line of questioning before it could be asked.

"Yes, I had him followed. As I am sure your father did, too."

"Bloody hell! There is no way to get word to my brother as they are on a ship." Edward closed his eyes and pinched the bridge of his nose, thinking. "I guess that is a good thing. We can get word to him as soon as they make port." He lifted the documents. "Is this correspondence in Melbrooke's own hand?"

"Indeed, it is."

"Henry, I will be asked how you came by this information. What do you want me to say?"

"Let me start with the truth. I broke into De Montrey's after I overheard him talking with someone at a ball last week."

Edward growled, "So, De Montrey is in on this, too? Who was he talking to?"

"He is being blackmailed by someone. I do not know who, and I do not know for what. I did not get a good look at the man who threatened him. I do not think De Montrey realizes what is in that book, nor how much danger he would be in for stealing it. Especially now that he has gone and lost it."

"He stole this?" Edward sputtered. "From Melbrooke?"

"Yes."

"Henry..." Edward feared the answer, but he had to ask. "What is your involvement with Lord De Montrey?"

His friend turned, hands on either side of his waist as he walked away.

"Henry, please."

His friend stopped and slowly turned back around. "The baron does not fancy women. I led him to believe that I—that *we*—shared the same preferences, and used him to get close enough to get the information I needed."

Edward fought to school his features. *De Montrey liked men?* "You did not—" He bit his tongue. Perhaps his best friend had been hiding more than having only been a mercenary. "I mean, if you prefer the company of—"

"Good God, man!" Henry exclaimed, looking shocked. "I let him get close, but not *that* close! I respect you like a brother, but even I have my limits as to how far I would go to help you." He guffawed.

"The fact that I let him fawn all over me was bad enough. I do not want *anyone* to know about my past involvement with Melbrooke. And I definitely do not want the *means* by which I tricked De Montrey into trusting me being discussed." Henry wagged a finger through the air. "Swear it to me, Edward."

"I shall take it to my grave." He nodded just as another pressing question entered his head. Why was the baron trying so hard to win over Morgan? Her dowry was not that great. "What did he want with Morgan, then?"

"That, I do not know either. He confided he was being blackmailed, but I was not sticking around to interrogate further once I had the ledger." His friend smiled wryly. "Again, I have my limits."

The sound of carriage wheels could be heard off in the distance. Edward's head jerked toward the noise.

"Ah, that," Henry said. "I might have called in for back up."

"What do you mean?"

"I was not going to come here and share this without securing a better foothold." He smirked. "I posted a note before I left."

"A note? To whom?"

"To Windsor Palace."

Edward brushed off his riding jacket the best he could as he and Henry made their way to the newly modified door. He disliked the idea of one of the Queen's advisors arriving to a manor in the midst of construction. The receiving section still smelled of smoke, but there was little be done about it now. The royal carriage had already arrived. A footman was tending to the horses as they passed.

Boswell opened the door for them with an unusual smile plastered on his face. Edward lifted a brow. Had he gotten into the sherry early tonight?

That was all he needed; a foxed butler. He tried to get a whiff of him as they passed over the threshold. The servant did not reek of alcohol, at least. *Small blessing.*

He could make out light laughter coming from the main study as Truman jumped in front of Boswell and rushed to open the next set of double doors. The action caused a snarl to emanate from Boswell. Those two would end up killing each other before the year was out unless Edward rectified the current situation.

What the deuced hell had he been thinking when he brought Boswell from the city? Lots of people retained separate staff at each residence, but only Edward Kingston, Earl of Wellington, had two.

Why? Because he was an idiot!

They entered the study and found Alex and Richard sitting in two wingback chairs that faced the doors. Morgan and Greyland sat just to the right on the damask sofa. Lady Vandicamp sat directly across from them. Everyone looked expectantly at Edward and Henry.

Edward frowned. The Queen's advisor had chosen the only seat in the room not directly facing them. Thus remaining completely concealed behind the high back chair. *Who was it?* His father and Melbrooke were her closest advisors. Edward knew, from Henry's assurance on the ride back, that Melbrooke was out of the country.

Every man in attendance rose when Edward stepped over the threshold. He nodded, and then smiled at his beautiful wife before turning his attention to his newest guest. *Still seated?*

The man would no doubt be important to the Queen, but no more than his own father, who had shown the expected *respect* of rising when the host entered the room. Just as he was about to clear his throat, in case the lord had lost some hearing...*and vision*...his father lifted the famous Kingston warning brow.

Edward hesitated. He had learned early on to shut up whenever that one elegant eyebrow arched high into his father's forehead. Completely flummoxed, he looked around the room once more. Surely there would be some indication in everyone's body language as to who was hiding behind that chair.

Alexander looked stately, showing no emotion whatsoever. Greyland could barely keep the smile from her face. Morgan appeared slightly uncomfortable, and Lady Vandicamp simply looked impatient. Edward walked further into the room.

Eyebrows be damned! *This man better start rising by the time he...* No sooner did the indignation hit, the unknown gentleman started to rise.

The first thing Edward noticed was that the man seemed to be wearing a lady's jeweled headpiece. The second visual disturbance was the ruby-red cloak that wrapped thin shoulders. The third oddity was abruptly dismissed when the refined profile of their Queen turned to face him.

Edward hit his knee to the floor, head bowed, in perfect timing with Henry. The Queen of England was in his house. The Queen of England was in his *burnt* house!

Richard agitated the brandy in his glass, reflecting on the events of the day as he stared into the flames crackling on the hearth. He had been set through his paces with a mix of emotions over the past two weeks. The Queen's unexpected arrival today had almost given him a heart attack. He was not sure how many more surprises he could take regarding his beloved family.

The Queen, thankfully, wasted little time getting to the reason for her unexpected visit. She had read aloud the missive she received from Henry. The letter was unexpected, but not startling. Edward's best friend had alluded, but not outright stated, who was behind a plot against the Kingstons and asked for their sovereign's immediate assistance.

Richard knew Henry would do anything for Edward; he just did not know how he had been able to collect the information when Richard's own hired professionals could not. Once Edward and Henry had finally arrived back at the manor, the puzzle began fitting together. It all began with Henry and Lord De Montrey attending the same ball last week.

At some point during said ball, Henry noticed the baron entering a side study. Not long after, he passed by the same study and heard a ruckus within. To his shock, he overheard Lord De Montrey being made the victim in an attempted blackmail. Whoever was threatening the baron was demanding he steal a ledger from Lord Melbrooke. Henry was just about to make his presence known when the mystery man told De Montrey the ledger he needed contained damning information regarding the Kingstons.

Henry, being a loyal family friend *and* loyal to his queen, decided he needed to find out just what was in those documents and return them to their rightful owner. He followed the baron to the palace and watched him enter. A short while later, Lord De Montrey emerged, a book under his arm, and in a hurry to return to his personal residence.

Henry then waited outside the other lord's townhouse, watching through the window as the baron consumed enough drink to eventually pass out drunk. Sneaking in through the servant's door, Henry quickly located the ledger in De Montrey's office, and purloined the book. With noble intentions of returning it to its original owner, of course. That was until he read the treason written inside the pages of the stolen documents.

Henry had realized right away that foul play was afoot, and that the Queen must be alerted to the contents of the ledger. Especially, now that it was clear Lord Melbrooke, her trusted counselor, was using the Queen to play a perfidious game of power in her court.

Richard had smiled at the admission of his son's best friend. There were more than a few gaps in his story, but Richard did not ask about any of them. Henry had his own reasons for relaying the story the way he had, so it mattered not. The outcome was the same— Melbrooke was finally exposed for the rat he was.

Richard took a sip of his drink. Perhaps one day, he would dig deeper into what exactly led Henry down this path. For he was certain that simply being in the right place at the right time was not the truth of the matter. Obviously, his son's friend had secrets he wished kept hidden. Richard could respect that. *They all did.*

Perkin probably most of all. He drew his fingers down his jaw to the point of his chin. *Secrets...*

Richard knew it was more than the Queen's love for his family that had placed her in that carriage today. He was not so old at sixty that he did not know what was going on. He had seen the way she looked at his eldest son, and he had heard the gossip at court.

He was just thankful that her husband chose to look the other way. Probably too busy with his own extracurricular affairs. The door opened behind him. Richard turned from the fireplace as the Queen glided in. She smiled warmly and surveyed the room before choosing her seat and nestling into it.

She patted the arm of the chair beside her. "Come sit with me, Your Grace. I am in need of your trusted advice."

Richard inclined his head and joined her. "What might I advise you on tonight, Your Majesty?"

Nonplussed, he watched her cast eyes down to stare at her clasped hands, twisting them together anxiously in her lap. He braced himself in preparation for what she might say next. Something told him this was more to do with Perkin than matters of state.

As if he needed more confirmation, she opened her mouth, then closed it tightly. *Dear Lord,* this was going to be bad.

"I am with child."

Richard wondered if the blood was visibly draining from his face.

"What splendid news." The sentiment could not be further from the truth.

"Yes, very," she said, but her eyes never lit on his. "It is just that..."

She turned her head to the fire, as if it would suddenly take over the narrative and explain the rest of the sentence for her.

Richard's mind raced. A million thoughts competed for supremacy in his head, all of them bad. He focused on the most pressing concern and clasped the Queen's hands, drawing her gaze back to him.

"I have always given you sound advice. That said, I must ask this of you: choose your next words carefully." He looked her steadily in the eyes. "We both know there is nothing that can be done now. Either way. However, there is much damage that could befall us all if these next thoughts are expressed."

She looked at him with sad eyes, searchingly. "You knew?"

Richard merely nodded and smiled weakly.

A tear rolled down her cheek. She brushed it away. "My country comes first."

"And your husband," he added.

Tears broke through the strong barricade of her lashes. "If only I had met him sooner."

Breaking complete protocol, Richard gathered her in his arms, as if she were one of his own children. If she were not the Queen, she likely would be. "I know."

He gently soothed her while she openly sobbed. He held her until she stopped shaking. Only then did he whisper, "He mustn't ever know."

She looked up. "He would not keep his distance if he knew, would he?"

A piece of his heart felt like it broke off and fell to the floor, but Richard confirmed her question. "No, he would not."

She looked at him with such extreme anguish that Richard feared she was not strong enough to carry this burden alone. His Queen was quite young and had so much at stake. She had to see reason.

Her husband might tolerate her indiscretion, but he would not allow another man's by-blow to sit on the throne. He would no doubt find a way to remove any *obstacles*. Especially obstacles that would possess more royal blood than all of England stacked together.

If the child was indeed Perkin's... *How could he be so careless?*

Just as Richard was about to speak, the Queen shook her head, silencing him. "I will love this child more than my own life. This baby will one day rule in my stead."

Then, with every ounce of strength Richard knew she possessed, she rose, a soft smile on her lips. "As it was always meant to be."

The water's gentle whisper became a louder, demanding voice the closer they moved to the fall's edge. Morgan instinctively squeezed Edward's hand as she risked a glance over, then turned back to look at him. His eyes seemed to change in color, something in them deepening, taking on a more feral glow.

He stepped forward, bringing one hand behind her head and pulling her to him. The immediate heat from his body engulfed her. He kissed her hard, like the river crashing on the rocks below. Feverishly; like the churning white water fighting for dominance against the edges of the solid bank.

She greedily took back from him, allowing her hands to explore the expanse of his chest. He deepened the kiss with a primal moan that vibrated down to the very core of her sex. Her legs grew shaky when he clasped his other hand around her waist, hugging her to him and claiming her with his kiss. Branding her as his and taking every last bit of her strength.

A gentle kiss on the nape of Morgan's neck pulled her slowly from her dream. She felt the goose bumps rise across her flesh as the second feather-soft touch skimmed the surface of her ear. From behind her, Edward's honey-coated voice intertwined around her senses.

"You are awfully fidgety for a person asleep." He sketched his skilled fingers up her spine slowly. "Can I help with that?"

Still wrapped in the quiet lullaby of the heated dream, caught in the blissful moment between sleep and alertness, she felt her body push back into his. *Yes*, this is still a dream. A dream that did *nothing* to rival reality. She smiled.

Her husband snaked his hand slowly over her hip bone and down her abdomen, his fingers seeking a new warmth. His other arm encircled her and his free hand roved upward to squeeze her breast. Morgan arched her back, pushing her ass against his readiness. The action elicited a guttural sound that emanated from his throat.

"God, I want you," he growled before lifting her thigh...*just enough.*

She felt the silky head of his cock against her sex and moaned into her pillow, her fingers curling around the sheets in anticipation. He bit down gently, but firmly, on the back of her neck as he slowly entered her. Her body fought to quickly adjust to his consuming size.

He was always so gentle at first, as if he feared he might hurt her. But this morning, Morgan intended to prove to him that she was not so fragile. She pushed back more, giving him the last few inches he needed to impale her to the hilt.

The sharp intake of his breath was all the confirmation she needed to know her message had been received. Her actions were all he needed, for he placed both hands on her hips and thrust harder into her. The sudden impact nearly sent her right over the edge. She cried out.

He continued the rhythmic pace until she was gasping and clinging to the edge of the bed. He moved one hand between her legs, so knowledgeable in what she needed. Her body began to tighten and tremble.

She reached back over her shoulder, tangling her hands in his hair and turned her face up to his. His mouth came down demandingly on hers. He drove into her relentlessly, over and over, until his cock swelled with his oncoming release.

He thrust one final time and filled her completely. Morgan began to shake, her muscles crying out and constricting around him as her own pleasure overtook her. She spiraled into carnal bliss as he groaned, breathless and ragged, into her ear. "Mine!"

The singular word that rolled over his tongue was as much an emotional release as the physical one. She *was* his. She was his in every way she could have ever hoped for.

He hugged her tightly to his chest and kissed the top of her head, as he always did. He was so loving, so tender. To think, under all the arrogance he had first shown her was actually the most honest, caring person she had ever met. Her heart expanded in her chest.

She knew he loved her, and she knew he would always have her best interest at heart. The complete, sobering clarity gave her strength. She felt one solitary tear rising in her eye.

With a blink, she let it quietly roll over the barricade of her lashes. That one tear represented more than any words could ever embody. It was a release from her past fears. A tribute to a new and wonderful life in this glorious man's world.

XVI

The next week seemed to sail by for Morgan. Greyland and Alexander had returned home to Greenshire Castle. Where, Morgan had learned, Bella, Greyland's best friend, and her new baby were also staying. Morgan would be making their acquaintance on the morrow when they traveled there themselves.

Apparently, Morgan would be meeting *every* pivotal person in the Kingston family in less than twenty-four hours, for a letter had arrived stating that the White Rose had made port. Edward's older brother, Perkin, Lord Dessmark, would be arriving forthwith. Accompanying him would be his best friend, Lord Ashlown, and Lord Kennington, Bella's husband and Alexander's best friend.

The thought of being introduced to a great many powerful lords and ladies in and of itself made Morgan nervous. What if they found her inadequate in her schooling? *Even worse*, what if they found her an ill fit for their beloved Edward? Morgan wished she could afford the time to wallow in that feeling of dread, but there was too much to do.

After tomorrow, they would have less than two days to prepare, before half of London arrived for Alexander and Greyland's planned ball. The confirmation letters had been pouring in. Amongst them were one from her stepfather, Lord Melbrooke, and one from Laird Davenport. The only person yet to respond was Lord De Montrey.

Morgan was still amazed every time she thought back on the baron's deception. The man really should find a place on the stage. *Maybe the gallows.*

She chewed her bottom lip. At this point, she might as well just start naming the butterflies in her stomach. For there was no point ignoring their existence.

By annoying contrast, Edward, Henry, and Richard seemed as calm as a quiet summer day. Morgan marveled at them. Either they were purely that confident, or they were masters at suppressing misgivings.

Even her aunt appeared unconcerned. As if the Queen's assurance that Lord Melbrooke and the others would be detained upon arrival was enough to guarantee their safety.

Just knowing her stepfather would be in attendance was enough to make Morgan want to start drinking at the noon day meal. She knew full well you could not arrest someone for being heavy handed with his wife. Additionally, Morgan had no doubt that Roderick would accompany him and try to make good on his threat. She had to find a way to remove both men, stepfather and stepbrother, from her and her mother's lives. *But how?*

Morgan suspired and resumed opening the pile of acceptance missives. She turned over the next letter and let out a small yelp. Eloise was coming!

Finally, a silver lining. Someone Morgan knew would be in attendance. She stood, letter in hand, and made her way to the study where Edward had gone with his father and Henry.

She heard their muted voices behind the thick wooden doors. She turned the knob slowly, so as not to disturb them, and slipped into the room. Three perfectly tailored backs were bent slightly over the large mahogany desk.

The men appeared deep in thought, contemplating something on the desktop. Still giddy from her news of Eloise's arrival, Morgan crept up behind her husband and circled his middle with both arms. He went rigid.

Richard and Henry swiveled their heads toward her, but Edward didn't turn. Morgan slowly released the hold she had on him, feeling instantly foolish. He was in a meeting, and she had interrupted. *So stupid,* she chastised herself.

She took a step back. A slow smile formed on her father-in-law's lips. Henry actually laughed out loud. Edward straightened, and one mortifying detail about the man she had just squeezed suddenly dawned on her...

He was a good two inches taller than her husband. She felt the blush rising in her cheeks as the strikingly handsome Perkin Kingston turned slowly toward her. *She could die now...*

"I see you have met my wife." Edward's voice came from the doorway.

She spun in place. Her actual husband, flanked by two other statuesque men, stood there grinning. One of his companions was huge, with bright dancing eyes and a smile that could rival her husband's. The other reminded her of a black panther she had once seen at a carnival, his moss-green eyes giving nothing away.

Morgan tried to locate her voice, but it had apparently gone into hiding. She was positive she was as red as a tomato.

"Ah, I was just getting the honor." A smooth-as-silk voice behind her answered.

Morgan gathered her strength and turned slowly back to face her new brother-in-law. *My word,* he was as stunning as— she shook off the thought before she could finish it.

"I am terribly sorry." The words beat a path out of her mouth. "It is just that you both look so similar from behind..."

One of his elegant brows lifted slowly, pulling with it the corner of his mouth. The same lopsided smile for which Edward was known. How on earth was this this man still single?

The man in question haphazardly slapped a royal decree in his palm. The action swiftly reminded her of his station and answered her previous puzzlement. Greyland had described her oldest brother as the serious one, involved with the court.

Interestingly, another woman had also given Lord Dessmark high praise. The Queen. No wonder she had smiled every time she had mentioned his name. Morgan had thought their queen merely concerned for him as a close representative of the crown. But, looking at him now, it was clear there was more to it than that.

Laughter erupted around her, and Morgan was pulled from her mental assessment. Perkin's smile grew in size, but he did not join in the laughter. Instead, he quietly took her in. Unlike Alexander's inquisitive study, she did not feel as if he were deeming her worthy. It was more as if he was getting to know her mind.

She smiled, albeit bashfully. He was bright, like the white chess pieces the bon ton had deemed him similar too. That thought brought her full circle. That meant the *panther* in the room was Lord Ashlown; the darker, contrasting one. And the jolly man was Lord Kennington. She had never been more thankful of her memory than right now.

The jolly one, who had to be *the* Thomas she had heard all about, spoke up. "You hear that, Perkin? Your rear end looks just like your brother's."

When they continued to laugh, Morgan found herself joining in. She felt familiar arms circle her waist and draw her into a tight hug. She looked up at Edward, lost to his own levity over the situation. Perkin Kingston was indeed regal, but her husband was still the most resplendent man she had ever laid eyes on.

Perkin cast a smirk in Thomas's direction, clearly used to the sibling-like banter. "I would beg to differ." He looked back at Morgan and smiled. "Welcome to the family, dear."

Richard reflected on how Edward held on to Morgan's hand and the way she clung to his every word. The slight incline of his son's head toward his young bride every time someone complimented her. The way she cast her long eyelashes to the floor, in an attempt to conceal her emotions, and when Edward would lean in and whisper in her ear.

Richard smiled to himself, truly enjoying the obvious love that had grown strongly between the two. Morgan was perfect for his son. She was lighthearted, but also solid and logical. She did everything a lady should do, but she was not so proper she could not keep up with Edwards's antics.

Morgan was also astoundingly astute. She was a lot like Perkin in that regard. That particular contemplation brought his gaze around the room to where his oldest sat engaged in a game of backgammon with Henry. Richard watched them.

Perkin's long legs were crossed at the ankles as he sat with them kicked out to the side of the table in a leisurely fashion. Clearly trying to cast the impression that he could care less he was winning. Henry, on the other hand, was drawn up tight over the board, elbows on the table in deep concentration.

Richard chuckled low. It was a good thing Henry did not use gaming as a strategic advantage in his past involvement as a mercenary for Melbrooke. The Queen had confessed Henry's past employment in private during her stay. She knew a good deal more of the goings-on around her than Richard had ever realized. His Queen held her cards very close to her chest. Just as a true monarch should.

Perkin did the same. It was no wonder she had taken to him quickly, and why now she might be carrying his child. This thought brought his brows together in worry. He hated that he must keep such a secret from his own son, but Perkin could not know. As long as Richard was alive, he would see that his son never discovered the truth.

Richard had made a solid promise to the Queen that he would serve as godfather to the child and if anything ever happened to him, someone from their bloodline would take over, bonding the child to his true lineage forever. It was not uncommon for a king or queen to choose a godparent from among their advisors, thus no suspicion could be cast.

His only concern was that the baby might bear the same features that ran so strongly through his family's blood. That would not raise any red flags for a while, but sooner or later, the child could grow to look more like his true father. Richard could only hope it was a girl. Unless she happened to take on Greyland's unique features. That might be even more obvious, he worried.

"What has you looking so concerned?" Dalton queried.

Richard did not bother trying to hide the fact he was, indeed, troubled. Dalton was too clever for that. "Does it not seem odd that Lord Melbrooke did not return with you?" Richard chose a different concern. "Did he say why he was taking another ship back?"

"He traded vessels in France when we made port there, claiming he had a correspondent he needed to speak with before returning home." The dark-haired lord sat down and took a swallow of scotch.

"It was a lie, of course." Dalton smirked, quietly calling out Richard's bluff for not having answered truthfully, in regard to what was really bothering him.

Richard smiled and raised a glass. "Well, here is to us finally exposing him."

Dalton clinked his glass to Richard's, then settled back into the chair. Richard could practically hear the astute gentleman's mind turning. After a good ten minutes of silence, Richard found his mouth opening on its own accord.

"Dalton, your loyalty to the Crown is unmatched by any, save myself and my sons."

"It is." He nodded. "As it always shall be."

"Yes, I believe you." Richard sighed and looked toward Perkin. "I am not a young man any longer. I guess I am just thinking out loud about England and the Queen's future. How things will be when I am no longer around."

Dalton's gaze followed the trajectory of Richard's, but he did not speak. Both men stayed rooted in thoughtful silence. There was no reason for either of them to say more. Richard knew the man at his side understood him well. He was Perkin's best friend after all. Not to mention one of the sharpest minds Richard had ever met.

"I need to know she will always be protected. No matter what the future should bring for England." Richard finished off the last of the amber liquor in his glass.

"Richard." Dalton drew his attention. There was not a wavering muscle in his body as he delivered the next words. "As long as I drag air into my lungs, she *and* her lineage shall be safe. You need not worry."

Richard did not answer. He did not need to. The understanding was etched in the air like carved stone. Solid, sound, and *unbreakable.*

XVII

*E*dward woke up early, kissed his sleeping wife on the head, got dressed, and made his way downstairs. He quite liked this unusual new routine of waking up and being productive. Funny, how the love of a young woman, *and threats of death*, kept at bay one's desire to sleep all day.

He smiled to himself as he rounded the corner into the dining room. By Jove, he was the first one up, it seemed. Edward sat down and took a moment to enjoy the silence.

The moment only lasted a second before bickering voices filled the air and his two butlers entered the room. Both Truman and Boswell stalled at once. "My Lord!" they spoke in perfect unison.

Edward nodded, hoping they would leave.

"My most trusted and exquisite master of the house, it is grand to see you on such a glorious day."

No such luck!

"It has come to my astute attention that there seems to be a small matter with a tenant on the west side of the property," Boswell continued.

Truman broke in, "Actually, I am the one who received the message this morning, my lord."

Boswell puffed up, looking as if he were about to let Truman have it. Edward dropped his head and held up his hand. "Where is the letter?"

Truman produced a piece of paper as Boswell huffed.

"Thank you." Edward took the message and quickly skimmed the note before sitting it back on the table. "Please have Elkinema saddled."

Truman started out the door, obviously intent on beating Boswell to said task.

The older butler spoke up once again, "Would you not wish to eat first, my truly magnificent lord?"

Truman stopped, turned, and rolled his eyes.

"No, it shan't take long to fix this problem." Edward nodded for Truman to continue in his pursuit of the stable boy.

"Might I suggest you take someone along with you?" Boswell offered.

"Not necessary. It is a short ride."

"Yes, sir, but with all the accidents..." Boswell let the sentence hang.

Edward looked up. It was the first time he had ever heard the man sound worried. "Why, Boswell!" He smirked. "Are you actually concerned for my well-being?"

Boswell sputtered, but before he could craft a condescending retort, Truman strode back in. "Your steed awaits, my lord."

That was fast. Edward stood and made his way outside, eager to see how ready a horse could be made in less than five minutes. The sun was just cresting the hill. It was going to be another beautiful day.

He turned and headed to the stables where there were *two* horses saddled and waiting. Just as Edward was preparing to question the groom, Henry emerged from the barn and smiled.

"You are not going without me. Even if it is only to settle a tenant dispute."

Morgan knew Richard had spoken, and she knew what he was asking. She simply could not fashion her words into any sort of response. The only image in her mind was of Edward and Henry, laying dead somewhere. The only voice that was clear was Roderick's. *"I will kill everyone you hold dear."*

*Except...*that was only if she did not comply with his wishes. Had he changed his sick mind? Panic gripped her. She began to shake so violently she had to tighten her grip on the reins.

A hand shot out and took her horse by the bridle. She looked over to see Lord Ashlown staring down at her. "You are going back to the house. Now," he stated for the fifth time.

This time, he seemed intent on making her obey his command. Morgan shook her head no, even as he turned Serenade around and began trotting both horses back toward the stable.

Richard flanked her other side. "I will take her back." He nodded to Dalton. "You focus on the search."

Dalton spun his horse around and galloped back toward the group of men riding east. Morgan's vision blurred, her eyes stinging with hot tears. Around her, torches burned like hundreds of stars drifting mere inches off the ground. In the outlying woods and neighboring fields, voices shouted out to one another across the expanse of the land. Men searching for her husband and his best friend.

Elkinema had returned hours ago without a rider. At first, it was surmised Edward must have gotten himself thrown and would surely come trotting up the lane at any moment, seated behind Henry. Perkin blew that theory right out of the water. Apparently, Edward never came off a horse, and Elkinema would never run far away from his master if he had.

It took less than a minute before the house turned upside down with apprehension. They started by checking at the tenant's residence where Edward had supposedly gone to handle some kind of issue. To their dismay, the family had no idea what they were talking about. There was not, nor had there been, a tenant squabble.

When Henry's bay was found in a nearby field an hour later, everyone in the house joined the search party, even Lady Vandicamp. Now it was black outside and still, no one had sighted them. It was as if they had vanished into thin air.

Richard reached out and patted her hand in an effort to console her. She felt the tremor in his touch; he was worried sick. The alarm that had flashed across his normally serene face the second that horse came back riderless had been chilling. He quickly schooled his expression, but she had seen it, and that memory would never fade.

A thousand emotions had raced through her very soul with that singular look, but the one that had taken root was the one of premonition. Richard Kingston knew something tragic was happening, too. There was absolutely no doubt in Morgan's heart that the next morning would be met with darkness and despair. Their futures were about to be shaped in a great and irreversible fashion.

Edward started to open his eyes and quickly slammed them shut. The pain that lanced through his head was blinding. His eyes snapped back open. *Henry!* There had been a shot. Right before Edward's world had gone black.

He narrowed his gaze in the dimly lit room, trying to adjust his vision. Where the hell was he? Where was Henry? Edward quickly surveyed the room, categorizing its details. It was small. Dirt floor. No windows. The familiar smell of horse and hay. The boarded walls, weathered. Clearly a barn, but by the hint of mold in the fetid air, not a well-kept one.

A sick dread began to scratch its way up his spine as his gaze landed on the mound in the corner. "Henry!"

Edward quickly scrambled to the crumpled form of a man; his fear confirmed. Henry was covered in blood, his breathing coming in ragged slow rasps, barely audible. Edward gently turned his friend's head to face him. Henry's eyes cracked open just under the lash line and he violently jerked away.

"Henry, it is me." Edward rushed to calm him.

"Ed?"

The frantic look in his friend's eyes began to subside, realization setting in. He drew in a labored breath and clutched his ribs. "Where are we?"

"We have to get you out of here." Edward quickly began searching his injuries.

Henry's rib was clearly broken. He had been severely beaten, but the gunshot to the left shoulder concerned Edward the most. He ripped off his own jacket and began wrapping it tightly over the wound.

"De Montrey," Henry wheezed, attempting to move.

Edward froze. "Is going to die," he growled.

A low chuckle echoed through the small space, bouncing off the tattered walls. Edward whirled around to find the shadow of a man standing in the opposite corner. "Is that so?"

De Montrey! He would know that smug voice anywhere. Edward was on his feet in a flash, but the baron produced a pistol with equal speed and aimed it at his head.

"Is this how you operate, coward? Shoot a man when his back is turned and then beat him when he is defenseless?" Edward spat.

The barrel of the gun preceded Lord De Montrey out of the shadow. "Your friend used me for information and then stole from me," he hissed. "I would have beaten you to near death as well, if I had not been instructed to bring you back alive. They have better plans for you and that little whore of yours."

"Who has plans?" Edward demanded as he took a step forward.

"Stay where you are!" De Montrey ordered.

"Are you not confident in your single shot?" Edward knew he was playing a dangerous game, but he also knew that the amount of anger residing in the baron was fragile and emotion-driven. His pride was wounded over Henry's use of him, and likely embarrassed that his secret was now out.

"Tell me, Martin, did you really think Lord Rockafetch had any true feelings for you?" Edward took another step closer. "I bet it is hard to live with that. Being used by someone with nary an interest in you to begin with."

"Shut up!"

"Ah, I have hit a nerve," Edward mocked. "It must be difficult not being successful at anything. Unable to secure a wife for appearance's sake. Never obtaining the affections you wanted so badly returned from Lord Rockafetch. And of course, losing your title."

The baron's face contorted. "I have not lost my title."

"Oh! They did not tell you?" Edward clucked. "The Queen knows everything. Henry told her right before he came here. He has not only used you, he has destroyed you."

"Why, you—" De Montrey swiveled the gun toward Henry.

It was all the time Edward needed. He lunged, knocking him backward and off his feet just as the pistol struck a spark, firing into the rafters. Edward was on him, raining down punches, before the man's back even hit the floor. All his pent-up hostility resolved itself with each new blow as the sounds and smells of fresh blood filled the air.

Henry shouted, but it sounded as if it were coming from somewhere far off in the distance. Edward kept slamming his fist into the baron. Over and over, his knuckles met with muscle and bone. He hit him for what he had done to his best friend. He hit him for Morgan. He hit him for liberating the beasts Edward had so tightly tried to corral within himself.

"Damn you!" he yelled.

Someone pulled hard on his shoulder, but still he attacked until blood ran down his fingers and dripped from his face. Only then did he fall back, releasing the lifeless body to collapse in the dirt. Henry's voice grew closer, penetrating the fog of Edward's rage.

He shook his head to clear the blackness from his eyes and

looked down at his hands. He felt nothing. He felt no anger, no anxiety, no fear...*nothing*.

Movement to his side. Henry was struggling to stand, his limbs uncooperative. Anger returned. Looking into Henry's bruised and battered face, Edward felt the darkness assembling anew. He scrambled over to his friend.

Henry coughed up a spattering of blood. "Listen, I can barely stand, my rib is broken, and I have been shot. Can you calm down long enough to get us out of here?" He wiped his mouth with his sleeve. "We have bigger problems."

His friend's words, combined with his efforts to move, injected just the right dose of logic into Edward's mutinous emotions.

"What do you remember?" Taking Henry under the arm and supporting most of his weight, Edward helped him limp toward the door. "Are there others?"

"Yes, Morgan's stepbrother was with him." Henry stopped moving and turned his head, looking Edward directly in the eyes and vocalizing Edward's greatest fears. "He has gone after her."

Richard surveyed the edge of the tree line as they approached. The estate was just on the other side of the small grove they needed to ride through. He did not know why, but the hairs on his arms stood on end as they drew closer.

Something was not right. He lifted his hand, a silent command for Morgan to still her horse. She did so immediately.

"What is it?" she whispered.

"We are going a different direction." He began to turn the horses.

A branch snapped.

"I don't think ye are." A low, sinister voice with a strong Irish accent came from the darkness of the grove.

Without a second thought, Richard slapped his hand down hard on the rump of Morgan's horse. It was all the prompting the mare needed. She shot off at a full gallop, just as a bullet buried itself deep in Richard's chest.

His horse shied, but he managed to stay on long enough to look down at the crimson staining his shirt. He found the wound with his fingers. *A perfect shot.*

His head became light, the landscape started spinning, and his limbs grew heavy with sleep. Richard slipped over his horse's shoulder, succumbing to the pull of gravity. He landed hard on the ground, but did not feel it. Not far enough away, Morgan screamed.

Colin McGreggor's face came into view, floating in the night sky above him. "I have been looking forward to this day for a long time, Kingston."

"Leave the girl alone," Richard managed to get the words out over the strangling blood flooding his throat. "She has nothing to do with this."

Colin chuckled. "I have no need of her, but my informant does." He knelt. "He is quite eager to get his hands on the lass, it seems."

The Irishman looked up at the sound of approaching footsteps. "And by the look on his face, he is glad to have her in his possession now. Although he may want to wait until she regains consciousness."

Footfalls crunched the fall grass not far from where Richard lay. He could just make out the back of a man carrying a woman's limp body. *Morgan!* Richard cursed and coughed up more blood. Colin threw his head back and laughed.

Taking advantage of his opponent's momentary distraction, Richard's hand located the blade hidden inside his jacket. He was going to die tonight, but so was Colin McGreggor.

The Irishman looked back down at Richard with a smug grin and leaned in closer. "You see, when you failed to give Greyland to me, you sealed your family's fate. However, we still need that heir to gain our claim to the throne of England. Once that child is born, all of Ireland will join our pursuit."

"You are truly deranged if you think either of my sons will bed anyone in your family," Richard ground out.

"They will when I threaten to tell the world that the Queen is carrying Perkin Kingston's child."

Richard felt his strength fading quickly. He clutched at the hole in his chest. He was not long left for this world.

"Is this how our families will continue it then?" Richard's voice quavered. "Our intersecting paths forever bent on revenge, a knife at each other's throat, fingers sweaty on the handle."

Colin guffawed. "No, for I intend to kill off every last one of your lineage. Starting with you." He moved to stand. "Melbrooke will pay a handsome reward for your death. Your reign is over, Richard Kingston."

Richard's head rolled to the side, blood continuing to fill his mouth. He was drowning in it. "Albus Draco," the words came out thinly veiled, a riddle unlocking a curse.

Colin froze. "What did you say?"

"Wrath is its own jailer, you fool."

"Enough with the tiresome limericks, old man." McGreggor dropped back down and grabbed Richard by his jacket's lapels. "What did you say before that?" He shook him hard.

Richard coughed, speckling the Irishman's face with blood. Colin angrily swiped it away. Richard grinned. "Your traitorous father never told you?

"Speak the words, old man!" Colin leaned in close, eyes blazing, saliva frothing at the edges of his mouth.

"Albus Draco!" Richard spit the words, coated in death.

McGreggor faltered, releasing his hold as his pupils grew round, seemingly paralyzed by the two words.

"One last piece of advice, boy." Richard smiled sagaciously and drove his blade up and into Colin's heart. "Revenge is only for patient men."

Two words. Two words that had been etched into Edward's memory since birth. *Two words* to represent a secret order created hundreds of years ago in support of his Plantagenet ancestors.

His father's voice echoed in his ears; a proverb repeated from childhood. *"To shape history, we must live beyond our lifetime."* Albus Draco...White Dragon.

No!

The ancestral blade sunk with a quiet resolve. The Irishman had only one breath left in which to make a gurgled gasp before falling into the grass, the weapon embedded deep in his chest. Edward knew his feet were moving, sprinting him to his father's side, but time seemed suspended, hung in the air.

He reached his father's side and fell to his knees. There was blood everywhere. *Too much blood!* Edward frantically pushed aside his father's thick jacket, searching past the saturated material of his shirt for the bullet's entry point.

His father took his hand, halting the investigation. "Son."

"No," Edward said stubbornly, locating the wound and pressing his hand firmly to the gaping hole. "We need to get you to the house."

"Edward." His father covered his hand with his own. "It is too late."

Tears blurred his vision. "No." Denial ripped from his throat.

"You have to save her," Richard said, locking his eyes on Edward's.

Edward's head shot up, his eyes frantically scanning the night. "Which way did he go?"

"East. Through the grove."

A battle like no other raged inside Edward's heart. "Father." His voice shook on the word.

"I need you to take over the safekeeping of a secret. You will find all you need to know hidden in my ledgers." His father gasped as another cough racked his body.

Edward nodded, his throat closing up on his reply. His father gently squeezed his hand. "Go get her."

"Father, please." Edward leaned in, placing a trembling kiss atop his father's forehead. "I love you." His voice shook as he looked back into the soft gray eyes he had known for a lifetime. "I need you."

His father wheezed. "They need you now."

Barely breathing, his father rolled his head to the side, unshed tears glistening in eyes that were dimming, growing distant. "I love you, son." His grip loosened. "I am proud of you."

His hand fell away, last words fading, carried away on the breeze as nature claimed its inevitable debt.

Morgan came to with a jolt as the horse she had been thrown across leapt a small creek. Unprepared for the landing, it felt as if she had been hurled from the sky onto a boulder. She gasped, her ribs burning as if they had splintered inside her chest. She struggled for oxygen, and for clarity.

Richard had sent her horse into a gallop without warning. There had been a gunshot. Roderick had appeared out of nowhere and chased her down. Morgan had kicked her horse as hard as she could, but his was faster. The last image she had was of him gaining on her.

The horse, whose withers she was slung over, slowed. "Enjoying the view?" Roderick bent over her and hissed into her ear.

She jerked at his nearness. He pressed his elbow into the middle of her back, caging her between his chest and the horse. "I would not dream of it, sister dear."

"Please, Roderick. I will do anything; just leave my family alone."

He loosened his grip on her and in one swift move, threw her off the side of the horse. The next thing Morgan knew, she was hitting the ground and gasping for oxygen anew. He was on her, straddling her and pinning her back to the ground.

"I am your family!" he ground out. "Not them. You belong to me!"

She felt a tear escape the corner of her eye.

"That's a good girl." He smirked sadistically. "I love it when you cry; it makes me desire you all the more."

He bent quickly and bit down on her bottom lip, drawing blood. She cried out and bucked beneath him, trying futilely to dislodge him. Between the physical pain, and the threat of agony yet to come, she had to get control of the situation. Any way she could.

What would Edward instruct her to do? Panicking would not be in the tutorial. She sealed her eyes shut.

Feel the dance. Let it lead you.

She was no match for Roderick's strength. Not if she continued to fight him. He would only work harder to break her. To make her bend to his will. She had to be smarter than his brute strength. Which meant becoming compliant.

With that singular thought, she forced her muscles to uncoil. If he was intent on taking her here, in the woods, she would lure him into the weakness of his physical desires. Morgan relaxed, compelling her mind out of its current prison.

As soon as she stopped struggling, he loosened his grip on her and became more focused on his end goal. Dragging his tongue along the edge of her bodice, he adjusted his position above her. He moved one of his legs between hers. She allowed it without resistance, but when he made the slight shift of weight to do the same with the other leg, she seized her only chance to topple him.

With his weight canted more to one side than the other, and his legs still spread, she brought her knee up hard and fast. At the same time, she rolled to the side and shoved him off balance. The combined effort worked, and he fell to the side with a sharp intake of air.

Morgan scrambled to her feet. The blasted horse had shied away when both riders left its back. She took off on foot through the woods. She heard Roderick's pursuit as he screamed out her name from somewhere behind her. Morgan pulled the material of her dress higher and ran as fast as she could through the night, thankful for the moonlight's well-lit path.

She glanced down to check her footing as she jumped a small

brook. Landing hard on the other side of the muddy bank, she scrambled up its steep incline. She reached the top, breathing heavy, and screamed.

A hand shot out and grabbed her before she could fall back down the embankment. "You are safe." Perkin stared down at her, eyes like daggers.

Morgan began to sob. He shoved her behind him and into another pair of uncompromising arms just as the foliage on the other side of the creek snapped and separated under the weight of a large animal.

She looked up to find Dalton glaring over her head at whatever had just broken through the bushes. Morgan did not need to turn to know who it was. She heard Perkin cock a revolver.

"She is mine!" Roderick, winded and sounding crazed, shouted.

She felt Dalton tense at the implication. "He is lying," Morgan whimpered. "I never—" Dalton put his hand to the back of her head, drawing her protectively to his chest.

"That is a very disturbing accusation," Perkin said flatly. "Especially considering she is married to my brother."

"He stole her from me," Roderick ground out, sounding closer.

"She was supposed to marry that simpleton, De Montrey, who had no stomach for preforming his husbandly duties." *Closer still.* Roderick was advancing. "Had they wed, he would have allowed me constant access to her."

"Why would a man share his wife with another man?" Perkin's question was calm and steady, as if he were dealing with a coiled snake. He was deliberately keeping Roderick talking.

Roderick scoffed. "He likes cock, you fool! He would gain our name in marriage and improve his standing in society. That is why. And he would be repaying a—"

The sudden and thundering sound of something trampling the earth silenced him. Before Morgan could look back over her shoulder, Dalton spun them both in place to face the opposite direction. Startled, she craned her neck to see around him.

Roderick had turned and was running back into the woods.

Everything was happening so fast. Only Perkin seemed unaffected. He held the pistol, its sight trained on Roderick's retreating back.

"I would not run if I were you," her brother-in-law yelled out.

Before Roderick could stop, or even reply, another man leveled him flat. Morgan gasped as the other man proceeded to pummel Roderick, delivering blow after bone-crushing blow. It was not a fight. It was not meant to simply subdue. *It was intended to kill.*

"Do not look," Dalton warned as he walked her backward, farther away from the violence.

But Morgan could not stop looking. Not when the other man was her husband. She pushed out of Dalton's arms and flew toward the creek, only to meet up with Perkin's unyielding grasp.

He snatched hold of her and yanked her to him. Morgan fought him with all her strength. She had to stop Edward.

This was why Ocman had regarded him so after that day in the parlor, when Edward had put his fist through the glass. The lifetime servant had been giving him the only comfort he knew how to give... the gentle understanding of silence.

This was his secret.

This blinding, all-consuming rage that plagued him.

He could not take Roderick's life. To do so would only validate his demons and reinforce the fear that they were inescapable. She could not allow hatred to consume him.

"Edward, no!" she shouted as Perkin walled her in, prohibiting her from going to him.

She looked up pleadingly at her brother-in-law. "You have to stop him."

He did nothing. How could he not see that this would destroy Edward? She frantically looked to Dalton for assistance. He, too, stood stock still, unwilling to interfere.

Morgan made another attempt to escape Perkin's hold, screaming as loud as she could, begging for the love of her life to hear her.

A distant bell rang out from somewhere in the dark, then faded into the black nothingness that surrounded him.

The singsong chime lit the cave once more, this time bringing a light that illuminated the edges, like a star burning brightly. The call was soft, yet demanding. Edward felt himself following its calming encouragement.

Slowly he drifted toward it, until the edges of the cave dissolved and the outer fringe of the surrounding woods began to take shape.

Suddenly, the bell became a terror-riddled scream and the whole picture painted itself clear, shaking him to the bone.

Morgan!

His wife was screaming his name with a desperation that was physically painful. He froze mid-swing, comprehension dragging him back to the present. He looked down and realized he was probably three blows shy of killing the man laying bloody beneath him.

Edward swiveled his head to the right. Morgan was clawing at his brother in an attempt to extract herself from his hold. Perkin did not budge, just shielded her, using his body to protect her from the grisly scene. The horror Edward was creating.

He stumbled backward. Something in his heart splintered. She had seen him, borne witness to what kind of blind, raging monster he could become.

She would hate him now. She would leave him. She would disappear from his life. Just as his mother, and now his father, had done. He looked up to the sky and cried out.

"Edward, please!" She'd called out again, but this time, the tone was different.

He turned back to where they were standing. Both Perkin and Dalton were watching him carefully, as if they were waiting to see the animal in him return. Morgan made one last attempt, and broke free of his brother's hold.

She bolted to the edge of the rushing creek and reached out toward him, tears glistening on her cheeks, her face an echo of his own pain.

She was the bell...

Edward pushed to his shaky feet.

Morgan had been the light.

He stumbled toward her.

She had fought off the demons.

He sloshed through the creek bed, and she flung herself into his arms. He held her tight, suddenly aware that she was his savior. *She was his soul.* She was his, and he was forever *hers.*

Edward had been her teacher. Now, she had become his. He fell to his knees with her in his arms. All hatred erased; all rage beaten back. A quietude he had never known wrapped around them like a cloak.

He knew something else as well. Without a shadow of a doubt, as Perkin and Dalton stepped back, giving them their space, someone else moved in. *His father was here.*

In this moment.

In this peace. In spirit...

He was with them.

The manor was abuzz with activity when Edward and Morgan stepped over the threshold. Perkin and Dalton had done as Edward had instructed back at the creek; Dalton took Roderick to the house for jailing, and Perkin rode into the village to collect the physician for Henry.

This provided Edward the time needed to relay the news of his father to Morgan. She was devastated, but collected herself before they arrived at the house some time later, allowing Edward to speak with Perkin in private. Thankfully, his brother was busy with the physician tending to Henry and did not see them enter.

Edward helped Morgan to their bedchamber and took the servant stairs back down. How could he bring himself to tell his brother?

Edward rounded the steps to the kitchen and took a hard right toward the back door. He couldn't. Not yet.

He slipped outside, summoning two footmen standing guard to follow. He needed a little more time to arrange the words. He certainly did not need Perkin riding off to exact revenge on their remaining enemies tonight, which was exactly what he would do. No, Edward would retrieve their father's body, and confide all when he returned.

He was just turning into the stable to collect the horses when Perkin stepped out of the shadows right into his path.

"Where are you going? And where is Father?" he demanded, a brittle accusatory tone in his voice.

Edward held up a hand to halt the others. "Leave us."

The servants retreated to the house.

"Where is he?" His brother advanced, eyes like chips of ice.

Edward shook his head dolorously. "Perkin…"

A sharp flash of fear lit Perkin's eyes, but he stood his ground, needing the words. "Tell me!"

"He is no longer with us, brother."

Perkin staggered back as if he had been physically struck. "No."

Edward reached out, but his brother shook him off and took a suspicious step away.

"Colin McGreggor shot him," Edward rushed to explain. "He was working with Morgan's stepbrother and Lord De Montrey."

"You left him?" Perkin ground out.

"No!"

Edward felt like he was circling a drain. He focused on his love for Morgan, he focused on his father's last words. He focused on the man standing, gaze hard and full of accusation, in front of him now…the brother who had always been the solid one.

A horrific fear nestled into Edward's chest. It was *his* turn to be the strong one. He challenged Perkin's mounting fear and stepped closer, his eyes locking on those of his older brother's.

He stripped his soul bare and fed it into his next words. "I was with him right up to the very end. He passed in my arms. He was not alone. I was there for him, Perkin. I was strong for him." Edward choked back the strangling lump in his throat. "I tried to be...you."

Unbidden tears glistened in his brother's eyes as he reached out and pulled Edward into a labored hug, weighted with loss. They cried, shrouded by the night, mourning the loss together. As their father would have wanted. As family did.

"Thank you," Perkin murmured, his voice harrowed with a despair Edward had never heard before. "Take me to him. Let us bring him home, together."

XVIII

TWO MONTHS LATER

$\mathcal{M}$organ ran her finger along the edge of the message from Eloise, smiling. Seemed she had grown quite fond of one Lord Rockafetch. She stole a glance across the table at her beautiful husband, who sat reading his own messages for the day, a similar smile on his face.

"Let me guess," she said.

He looked up.

"That is from Henry?"

Edward nodded and then waved her over. She stood and walked around the table. He pulled her into his lap, playfully nipping her earlobe. "Seems the self-proclaimed bachelor has met his match in your lovely friend."

Morgan giggled. "It would appear that way, my lord."

Edward cradled her in his arms, his low chuckle vibrating off his chest like lapping waves on a shore. She would never forget how badly she had wanted to hear and witness this man's joy—only a short time ago. Back when he was her teacher in her aunt's ballroom.

Since then, her husband had shown her how many layers he truly did possess, and how much love he could give. They had come so far, grown so much, and fallen so completely in love. Morgan smiled, growing reflective. So much transpired after the day the Earl of Wellington walked into her life.

They had lost so much on the day Richard was stolen from them. He had been lain to rest in the cemetery outside Westingham Castle, his home, and the resting place of many of the Kingston ancient bloodline. The Queen had attended, and the country had wept for the loss of one so loved as Richard Kingston, Duke of York.

Morgan's mind wandered further back, to the day after the attack. Perkin had ridden straight to Greenshire Castle to inform Greyland and Alexander, and Edward had obsessively poured over documents from his father's safe. Sometime in the middle of the night, he had come to her and revealed the secret he was now honor-bound to keep.

The Queen was expecting a child. The news was earth shattering for Edward. But moreover, had been the knowledge that he must hide the secret from his brother. Morgan talked with him until the wee hours. Afterward, they had fallen asleep in each other's arms. When they woke the next morning, it felt as if the burden was somewhat lifted for her husband.

A new understanding had grown between the two of them, an awareness that was solid and strong, unwavering, and safe. Since that night, Edward had told her every fear, every dream, every hope he'd ever had. Although, some of it was hard to stomach, she knew he must purge it all.

He had repressed so much, and unknowingly, she had been doing the same. She told him everything that happened with Roderick, and every cautious step she had taken...along with the few rebellious ones. The only topic Morgan did not ask about, and he did not offer, was the words she heard him speak to Perkin, Alex, and Greyland after the funeral.

Morgan had been passing the study. The four had been holed up all morning hashing out the last details regarding the inheritance. She had decided not to interrupt them and continued down the hall, but not before she heard two distinct words: *Albus Draco.*

She remembered enough of her Latin to translate the words

quickly into White Dragon. She'd thought it odd at the time but did not inquire as to the meaning. If it was something Edward someday felt he needed to share, it would be his choice.

Roderick had been taken into custody at the Tower of London the day after the attack. Morgan's mother was granted permission for a divorce by the Queen and was currently residing with her aunt in London. Lord Melbrooke had not been seen or heard from. It was rumored he had sought passage to America. Lastly, they were assured an investigation into Davenport was underway. It seemed all wrongs were being set right.

As far as Morgan's new family was concerned, they drew in even closer, finding strength in the tight family unit and comfort in each other's presence. It was everything she had ever wanted, and everything she would die to defend. These were *her* people. This was where she belonged.

The only one who appeared not to be faring well was Perkin. He hid his pain skillfully, but Morgan was more perceptive than most. Her brother-in-law was deeply affected by the loss of his father.

She could tell by subtle things. Such as the way his eyes would grow despondent when he thought no one was watching, but never to a depth that would give himself away. He could reengage at a moment's notice in conversation, his brilliant mind masking the hurt that clearly chewed at him from the inside.

This worried Morgan most because it could not be healthy. He was not allowing himself to grieve. Instead, Perkin was fighting to shoulder this weight all by himself, diving into his work with Parliament, affecting the image he was *still* the world's ever-present shining example of a rock. When the truth was it was all an act. One Morgan was sure he could not maintain forever.

The only other person who seemed to understand this was Dalton. He stayed glued to Perkin's side, never giving away his best friend's secret and ever watchful of him. He remained the one constant pillar in her brother-in-law's life. For that, Dalton had Morgan's undying gratitude.

Edward pulled her from her musings by kissing her neck softly.

She turned to butter in his hands as she always had done. The man truly was a master at seduction, but that was no new revelation. Edward Kingston was a master at most things, and he had taught her so much.

He had led her into a life she never imagined she could have, guiding her through his vast experience and teaching her what it meant to be truly loved. In turn, she had followed him into the pits of hell, fought tooth and nail beside him, and proved to him that true love could indeed conquer all.

They were each other's compass. One another's careful and steady guidance. Both of them weathering life's storms and emerging stronger when the clouds did lift. Because of each other. Because of love... and scars.

Edward brushed back a strand of her hair, which she always kept loose now, and whispered in her ear the words that started their journey together.

"Shall we dance?"

PREVIEW

PERKIN'S STORY

IRELAND 1840

*A*t half-past five, the majority of inebriated guests made their wobbly way across the lawn to their waiting carriages. The minority in attendance, those most favored, dragged themselves, stumbling over their own feet, up to appointed guest quarters.

Perkin glanced down at the pocket watch in his hand and rolled his eyes. He could literally set a clock by the laird's proceedings. For two weeks, this had been a nightly occurrence.

The wealthiest and most influential would arrive just after ten p.m. for an evening of lavish entertainment, extravagant food, and fanciful dancing. The partygoers would then imbibe greedily on the widower's hospitality until the wee hours of the morning before falling out the front doors and onto the castle grounds.

Some called it grieving, but most knew better. Content to reap the benefits of loss, the guests simply drank the wine and ate the food and called it nothing. This was Ireland, after all.

Confident in his ability to go unnoticed, Perkin began his trek up the curving, candlelit staircase, his footfall treading lightly on the ancient stone steps. A quick look down the hall confirmed the coast was clear and he resumed his pace, pausing only when he stood in front of the bed chamber's large double doors.

He leaned in closely, listening to the soft giggles coming from within and waited. As soon as the feminine voice said, "Oh my!" he opened the doors and slipped inside the chamber.

The laird was exactly where Perkin had hoped to find him. Flat on his massive ass in the middle of his four-poster bed, a curvy brunette bouncing up and down wildly on his ruddy, engorged cock.

Perkin moved further into the room, his presence concealed by the exaggerated meows and purrs of pleasure. He had to give credit where credit was due—the girl was worth every shilling Perkin had paid her.

He crossed to the end of the bed and waited until the laird's grunting and thrusting became frenzied, signaling his near completion. *But not quite...* "Is this how you honor your dead wife's memory?"

The whore took a solid knock to the side as Davenport sprang straight up in the bed. "Guards!" he bellowed.

Too bad most of them had already been drugged by Dalton. Perkin smiled and unsheathed his sword.

"Kingston!" the laird growled. "Come to kill me when I am unable to defend myself?"

Perkin took two steps over to a chair near the end of the bed and grabbed Davenport's own sword to toss it to him. The laird caught it haphazardly, sputtering as he hastily made to stand.

"You should be on your way now." Perkin nodded the girl toward the door. She wasted no time, snatching up her gown and scrambling out of the room.

Davenport's eyes narrowed into slits as he quickly pulled his nightshirt over his head. "I knew you would eventually come. I had hoped it would be a duel at dawn with pistols. Like proper gentlemen. Leave it to a Kingston to take the barbaric approach."

"You may address me as Sir Kingston." Perkin slowly advanced.

Davenport stepped to the left, adjusting the sword in his grip before lunging forward. Perkin sidestepped and, with a quick arching blow, swung his blade down on the fat man's forearm. The laird hissed and lunged again. Perkin brought his sword up and both weapons clashed in a fight for dominance; the cold, angry metal singing out in the still room. Perkin rotated with a downward twist and sent Davenport's blade spinning across the floor.

"Sir Kingston, His Grace," Perkin added as the other lord made for his weapon.

Perkin felt his lips curling into a sarcastic smile as he extended his sword again. He tossed it between hands, checking its weight as he paused for his opponent to regain his stance. Davenport snorted in reply and charged once more, bringing his weapon up high before cleaving it down quickly toward Perkin's throat. Perkin stopped the blade mere inches from his flesh, spun in place, and sunk his sword between his enemy's ribs.

Davenport sputtered, a look of bewilderment moving from Perkin's eyes to the hole in his chest before returning back to Perkin's stare.

"Now..." Perkin leaned in and looked right into his enemy's eyes as he twisted the blade. "Duke of York."

A wet gurgling sound pushed its way over Davenport's pursed lips and a bloody froth bubbled up around the edges of his mouth. The sound of death. Perkin kicked the fat pile of flesh off his blade and watched it collapse in an undignified heap on the floor.

It was everything Perkin had hoped for. Planned for. Everything as expected. Except for the distinct sound of the doors bursting open behind him.

Perkin stood, shoulders square, his back to the new arrival. Whoever it was, and whatever would happen next, would not sway him from the satisfaction of this moment. The eradication of everyone who had played a part in his father's death.

Without turning, he reached out and yanked a decorative tapestry off the wall and used it to wipe clean his weapon. An oddly timed observation—*the blood was still warm*—crossed his mind as his hand methodically followed the steel blade to the tip.

"Put that down!" A feminine voice flared at him from the doorway.

Perkin turned slowly. There, framed between the double doors, bathed in the hallway's soft candlelight, hands on hips, blonde hair falling artfully around a delicate heart shaped face, stood what was quite possibly the most beautiful young woman he had ever seen. And she was currently drilling holes through his skull with her crystal blue stare.

"That tapestry is more than a century old, you fool!"

Book Three, Under His Discretion, is available now at all online retailers!

ABOUT STACY VON HAEGERT

Stacy grew up in Nashville, Tennessee, daughter of a singer-songwriter and an equestrian enthusiast. When she was not tagging along with her father into music city staples like the Blue Bird or riding her mother's Arabians at breakneck speeds over the Tennessee countryside, she was writing short stories and poems. She is obsessed with old houses, good literature, and boogie boarding.

Her passion for words grew and in 2013, Stacy released her first book, 'Under his Protection,' that raced up Amazon's charts landing at #2 in the US and #1 in the UK.

Stacy currently lives in historic downtown Franklin TN where she writes by day and teaches ballroom dance in the evenings.

Don't forget to stalk me on social media!

Made in the USA
Middletown, DE
03 January 2025

68763721R00156